TRIAGE

A Novel

TRIAGE

A Novel

Elisa M. Speranza

BURGUNDY BEND

Triage

Published by Burgundy Bend Press

BURGUNDY BEND

Learn more at: www.elisamariesperanza.com

Human Authored Reg #: 8792807
https://authorsguild.org/human

Cover art by Jon Langford
Book design by Kim Leaird
Author photo by Cheryl Gerber

Library of Congress Control Number: 2026900508

ISBN (hardcover): 979-8-9944991-0-8
ISBN (paperback): 979-8-9944991-1-5
eISBN: 979-8-9944991-2-2

Printed in the United States of America

For my sisters

"We all cry in private. But not in front of the boys.
Never in front of the boys."

—First Lieutenant June Wandrey, R.N. (1920-2005),
U.S. Army Nurse Corps, 1942-1946
Author of *Bedpan Commando*

TABLE OF CONTENTS

PART ONE

New Orleans, 1951

CHAPTER ONE

Laura wakes up with the war in her bones. The weak, pre-dawn light seeps in around the edges of the curtains. She sits up, registering familiar shadows: vanity, chair, wardrobe. She listens for planes and explosions but hears only birds beginning their morning songs outside and Nicholas snoring lightly beside her. She brushes his back with her fingertips to reassure herself. He is real. She is safe.

She's sweated through her bedclothes. Rising, she gropes for a fresh nightgown and panties in her dresser drawer, touching the corner of the envelopes she'd received the day before, tucked under her lingerie—the devastating letter from Frances's mother, the unread one from Frances herself.

In the bathroom, she strips and splashes cool water on her face, then pulls on the clean clothes. But it's no use, and she sits down heavily on the closed toilet lid. The room spins as a high-pitched whine assaults her ears; she ducks her head between her legs to keep from throwing up.

The war is six years behind her, but sometimes in her sleep, and even awake like now, she's back at the front. Her back is stiff, her hands like claws from gripping forceps and clamps, her shoulders strained from working for hours at the doctor's elbow. The terrifying, ceaseless clatter and boom of the artillery is so close the hospital tent quakes. The stench of the dead and dying. The sharp, antiseptic tang of alcohol, the metallic smell of blood, the gut-wrenching odor of infected gas gangrene wounds. A boy's desperate, clammy hand is clutching hers, its grip fierce, missing his family, his limb, his mind. His youth.

She breathes deeply, trying to keep her eyes open so she won't see their tortured expressions, their disfigured bodies, their burns. *You'll be good as new in no time*, she'd lied. To them, to herself. Frances said they'd needed her, or at least the idea of her—a woman's touch, a soft voice, a soothing smile, absorbing their pain. And she'd tried. But she could never offer them the one thing they all wanted so desperately: for the war to be over, to be home.

Her left hand is shaking now. Along with the night sweats and terrifying dreams, the news about Frances has triggered the tremor's return. She puts two fingers on her wrist, counting off her pulse—the old habit: one one-thousand, two one-thousand, three one-thousand. Breathe. *You survived,* she tells herself.

"Are you OK?" Nicholas calls through the closed door, his voice thick and drowsy, startling her.

"Fine," she answers.

"You sure?"

"Yes. Go back to sleep." She grips the sides of the toilet and tries to focus on the solid, mundane artifacts of her everyday life: the bathtub, the towel, the soap, and their toothbrushes sharing a glass. *This is your bathroom, in your house, in New Orleans—your city—where you live with your husband. In a couple of hours, you'll be back at the hospital, where your patients are counting on you. You're a good nurse.*

She creeps back to bed, then curls herself against Nicholas's strong back. She inhales his musky scent, lets his warmth calm her, and matches her breath to his. She clings to her memory of Frances's voice, knowing she'll never hear that Texas drawl again: *You're alright, kid. You did the best you could.*

Laura slumps against the passenger seat and closes her eyes, her head throbbing, sweating out alcohol and nightmares. She rolls down her window as Nicholas pulls the big Chevy out of the driveway. Seven a.m., and it's stifling already. August, the month the swamp underneath the city threatens to drag them back into the ooze.

Her head throbs. While Nicholas was at the VFW the night before, she drank too much wine and opened the letter from Frances's mother. *Our darling Frances is gone.* Laura's best friend from the war, dead by her own hand. She'd read the letter twice but couldn't yet bring herself to open the second letter, her name in Frances's handwriting on the sealed envelope. Even though they'd lost touch, a world without Frances in it was unthinkable. Incomplete.

She should tell Nicholas about the letters, now nestled in her purse like ticking time bombs. But she needs to absorb the pain on her own first. Does her distress even register with him? Most of the time, he's self-contained, like the good surgeon he is. Sometimes, though, he tosses and turns himself, muttering and whimpering in his sleep. He served on the front line just like she did; he must have his own ghosts. Does he see them in his dreams, too? She never asks. He never says.

"You're in the general ward today, right?" Nicholas says.

She snaps back to attention. "Uh-huh," she replies. "Assholes and elbows." Maybe she'll tell him at dinner tonight, and they can read Frances's letter together. She wasn't brave enough to read it on her own after reading Mrs. Harris's letter. "Meet me for a sandwich later?"

"Afraid not. Wall-to-wall today," he says. "They might have to feed me through a tube."

Though she sometimes resents his schedule, she has to admit she's proud of him. He'd parlayed his Army experience to become a highly in-demand trauma surgeon. With his salary and help from the GI Bill, they'd been able to buy a single-family house in Mid-City and move from the half-double they rented from her sister Rose after the war. It's a nice life, comfortable, with no need to ever worry about money. So different from how she grew up—with her parents and her sister and brother crammed into a small apartment above their grocery store on the Sicilian end of the French Quarter.

Nicholas reaches to turn up the radio. The morning news talks of Charlie, a "killer hurricane" making landfall on the Mexican coast. Laura only half-listens. She'd stopped paying attention once the storm took a left in the Gulf, though she wishes those people well.

He gently lets out the clutch and changes gears, the big chrome steering wheel sliding through his hands. He is tender with the car, a Bel Air coupe, mint green with a white roof, another luxury his salary affords. He'd been like a kid at Christmas when they picked it up a year ago. Maybe it fills a void for him.

She taps her foot and hangs her arm out the window. She craves a cigarette, but Nicholas doesn't allow smoking in the Chevy. In the side mirror, she notices dark circles under her eyes and a few broken capillaries on the tip of her nose. She looks over at him. Despite the wisps of gray at his temples, to her, he's still that young Army doctor: navigating a jeep through the dunes, his broad shoulders and muscled forearms tanned from the desert sun. *Doctor Dreamboat,* Frances used to call him. She wonders what her husband sees when he looks at her—certainly not the fresh-faced young nurse she'd been when they met in North Africa.

Nicholas maneuvers around parked cars and potholes. The traffic is thicker near the Charity Hospital complex. Other nurses and doctors make their way along the sidewalk as the letter's words replay in Laura's head like a sad dirge. *Our darling Frances is gone.* She longs to reach out to Nicholas, to tell him their friend is dead. Maybe he'd help her make sense of it, tell her there was nothing she could have done. But lately, there's a wall between them she can't seem to scale. Besides, they're almost at the hospital; if she tells him now, she'll disintegrate.

She forces her thoughts to the upcoming workday and the ongoing gossip around staff changes. She's heard rumors she might be named supervisor of the post-op ward when it opens, now that the construction of the new wing is almost complete. She wants the promotion more than she'd like to admit—a reward for all her sacrifices, a recognition of what she went through in the war. A chance to prove she's still worthy, capable. As far as she knows, she's the only one in the running with combat training. The not-knowing has been driving her crazy.

She turns the radio down. "I hear they're going to announce the post-op supervisor position any day now."

"Do you think you'll get it?" Nicholas asks.

"Do *you* think I'll get it?" She can't help thinking he knows more than he's letting on. Surgeons are at the top of the food chain at Charity. Along with the GIs, the surgeons came back from the war to a hero's welcome. Meanwhile, nurses like her were patted on the head and sent on their way as if they hadn't been right in the thick of it. As if they had all made it home safely.

"I have no idea," he says. "I mean, you *deserve* it, of course. But sometimes that doesn't matter. Hospital politics. You know how it is."

She does know. She presses her palm against her thigh to stop her left hand from trembling.

"No sense worrying about what you can't control," he adds. His unsolicited advice is irksome—as if her career were as inconsequential as the weather, a surprise rainstorm.

They pull into the garage and park. He walks behind her toward the wide granite steps leading to the hospital's front entrance. Thunder rumbles, and Laura scans the sky for trouble—an old habit from the war—but she sees only gray storm clouds gathering and pigeons perched on the hospital's ornate carved ledges. The concrete and stone towers soar twenty stories. When Frances came to town, Laura had been so excited to show off her hospital. Frances had stopped on these steps and pointed to the metal grillwork above the entrance depicting life in Louisiana. "Where are the women?" she'd asked. "Only a dancer—the rest of them are cooking and sewing." They'd had a good laugh over that.

Nicholas touches her elbow, stopping her. "You OK?" he asks. "You seem a million miles away."

She musters a smile, reminding herself that she loves him. "I'm fine. Didn't sleep very well."

"Another bad dream?"

"Maybe. I can't remember," she lies. She can't hold his gaze, or it'll all spill out: that Frances is gone, that she's never felt so alone. That she wants him to take her in his arms and tell her it's going to be all right—the way he used to back at the front, when she was afraid all the time.

Hospital staff scurry past them in ones and twos, smiling and laughing, looking cheerful and eager to meet their workday. A doctor they know waves, then slinks away as if he's interrupted a tender moment between husband and wife. If only it were true.

"I'm going to stay out here for a smoke before I head in," she says, pulling a pack of cigarettes from her purse, along with the battered green metal lighter she's kept since the Army. "Try to wake up a little."

Nicholas frowns—he gave up smoking years ago and has made no secret of his desire for her to do the same. "You're off at three?"

She has to think. "Yes." She cups the flame with her hand to light her cigarette, then takes a deep drag and holds the smoke in her lungs until it burns.

He hands her the car keys, waves away the cloud of smoke she exhales, then leans down and kisses her on the cheek. "Take her home. I'll hop on the streetcar and see you for dinner later."

"Thanks," she says, tucking the keys in her purse. "Leftovers all right?"

"Sounds good," he answers, already walking away.

"*Ti amo*," she says, though she guesses he can't hear her over the wail of an incoming ambulance.

CHAPTER TWO

Laura spends the morning in the general ward—nothing's urgent, just minor wounds, breaks and sprains, and curable infections. She loves the familiar smell of disinfectant mixed with humanity, the murmur of nurses calming upset patients, the flow of people in and out, most patched up quickly and sent on their way. It's not the most exciting rotation, but she's grateful for the work and the distraction, remembering what her commanding officer, Captain McCarthy, used to say when things got tough: *Do your job*.

She visits each bed on the ward, making sure everyone is taken care of, then slips into the nurses' lounge for a break. She holds the door for two women exiting; she can never remember their names. The hum of voices and rolling carts in the hallway recedes as the heavy door swings shut. She has the lounge to herself and settles into one of the armchairs. This room hasn't changed much since Laura's student days: the faint antiseptic smell of cleaning products, drab beige walls, a brown vinyl sofa worn at the armrests, and two boxy, metal-framed chairs. Charity's founding mother, Sister Stanislaus, scowls from a framed photo on the wall in her enormous white winged headpiece.

She pulls the two envelopes from her purse, brushing her fingertips over Mrs. Harris's looping penmanship. The postmark reads Dallas, Texas. She unfolds the letter for the third time. The writing is neat and clear on the single sheet of white lined paper, as if Frances's mother had copied it over until it was perfect. She reads the letter once again, parsing every sentence in case she missed something the first two times through, in case the words had magically changed, and Frances was alive and well.

Dear Laura,

I hope this note finds you. It took me a little while to track down your address, and I sure hope this gets to you. I am Frances Harris's mother, and I have some sad news to share. Our darling Frances is gone.

She was doing pretty well when she first came home from the war. She had a great job and was dating a nice fellow. But over the last year or so, she began to struggle. She took her own life in May. God forgive her. We're devastated to lose our only daughter but comforted to know she's at peace.

Frances did not like to discuss her time in the service, but she did mention your name to us often, always fondly. She was raised in a God-fearing home, and we taught both our children to walk in Jesus's path—to be kind, thoughtful, and loyal—and to help others, especially through the hard times. I hope she was as good a friend to you as I know you were to her.

I would be so grateful if you could drop us a line to let us know this letter found you. Throughout so much of her life, I was somehow unable to help Frances. It would mean a great deal to feel as though I'd done something for her.

If you ever get to Texas, I hope you'll come and visit. Earl and I would love to hear more about your time with Frances in the service. Meanwhile, please take care of yourself. You girls went through so much. I know you didn't get the credit you deserved. You saved a lot of lives. There ought to be some solace in that for you, and I'm sure your parents are as proud of you as we are of Frances.

God bless you,
Mabel Harris

Laura swipes away her tears. She doesn't want to have to explain herself if someone walks in. She also knows Frances would be the first to tell her to stop blubbering. In Laura's mind's eye, Frances stands tall in the triage ward in Tunisia in those early days, blond curls piled under her cap, somehow glamorous in rumpled fatigues, kidding around to lighten the mood while moving from patient to patient, calm and competent. Laura had been in awe of her unflappable strength, wanting it for her own.

She holds the unopened envelope from Frances but hesitates, afraid of what Frances might have written, of the memories that might get dredged up—thoughts and feelings she's worked hard to stifle since she came back from the war.

The door opens, startling her. Three nurses come into the lounge, whispering in gossipy tones. They spot Laura and abruptly stop their chatter, moving past her with a curt nod on their way into the adjoining lavatory. Some of the nurses are friends outside of work, hanging out at Joe's Bar across the street after their shifts, drinking and flirting. Laura prefers to keep things professional; she goes to Joe's too, but only with Nicholas.

"Boss lady's looking for you out there," one of the women says over her shoulder. Laura returns Frances's unopened letter to her purse.

Laura spots her boss at the nurses' station. "There you are," Phyllis says. "I could use your help in the storeroom. I'll meet you there in a bit."

The windowless storage closet is stuffy and cramped, its shelves overflowing with supplies and cardboard boxes stacked precariously. Laura wonders what could be so urgent about a routine supply chore. She reaches for the small radio on the shelf and waits for the tubes to warm up, then turns the dial to WNOE, the Rhythm & Blues show. Music always helps calm her; she grew up with the radio always playing in her father's grocery store. Ruth Brown sings "Teardrops from My Eyes."

She opens a shipping carton and starts stacking boxes of bandages on a shelf. Snippets of Mrs. Harris's letter replay in her head. *God forgive her*. It's morbid, but Laura can't help wondering how Frances did it. Pills, she suspects. Or hopes. She can't bring herself to think about more gruesome possibilities. Not that it really matters. Gone is gone.

Phyllis enters, closing the door behind her. "Are you alright?"

"Of course, why?" Laura tries to keep an even tone. With the door shut, the storeroom becomes even more stifling.

"I couldn't find you anywhere." Phyllis stands with her hands on her narrow hips, a mix of concern and irritation on her face. Phyllis and Laura are around the same age. With her short, dark hair and wiry build, Phyllis reminds Laura of a coiled-up spring. They are friendly, but not outside of the hospital.

"I was just in the lav," Laura says, touching her stomach. "Something I ate." Her hand starts to shake, and she stuffs it into her pocket.

"What's that all about?" Phyllis says, pointing.

"Just an old war injury. It flares up sometimes."

Phyllis crouches down to make room on a shelf in a lower cabinet. She uses a box cutter to open a carton of syringes. "Maybe you should see a neurologist."

"Thanks for your concern," Laura says, anxious to change the subject. "It's nothing, really. Is that why you pulled me in here?"

"Actually, I wanted to update you," Phyllis says. "I think they're getting closer to opening the new wing. Maybe right after Labor Day, I'm hearing."

Laura gathers up the crumpled packing material and throws it in the trash barrel. "Not a moment too soon. The ceiling's leaking again in the old post-op area. Even when it's not raining."

Phyllis laughs at this and unloads more white boxes of syringes, stacking them into the cabinet. On the radio, Fats Domino sings "Right from Wrong." His smooth piano and bluesy voice rekindle Laura's sadness. She turns the radio off.

"What about the supervisor job?" Laura asks. Few secrets last long at Charity, and everyone knows Phyllis is advising the hiring committee. She'd already told the staff she wasn't applying for the new position—a lateral move, she'd said.

Phyllis grunts as she slices open the last box of supplies, but doesn't answer.

Laura sits down on a low footstool, her back against a carton. Her face heats up. "Do you know something you're not telling me?"

Phyllis purses her lips. "I shouldn't say anything."

"What? Come on!"

"I heard you're a finalist. But don't tell anyone I said that. It's still not decided."

Laura makes a zipper sign across her lips.

"I've made my recommendation, of course," Phyllis says. "I think you'd make a great supervisor, and you've about reached your limit over here."

It's true. Laura will never be promoted unless she moves out from under Phyllis. "Thanks for that," she says. "I'm sure your word carries weight with the committee."

"They asked me if you planned to get pregnant again," Phyllis says. "I told them I didn't think so. Am I right?"

Laura bites her lip. "No plans."

"That's one reason I was concerned about the shaking," Phyllis points to Laura's hand. "Don't let anyone else see that. You don't want to raise any...unnecessary questions."

"Got it," Laura says. The room is overheated now. She's not sure what kind of questions Phyllis means, but doesn't ask. She'll quit while she's ahead.

Back on the ward, Laura performs her rounds. At her mid-afternoon break, she heads up two flights for a quick smoke. From the roof, she can see all of downtown. There'd been a downpour since she came in this morning, the usual fast-moving New Orleans summer thunderstorm. The worst of the weather seems to have cleared out, and gray clouds race across the bruise-colored sky. On the horizon, it's brighter up by the lake. Traffic crawls through the streets below, the stormwater swirling down into the drains.

The pebbled tarpaper floor is littered with all manner of wet refuse scattered among the puddles—surgical masks, sandwich wrappers, somebody's t-shirt. She takes off her nurse's cap, shaking out her hair, then lights a cigarette and takes a long drag, replaying the conversation with Phyllis and angry all over again that her pregnancy plans should be a consideration in her promotion. She's sure Nicholas has never been asked about fatherhood, though he was the one pushing for a child as soon as they got married. It took a few years, but Laura remembers the unexpected thrill when she found out she was pregnant, even after Charity forced her to leave the job she loved—hospital policy.

Their baby boy lived for only a few minutes after Laura gave birth. He'd come two months early. They'd named him Michael, after the Archangel, the patron saint of soldiers. They wouldn't let her hold him or even see his face. They sent her home, empty-handed. Later, the priest had mumbled a simple blessing before they slid Michael, unbaptized, into the mausoleum. Laura had wanted to follow him, to curl up beside the tiny white coffin, to sleep there forever.

The clouds swirl overhead, and a breeze riffles her hair, which she re-pins under her cap. She looks at her watch and realizes she's overstayed her allotted break time, and she's overdue for her accident room shift. Two more hours before she can clock out. She crushes the cigarette butt under her heel and returns Michael to the hidden chamber of her heart, where she keeps him to herself.

CHAPTER THREE

The accident room is chaotic as usual—ambulance attendants rushing in with patients on stretchers, moaning and occasionally screaming in pain. Others, less severely injured, grumble about sitting too long on the uncomfortable benches in the waiting area. She's grateful to be working days, though. The overnights are far more frantic: knife wounds, gunshots, Bourbon Street revelry gone awry.

Shortly before she's due to clock out, Laura spots a man reading by the window in the ER waiting area. Short hair in a military-style cut, in need of a shave, his left arm gone below the elbow. He's about the right age to have served. A tattoo peeks out from the rolled-up sleeve of his good arm. She has a soft spot for these veterans. They don't get many at Charity; mostly, they go to the VA around the corner. She decides to take one more case before she calls it a day.

She touches him lightly on the shoulder. "Sir? You can follow me."

He looks up from his paperback—Carson McCullers' *The Heart is a Lonely Hunter.* He rises and tucks the book into his back pocket, running a hand across his sandy brown hair. She draws a privacy curtain around them.

"What's the trouble, Mr. Boyer?" she asks, reading his name on the form.

"I'm not sure," he says. "My arm just aches. I can't sleep either. Bad dreams. I was hoping I could get a little something to help." His voice is low and steady, with no accent she can detect. He's not from here.

Her first thought: phantom pain. Her second, he struck out at the VA, looking for drugs. She can smell the alcohol on him.

"Well, let's take one thing at a time, all right? Hop up for me."

He hoists himself up onto the exam table. Laura peels his shirt off. The stump of his injured arm is red and inflamed, clearly infected. "Let's clean this up a bit." She takes her time, swabbing the wound gently with soap and water, aware of him watching her hands. Then she douses cotton batting in alcohol. "This will sting a little."

"It's all right. I know the drill."

She applies antibiotic ointment, then tapes a gauze pad over the stump, and re-pins the empty sleeve. "I'm going to give you some penicillin, just as a precaution."

She rolls up the sleeve of his good arm to administer the shot. She touches her finger to the intricate tattoo: a woman with dark hair spilling from under a Red Cross nurse's cap, her cheeks and lips in a rosy pout. Her dark eyes are full of sorrow. "Who do we have here?"

"Rose of No Man's Land," he says. "I got it on Bourbon Street when I moved here. There was a nurse in the war...long story."

Laura had known some Red Cross nurses in Italy—every bit as brave and capable as the Army nurses. She administers the penicillin shot and puts a band-aid over the injection site. "Where did you fight?"

"In France—Utah Beach. Later, the hedgerows," he whispers. She leans close, hearing the anguish in his voice. "We liberated Periers and St. Lo...then...well, then all hell broke loose. She helped me a lot, that nurse, when I thought...maybe I didn't want to go on like this, you know?"

She does. She fights the urge to tell him about the men just like him she'd seen suffer, about the friends she'd lost over there, about how Frances pulled her through the lowest points. "I can't imagine," she says instead. They're not supposed to share personal information with patients.

"The pain," he says. "Can I get something for it?"

"No prescription, I assume?"

He shakes his head.

How hard it must be to navigate through life with one arm, though he'd reject the pity. Wounded in visible and invisible ways. "Stay here. I'll see what I can do."

She takes a small glass sample bottle of low-dose morphine pills from the medicine supply cabinet. Without a prescription, it's against the rules, but everyone does it. Maybe he's playing her, but if she can ease his suffering, she will.

Back behind the curtain, she tucks the tiny vial into his warm palm. "These are samples. Four of them. Take just one per night." She curls his fingers around the bottle, closing his fist with both her hands. She's startled by his electric blue eyes but holds his gaze. "You shouldn't drink alcohol with them," she adds, releasing her grip.

He rubs his hand across his stubbled growth of beard, his eyes on her name tag. "Thank you, Nurse Bruno."

"And keep that wound clean, OK?"

"Yes, ma'am." He tucks the pill bottle into his shirt pocket. "I'm grateful."

She watches him make his way out. He's well-built, solid, with broad shoulders—the type of man Frances always went for. She can almost hear her quip: *I shoulda gotten his number.*

Laura signs out at the nurse's station. Outside, steam from the earlier rain shower rises off the hot pavement. A bus passes by belching exhaust, adding noxious fumes to the late-summer funk of oily asphalt and rotting vegetation. Nicholas will be working late, so she has a couple of hours to kill. She's exhausted and should just go home and rest, but something about the one-armed veteran has left her unsettled. Just one beer at Joe's Bar, she thinks. To take the edge off. Joe always knows how to make people feel better.

Joe Raviotta's Lounge sits on the first floor of a two-story green stucco building on the corner across from Charity. Inside, Laura's eyes adjust quickly to the dim light and the blue haze of cigarette smoke. The arctic blast of the air conditioning from the big, noisy unit on the wall evaporates the sweat on her skin.

The jukebox in the corner plays Smiley Lewis's "Tee-Nah-Nah." She's comforted by the sticky floor, the warm wood paneling on the walls, and the Christmas garland that stays up year-round. Above the mirrored bar back are two carved wooden signs: *Joe's—An Rx for what Ales You* and *Unescorted Ladies Not Allowed*, underneath which someone has taped a note that says, *Except Charity Nurses*. Everyone from the hospital staff goes to Joe's, even when they're on-call and pretending to drink Coca-Colas.

"Afternoon, cuz," Laura calls to Joe, who's polishing beer mugs behind the bar. They're not really blood relations, but she's known Joe forever. Their fathers are longtime friends from the Italian Club.

"Laura! It's been a while," Joe says. Short and stocky with dark curly hair, he wears wire-frame glasses, the lenses bottle-thick.

She settles onto a barstool. "Too long." She and Nicholas used to be Friday night regulars, but since Nicholas started spending more time at the VFW, they haven't been back much.

"What can I get you?" Joe waggles his bushy eyebrows.

"I'll take your coldest beer, please."

"You got it." Joe pours a bottle of Jax into a frosted mug, then places it in front of Laura on a cardboard coaster featuring a drawing of a scantily-clad woman sitting in a cocktail glass.

Laura doesn't recognize either of the crusty-looking day drinkers sitting at one of the tables. She takes a long sip of the beer. "*Va bene*," she says, already more relaxed.

"How're your folks doing?" Joe asks.

"Fine. The same, I guess. Mama spends a lot of time with Rose's kids when she's not driving Papa crazy at the store."

Joe laughs. "They must be very proud of you, of both you girls." He wipes the counter with a damp rag. "And you? How've you been? You look tired, if you don't mind me saying."

Sweet Joe. "Oh, I'm alright," she says. "A little sad. I just treated a wounded veteran. Made me think of all my pals over there. Some who made it home, some who didn't."

"I hear you. It was frustrating being 4-F," Joe points to his eyeglasses. "I lost a couple of close friends. Your brother, of course." Laura's big brother, Giovanni, was killed in the Pacific back in 1944.

"I thought it would get easier," she says.

"Seems like the sadness goes on, war or no war." Joe's eyes tear up. His mother passed a few months back; Joe broke down crying at the wake.

"It does," she says. "We see it every day at the hospital, of course."

"But it's different when it's people you love."

She wipes a few tears from her own eyes. True, she thinks, and kicks herself for not reaching out to Frances. She could've started over in New Orleans. Charity was always hiring nurses. Maybe if Laura had made more of an effort, she and Frances would be sitting here drinking a beer, side-by-side, right now.

Joe pats her hand. "Life goes on, though, right?"

He moves down the bar to wait on another customer. Laura lights a cigarette and washes the smoke down with the last of her beer. She thinks about the one-armed veteran, who somehow kept going, and Frances, who could not. She fishes a dollar bill out of her purse and leaves it on the bar.

"*Grazie,* Joe," she says, climbing down from the stool. "Give my love to Gert and the boys."

"*Ciao, cara,*" Joe says. "You've got an important job over there. They're lucky to have you."

She makes her way out into the late afternoon glare. For a moment, Joe's words feel like the truth.

CHAPTER FOUR

At home, she finds Nicholas in the kitchen, tie loosened, sorting through some envelopes he's brought in from the mailbox. "I thought you'd beat me home," he says. "Weren't you off at three?"

"Sorry, I got hung up at work," she says. "Late case in the ER." The white lie comes easily. He wouldn't like her drinking alone at Joe's.

"Wish I'd known. I would've waited and caught a ride with you." He removes one letter from the stack and lets out a small grunt.

"What's that?"

"Work," he says vaguely. "I've got poker tonight—I'm going to shower and change." He heads toward the bedroom, taking the envelope with him. He hadn't even kissed her hello.

"Right. Wednesday. Cards," she sighs, trying to keep the shrew out of her voice. It's the second night in a row he's spending with the boys at the VFW. She'd thought she'd break the news to him about Frances, that maybe it would be easier to read her letter together. But now she's glad she'll have the house to herself instead.

Fifteen minutes later, Nicholas comes back into the kitchen, freshly dressed in khaki pants and a blue short-sleeved shirt, his hair damp—without the mystery envelope. He takes the cork out of an open bottle of red wine and pours glasses for them both.

She ladles red sauce onto the pasta and plates it with some leftover *braciola*. "I had a chat with Phyllis today. Sounds like the new ward will be open right after Labor Day."

"That's what I'm hearing, too."

She waits for him to say something about the supervisor position, so she won't have to pry it out of him. But he just keeps eating.

She puts down her fork and sits back. "She said she put in a good recommendation for me."

"Really?"

"You sound surprised."

"Well, you always talk about Phyllis not being very supportive."

She takes a small sip of the wine. She waits again for him to say something encouraging, for him to be on her side.

"I guess we'll see," is all he says before recounting the details of a challenging operation from his day. He finishes eating and leaves his dirty plate on the table. "I'm late," he says, picking up his keys. "Don't wait up."

The growl of the Chevy's motor recedes as Nicholas pulls away. Laura clears the dinner dishes, pours the last of the wine into her glass, and takes it to the bedroom along with her purse.

She washes up and changes into her nightgown, then flicks on her reading lamp. Curling up on the bed, she takes a long sip of the wine. She brushes her hand across the front of Frances's letter, unsure she's ready for whatever is inside. Her left hand trembles as she slides her fingernail under the flap and pulls the letter free. The words are written in different-colored pens, some crossed out and smudged. No date.

Dear Laura,

If you're reading this, it means I'm gone. Wipe those tears off your face, kid. We all have to go sometime, and I've had a more eventful ride than most. Too many years have passed, my friend. I hope you and Nicholas have a houseful of kids by now. He was always kind to me, and I appreciated it—that, and his love for you—one of my happier memories from the war. God knows there weren't enough.

When I first got home, I tried to stay busy, worked hard, and played hard (of course)—at least as much as this backwater Texas town allowed. But after a while, I couldn't help feeling disconnected from everyone—my parents, boyfriends, even you. Maybe I just missed the adrenaline rush, you know what I mean? Back at the front, I knew who I was and why I was there. It sounds crazy, and maybe it is, given how much danger we were in most of the time, but I guess part of me didn't want the war to end. I was even thinking about signing up for Korea, but couldn't get it together.

I know you had your reasons for not responding to my letters after that disaster of a visit to New Orleans, though I won't pretend I wasn't sad about it. You're the best person I know, Laura. I'm sorry I was so terrible to you toward the end, back in Germany. Jealous, I suppose. You were so in love. I'd lost mine. You had a clear future. Mine was murky at best. I hope you can forgive me for that—and for my behavior at Mardi Gras with that moron I was dating.

We had a lot of fun times, too, though, didn't we? I hope you still have the Good Thing. If so, take a swig for me. And never forget: we did the best we could.

All my love,

Frances

Laura lowers the pages into her lap, tears spilling down her cheeks. She reaches into her nightstand for a pack of cigarettes and lights one up. Nicholas will object to the smell later, but she doesn't care. He's not here. She wipes her eyes with the edge of the sheet and thinks about the last time she'd seen Frances, during Carnival over three years ago. Laura had taken time off from work and made all kinds of plans—dinner with her family, parades, beignets at Café Du Monde. One morning, while the boyfriend, whose name Laura had long forgotten, was sleeping off a hangover, she took Frances to Charity. She introduced her around as if she were a visiting celebrity.

Laura was thrilled to have time with Frances, if a little annoyed to have to share her with the lout she'd brought with her, drunk most of the time, loud and obnoxious. He had all kinds of ignorant opinions about New Orleans and wasn't shy about sharing them. The worst part was how Frances would defer to him, almost as if she was afraid he'd leave her and disappear into the Mardi Gras throngs. The Frances she'd known in the war would've told him to go to hell.

Laura held her tongue until the end. "I hope you don't end up with this jerk," Laura said as they walked into the train station. He'd gone ahead of them, not even helping Frances with her suitcase.

Frances glared at her. "Sorry if I embarrassed you in front of your family and friends. We can't all have a fairytale life like you."

"It's not you," Laura said. "Just your poor choice in men."

"I guess some things never change."

Laura touched Frances on the arm. "The point is, you can."

"I didn't mean *me*, Miss High and Mighty," Frances said, shaking her head.

They caught up with the boyfriend, who was impatiently pointing to his wristwatch. After an awkward pause, Frances took his arm. "Goodbye, Laura. Thanks for everything." The boyfriend smirked, and they turned their backs and walked away.

They hadn't spoken since, despite Frances's attempts to reach out with a heartfelt letter of apology. Laura never responded, not even when she got pregnant, thinking that would just be one more accomplishment Frances would resent. She ignored a second letter. Now it's too late. The guilt hits her hard—for not knowing how much pain Frances had been in when she got back from the war, or not wanting to know. She'd written off the best friend she'd ever had. Over what? Too much booze? A stupid boyfriend who probably didn't last the train ride home? There must've been something she could've done to make a difference for Frances, instead of lying to herself that it wouldn't matter. Now she wishes she'd walked back across that burning bridge.

She checks her alarm clock. Nicholas won't be home for another hour at least. She pulls a stool out of the utility closet and steps up to open the attic door in the hallway ceiling. As the rickety stairway unfolds, she swats at dust and cobwebs. Her pulse quickens as she climbs—she hasn't been up there since they moved into the house. The musty smell of mildew and memories makes her gag, and she holds her breath for a moment before hoisting herself the rest of the way into the sweltering space. She bangs her head on the door frame and curses. Her hand gropes in the darkness, then pulls the cord dangling from a naked bulb. The small pool of light does little to illuminate the shadows in the rest of the attic, cluttered with unidentifiable shapes. She pushes aside a few boxes, trying not to think about any vermin who might have made their homes up there.

As her vision adjusts to the dim light, she's surprised by the beautiful white wicker bassinette, never used, glowing in the corner. She'd asked Nicholas to get rid of it. The thought of him carrying it up here while she was recovering in the hospital overwhelms her with sadness.

The corner of her green Army footlocker peeks from under a moth-eaten quilt. She dusts off a wooden ladder-back chair and drags the heavy box over to it in the light, then spreads the quilt on the floor. She puts her hands on the metal, warm from the attic's heat and humidity. Her left hand shakes a little; she closes her eyes. She hasn't looked inside since she packed it up, before shipping home in March of '46.

She opens the lid slowly, as if something might escape, something she can't control. Her dress uniform, pressed and wrapped in tissue paper, sits on the top layer. She takes it out and leaves it folded, placing it gently on the quilt. Her throat tightens at the sight of a bundle of letters from her sister, tied in a pink sateen ribbon. She'd read each one over and over back then. She brings the packet to her nose, imagining she might still smell the lavender fragrance Rose used to spritz on the pages.

A small wooden toy sheep she'd bought at a bazaar in Morocco makes her smile, thinking of those early days. Next to that is a crudely-made angel, cut from a red tin plasma can for a makeshift Christmas decoration in '43. She opens a small wooden box, lined in satin, containing her service medal—they all got one after Anzio. She rubs her forefinger over the bronze depiction of soldiers and a landing craft on one side, an American eagle on the other. A memory threatens to surface: the triage tent quaking while they worked through a bombardment. She refuses it.

Under a May 1945 issue of *Life* magazine, she finds the leather-bound journal Aunt Inez had given her as a going-away present when she shipped out. Laura had scribbled in it throughout the war, details she couldn't write in her letters to Rose or in her postcards and V-mails to her parents. She rubs her hand across the journal's worn brown cover, then leafs through it quickly. The front part— early days in training camp, later in North Africa—is written in neater penmanship. The later pages, written in Italy and Germany, look like random scribblings. She flips to the back of the notebook to find the list of names she'd kept—a grim roster of the men they'd lost in the hospital tents.

As she turns those pages, a small photograph flutters out and lands on the floor. Her breath catches as she holds it up to the dim light. She and Frances, in their bulky fatigues, were leaning back against a jeep, Frances's elbow resting on Laura's shoulder. She was five-nine in stocking feet. *Not counting my hair*, Frances always said. Scrawled in the margin: *December 1943*. Fondi, Laura thinks—a brief respite in the small market town south of Rome. Laura looks at her own younger smile, open-mouthed and wide, no doubt laughing at a joke Frances made just before someone snapped the shutter, the quip long lost to memory. Nobody could crack her up like Frances, before or since.

She tucks the snapshot back inside the journal. She finds a small cloth pouch containing a Virgin Mary medal on a gold chain. Rose had given Laura her own Miraculous Medal the day she shipped out.

To keep you safe, she'd said. Finally, at the bottom of the trunk, under a few old movie magazines, she finds what she's looking for: the small silver flask, engraved with a western-looking filigree design—the Good Thing. When Frances bequeathed it to her at the end of the war, she'd joked that the flask was the root of many bad decisions. But Laura thinks it was a life-saver as well, passed back and forth between them—a spot of relief back when every day was a horror show.

She repacks the trunk, then brings the flask, the medal, and the journal downstairs. In the kitchen, she wets a dishtowel and pats her sweaty face and neck. She unscrews the top of the Good Thing, disappointed not to smell the booze they drank from it. She rinses it out, then carefully fills the flask with vodka from a bottle they've kept in the freezer forever. She wets the corner of a dish towel and pats her sweaty face and neck.

Back in her bedroom, she opens the journal to an entry from early in the war, shortly after her unit landed in North Africa. She'd been so naïve then, so innocent. She takes a swig from the Good Thing and coughs. It's been a while since she's had stiff stuff. She takes another swallow. Her throat is on fire, but the pain feels true, like what she deserves. She'd broken the first rule of combat—never leave a fallen comrade behind.

PART TWO

North Africa, 1943

CHAPTER FIVE

.

The night before they landed on the Algerian coast, the nurses of the 48th Evacuation Hospital waited offshore, terrified and clinging to one another. They'd been told the Axis forces might be lying in wait for them and that there could be some live fire. Laura joined in with some of the other Catholic girls as they recited the Rosary while the men of the First Division went ashore.

Just before dawn, the guns started booming; the noise was monstrous. "This is it, ladies," Captain McCarthy shouted. "You're about to be part of history."

The landing craft pulled up alongside their transport and hooked a ladder to the side of their ship. "Unbuckle your chinstraps and leave your boots untied," an enlisted man shouted over the crashing waves and explosions from the beach. "If you go overboard, dump everything. Try to save yourself."

"Go, go, go," Captain McCarthy said, guiding each of them by the shoulders. One by one, they climbed down the swaying ladder onto the deck of the smaller boat, pitching in the waves.

The boat swung its ramp down into the surf as they approached the beach, then they waded ashore in waist-deep water. Laura struggled to hold her pack over her head, determined to keep the clothes, books, and all her worldly possessions inside dry. Soldiers carried some of the prettier girls to shore—one of them picked Frances up like she was a rag doll and threw her over his shoulder. She waved as Laura kept slogging.

That night, they bivouacked on the beach and hunkered down, wet and miserable, too scared to even be hungry. The guns raged all night, frighteningly close. Laura stayed glued to Frances and dozed off once or twice from sheer exhaustion, but couldn't sleep for more than a few minutes at a time.

At dawn, the nurses climbed into trucks and set off for their first encampment—50 officers, 60 nurses, 275 enlisted men, equipment, and supplies. A hot, dusty wind swirled around their convoy, sometimes threatening to swallow them up altogether.

"At least it's a dry heat," Laura said, thinking of the oppressively humid New Orleans summers.

"That's what the witch told Hansel and Gretel," Frances said.

Some of the girls had spread items of wet clothing on the truck railings to catch the sun. The parched, sepia-toned landscape unfolded behind them: beige dunes, darker mountains in the distance, making Laura think of the Old Testament stories she'd learned as a girl. Pharaohs and Israelites. Moses and the Red Sea. The occasional palm trees reminded her of home.

When they arrived at Arzew, Frances jumped out of the truck and spat onto the ground. "Grit in my teeth," she said. Laura felt it too; sand had made its way into her eyes and hair. With the help of a couple of enlisted men, they pitched a four-person tent with their new tent-mates, Mildred and Avis. Mildred immediately endeared herself by lighting sandalwood incense to cover up the aroma of their unwashed bodies and the stench already emanating from the latrines.

A siren wailed, waking Laura from a deep sleep. She was disoriented for a few seconds in the pitch dark of the tent, still wearing the rumpled fatigues she'd had on when she lay down. She'd slept for two hours after dinner; she could sleep another twenty-two. Her spine ached from the hours on the back of the truck. She'd been in the war less than a week and hadn't seen much action yet, but already she couldn't imagine how she'd make it for the duration.

"What time is it?" she mumbled.

Frances clicked on a penlight. "Nine o'clock," she said, looking at her watch. "P.M."

Mildred and Avis's cots were made up, their belongings neatly tucked underneath. Laura swung her legs over the side of her own cot, hunching her sore shoulders up and down to loosen them up. "What was that alarm about?"

Frances stepped into her boots. "I don't know, but that siren interrupted a perfectly good dream. Me and Donny were just getting to the good part."

Frances's fiancé, Donny, was fighting in the Pacific. Laura was pretty sure Frances worried about him more than she let on. "I feel like death warmed over," Laura said.

Frances shone the tiny light on Laura's face. "You look fresh as a daisy. Run a comb through that hair, and you're good to go. You might want some of this, though." She tossed a tin of tooth powder to Laura.

"Thanks." Laura brushed her teeth with her finger and rinsed the grit with a swig from her canteen, pushing aside the tent flap to spit.

They walked through the dark camp, the silent desert night already cooling the day's sweat. Laura kept her hand on Frances's elbow to keep from stumbling over tent pegs. They'd been thrown together in neighboring bunks at training camp. Frances grew up outside Fort Worth, Texas, with strict Baptist parents— "holy rollers," she called them: no drinking, no smoking, no dancing. In the Sicilian enclave of New Orleans's French Quarter, where Laura was raised, there was never a shortage of wine, cigarettes, and music. And yet it was Frances who seemed bold and worldly-wise. Audacious. She seemed determined to make up for everything she missed in her sheltered upbringing, and to bring Laura along for the ride.

The temperature had plummeted since sunset, and the night breeze carried the earthy scent of sand and dust along with a slight fragrance of sagebrush. So different from New Orleans, where the jasmine and sweet olive perfumed the muggy air, streetcars rattling by, fruit and vegetable peddlers with their mule-drawn carts clip-clopping down cobbled streets. The cacophony of home.

Inside the cavernous, dimly-lit triage tent, stations were set up along the sides—instrument trays next to each bed, IV poles, rolling carts with shelves, portable lights, and units of plasma ready to go. Their unit was joining a group of nurses, doctors, and enlisted men the departing 56th Evacuation Hospital had to leave behind to tend to patients who couldn't be moved. She and Frances jostled their way through the crowd to get closer to the front, where Mildred and Avis stood near Captain McCarthy.

Mildred was short and solidly built, with a round face, a blunt chin, and brown hair she kept pulled up in a bun. Avis was tall and lean, with slim hips, a prominent nose, and short, dirty-blond curls. "Mutt and Jeff," Frances called them, after the cartoon characters. Laura was shocked when she said they were a couple and had been together since training camp. Laura didn't think she'd ever met any lesbians, though a few girls from her Catholic school days came to mind. Not to mention some of the nuns.

Captain McCarthy clapped her hands together, and the women stopped their chatter. "Ladies, ladies…settle down now. I've had a briefing from the Colonel."

A tough-talking New Yorker, Bridget McCarthy had field experience, having served as a young nurse in the Great War. She reminded Laura of her old high school principal, Sister Mary Arnold: tough but fair. Laura and Frances had been with her unit since day one of training. They proudly considered themselves "McCarthy's Girls."

Captain McCarthy clapped her hands again. "Listen up. Here's what we know. The good guys have Casablanca surrounded, but the field hospital there is overloaded. They're shipping some casualties to us, so, those of you in triage: don't get bogged down. Remember your training: solve your worst problem first. Assess, bind up anything gaping, stop obvious bleeding, and move 'em over to surgical or off to recovery if they can hang on."

She pointed to a stocky young man with dark hair standing in the back. "Freddy Gomez over there's your chief medic." The man raised his hand and waved. "Freddy and his crew are here to run supplies and transport the patients, along with the litter-bearers. If you're real nice to him, he'll bring you a Coca-Cola."

The women chuckled. Laura made a note to remember Freddy's name. Back at Charity, she'd always gone out of her way to befriend the orderlies. They worked hard but got so little recognition. It couldn't be too much different here.

"We have twenty doctors in triage and fifteen in the surgery tent. They've been reminded you are fellow officers, not maids," McCarthy said. "And just to save you the speculation, they're all married." More laughter rose from the nurses. "Seriously, though. I have high expectations for you all. You're trained professionals, you're ready. The wounded men coming in tonight are counting on you. They've done their part. Now we *do our jobs*. Understood?"

"Yes, ma'am," the nurses mumbled.

"I didn't hear that. What are we going to do?"

"Our jobs!" the women shouted in unison.

"How many of you are on your first night of duty?" About half the hands went up, including Laura's and her tent-mates. "Those of you who've been through it, I want you to pick a partner from the newbies." Nobody moved. "I mean NOW!"

Frances paired off with another nurse and gave Laura a little wave, mouthing, "Good luck."

A tall nurse with brunette curls framing a pretty face extended her hand to Laura, smiling brightly. "I'm Ellen Ainsworth. I was with the 56th Evac, but I'll be sticking around here for now. I have a whole two weeks under my belt. Where you from?"

"Laura Marino. From New Orleans. Nice to meet you."

"New Orleans! That sounds like a lot more fun than Glenwood City, Wisconsin."

"I've only ever worked trauma in the ER back home." Laura pictures the clean, brightly lit emergency ward back at Charity, bustling with all manner of locals and tourists having a bad night. She'd taken it all for granted. Now those days belonged to another lifetime.

"Yeah...it's not going to be like that," Ellen said, leading Laura to their station. "Just stay in the moment and try not to flip your wig. Let's get our bandages ready."

The scene in the triage tent reminded Laura of her nursing school days, before the old Charity Hospital had been rebuilt. "Looks pretty primitive," she said.

"Hah! This is the lap of luxury compared to where I was a few weeks ago," Ellen said. "Out with a mobile unit. We were making dressings out of ripped shirts at one point."

They rolled their bandages into neat rows and inspected their station. The instruments were the same as they were at home, only in a tent. Laura told herself she could do this and felt her heart rate slow a bit. After all, she'd been a star student at Charity Nursing School, and a model employee for a year after that. Captain McCarthy was counting on her; the boys were, too.

"Let's go get a breath of air while we can," Ellen said.

They stepped outside into the crisp darkness. Muffled sounds of fighting echoed from beyond the mountains. Ellen waved a pack of cigarettes, "Want one?"

"No, thanks," Laura said. She jammed her hands into her pockets against the cold. "I don't smoke."

Ellen lit a cigarette, cupping her hand to hide the flame. She choked out a laugh and a smoky cough at the same time. "You will."

The *BOOM BOOM BOOM* of distant fire echoed across the mountains, followed by flashes of light illuminating the jagged peaks.

Laura had thought so much about what the war would be like. She'd heard stories, but now it was real.

"Artillery," Ellen said. "Big guns. They're going to tear some things up."

Laura had seen photographs of the various weapons and the wounds they would inflict during her training. The men would be coming at any moment. Suddenly, she doubted she had even a fraction of the medical knowledge she needed to be here.

A different sound reverberated from the desert: *rat-a-tat* in rapid succession. Laura looked at Ellen, raising one eyebrow.

"Giant machine guns." Ellen patted her on the back. "Don't worry. You'll get to know them all. A real symphony of destruction the Krauts put together."

Laura marveled at Ellen's calm attitude. She couldn't imagine this becoming routine. A flash from a distant explosion lit up the camp briefly, and Ellen's face was visible in full, her jaw set, her eyes closed. Three ambulances approached, fishtailing in the sand with their headlights dimmed.

Ellen flicked the butt of her cigarette to the ground. "Here we go."

CHAPTER SIX

"Showtime, ladies," Captain McCarthy shouted. Ten stations lined each wall of the canvas triage tent, a supply station at the far end. "Gloves and masks."

Laura and Ellen found their station, and Ellen did a quick survey of the equipment. She tucked a pencil behind her ear and handed one to Laura. "Sometimes the medics mark the triage tags, and we just confirm or update them," Ellen said. "If there's nothing, we have to categorize them: red for heavy bleeding, open fractures, critical internal injuries. We send those to surgery. Yellow for the serious but stable. Green for minor wounds and abrasions." The final category, black, was for those with injuries so severe they were unlikely to survive. It had all seemed so simple and organized back in triage training—now it was anything but.

A doctor approached them. "Isidor Tolpin," he said, holding up his gloved hands and pointing his masked chin at the nurses. "Good to see you, Ellen. Who do we have here?"

"Laura Marino, from the 48th," Ellen said. "It's her first time."

"Well, then," Dr. Tolpin said. "We'll try to go easy on you." The crinkles around his eyes and wisps of gray hair peeking out from his cap were reassuring.

The ambulances made a racket as they pulled up outside—no sirens like at home, but a loud grinding of gears, then shouts. The tent flaps suddenly opened, and litter-bearers began carrying patients in on stretchers. Six. A dozen. Laura lost count. Dr. Tolpin motioned for a litter-bearer to help transfer a yellow-coded man from a stretcher onto their station bed. "Cut away the uniform," the doctor said in a low, steady voice. "I'll be back." The six doctors in triage worked multiple stations, rotating as the nurses processed the incoming wounded.

Laura used a pair of surgical scissors to gently snip away the man's tattered shirt where shreds of cloth had worked their way into a jagged gash on his chest. The wound was not too deep, but he'd lost a lot of blood.

"It hurts like hell," he groaned in fear and pain. "One minute, I was fine. I picked off at least four Krauts, then the next thing I knew: BOOM, like a hot poker."

Ellen leaned over and pressed his shoulders down firmly. "I've got you, soldier," she said in a soothing tone. "We're going to take good care of you."

While Ellen started an IV infusion of plasma, Laura flushed the wound with saline, then took a damp cloth and wiped the area around the laceration. She poured hydrogen peroxide onto a large piece of cotton. "This is going to sting. Ready?"

"Ready," the soldier said, squeezing his eyes shut and gripping the table on either side of him. Laura patted the cotton directly onto the edges of the wound. He inhaled sharply through gritted teeth. "God damn."

Between patients, there was a commotion as an IV pole toppled over and someone shrieked. A nurse lay on the floor, surrounded by broken glass, and fluids forming a pool beneath her. The nurse was part of their unit, a quiet mouse of a girl, so timid that Laura had never heard her speak. Captain McCarthy knelt by the girl, patting her on the back. She sat up, sobbing loudly, and the Captain quickly got her to her feet and out of the tent as two enlisted men cleaned up the mess.

"Hope she's OK," Laura said, feeling the girl's pain.

Ellen kept cleaning up their station, readying the instruments for the next patient. "Better to weed her out now if she can't handle it," Ellen said.

Before Laura could respond, a grim-faced medic brought them another man to assess. Laura drew a deep breath. His legs were missing from the thighs down. Laura put her fingers on his wrist and counted. "Weak pulse," she said, reading the patient's tag. "Code red."

Ellen shook her head. She changed "red" to "black." Laura swallowed hard as the litter-bearer took the man away. Ellen patted her shoulder. "No sense wasting medication or time, cruel as that sounds," she said. "Catch and release."

Laura waited for more of an explanation, but Ellen remained quiet as she prepared the suture tray for the next patient. It all seemed so subjective, so arbitrary. What made Ellen, or any of them, qualified to decide who got help and whose life would end right there, in a triage tent in the middle of a foreign desert?

The rest of the night passed in a blur. Patients came across their table far faster than the Charity ER on a busy Saturday night. Laura and Ellen worked with Doctor Tolpin to patch torn-up arms and bellies and prepped two men for amputations before sending them off to surgery. Laura's stomach lurched at the first few gruesome wounds they treated. Twice the stench of infections drove her outside the tent to retch. She heard more than one deep sigh from Dr. Tolpin when she ran from the bedside, bile rising uncontrollably in her throat. Captain McCarthy came out to check on her the first time. "You all right, Nurse Marino?" Laura managed a nod. It was a lie. She was mortified to have abandoned the patient, but couldn't control her stomach.

Back at her station, Laura apologized to the doctor. Ellen's eyes were kind over her mask. "Just keep going. Focus," she told Laura.

The man on the stretcher before them appeared perfectly fine: no marks on his body, a slight smile, his eyes open wide. Laura waved her hand in front of his face; he didn't blink. "Is he hurt or not?" she whispered.

"Blast wave from an explosion. The pressure rattles the brain. Shell-happy."

Laura wondered if the man could hear them, whether he'd snap out of it at some point, or whether he'd have long-term problems. "What can we do for him?"

Ellen marked an "M" on a patient's forehead so they could keep track of who'd already had morphine. "Nothing. He just needs to rest. Shock ward."

The parade of stretchers slowed to a trickle just as the dawn light leaked through the tent flaps. Ellen snapped off her bloody gloves and threw them in a pile to be washed and reused—nothing went to waste here if they could help it. Laura did the same, putting her hand on the small of her aching lower back.

"Had enough?" Ellen asked.

"More than enough," Laura said. "Are we done?"

They glanced over at Captain McCarthy, who was assisting another doctor across the room. She made a shooing motion with her hand.

Outside the mess tent, Ellen shook a cigarette from her pack. A rosy glow lit up the mountains on the horizon. A mournful chant floated on the breeze and caught Laura by surprise, the otherworldly music a welcome break from the gunfire.

"The Muslim call to prayer," Ellen anticipated her question. "Must be a mosque in a nearby village."

"Is it like this every night?" Laura asked, trying to keep the panic out of her voice. She couldn't imagine being back here in just a few hours to do it all over again.

"Well, not *every* night." Ellen took a drag. "Don't worry, you get used to it."

"I threw up twice."

"Next time you won't." Ellen exhaled and tried to wave the smoke out of Laura's face. "Sorry."

"It's OK," Laura said. The tobacco scent reminded her of her Aunt Inez, who always had a cigarette going; Laura was hit with a jab of homesickness.

"Let's get some breakfast," Ellen said.

"All I want to do is collapse on my bunk."

"You won't sleep," Ellen said. "Trust me. You need to eat and to get your heart rate down a bit. Otherwise, you'll toss and turn."

The mess tent buzzed with personnel. Some were fresh and ready for the day shift; others looked as rough as Laura felt, sticky with sweat, her uniform stained with various bodily fluids. She re-twisted her hair and pinned it back into its bun. The first chance she got, she'd have it cut short like Ellen's.

They picked up powdered eggs and cold toast in the chow line. Frances filed in, and the three of them sat together. Ellen and Frances began chatting, comparing notes. Laura half-listened and picked at her food. People around her were just going about their day, laughing and joking, eating their breakfast as if they hadn't all just been through the wringer.

Frances was eating with gusto, talking with her mouth full. "I think I was made for this. Is that crazy? Blood and guts everywhere, guys moaning in pain. But some were on their way to getting better. In a million years, I'd never have a night like that back in Fort Worth."

Laura was startled. It was as if Frances was speaking in tongues. She sounded so excited; meanwhile, all Laura could think about was that she'd made a terrible mistake by enlisting.

"The rookie high," Ellen said, taking a swig of coffee. "I felt the same way my first night. Hold onto that energy—you'll need it when the adrenaline rush wears off."

"It's like everything I've learned was just…" Frances paused, "A rehearsal for this."

"We barely treated some of those guys before moving them along," Laura said, sharper than she meant to. "And we lost three." She pulled sheets up over their still faces, then filled out their death certificates, their names seared into her memory.

"Just toughen up and don't get sent home," Frances said. "Y'all saw that girl lose it?"

Laura pictured the young nurse, her uncontrollable sobs.

"I've seen a couple of people get sent home already," Ellen said. "It happens fast. You can either handle it, or you can't."

Laura shuddered, thinking of her own retching. She couldn't let that happen again. Even if she doubted her choice, the thought of being sent home was unbearable. It would only prove her mother right. *Never*, she told herself.

They stood and cleared their trays, then headed out into the morning, the sun well above the horizon now and the desert heat creeping into camp. "Time for some shut-eye," Ellen said, heading off with a wave. "Catch you later, ladies."

Back in their tent, Ellen's words replayed in Laura's head as she got undressed in the dim light coming through the tent seams. Mildred and Avis weren't back yet. "What if I'm not cut out for this?"

Frances lay on her cot and pulled her blanket up to her chin. "So you yacked a couple of times. It's not the end of the world," she said. "The only way through it is to put the last shift in a box and move on. Like the soldiers have to."

Laura wasn't sure she had any of those boxes. "Do you know if they sent that girl home?"

Frances yawned. "What I know is that it'll never be me."

"Me neither," Laura whispered. Her mother had been dead set against her enlisting. *Your place is here with us. Besides, you'll never find a husband that way.* The day she shipped out, her mother had refused to come see her off. On the dock, her father had pulled her and Rose into a sweaty hug, tears in his eyes. Thinking about it now, she could almost smell his cigar and feel the softness of her sister's blouse. She'd waved to them from the top deck, still searching for her mother in the crowd below as the crew threw off the lines and the big ship slid into the brown churn of the Mississippi.

Frances was asleep in minutes. Laura couldn't stop thinking about the three boys who'd died on her table. She pulled out a penlight and held it in her teeth so she could see to inscribe their names in the back of her journal. She offered up a small prayer for them; it was the least she could do. She thought about her brother Giovanni, somewhere in the Pacific. She hoped he wouldn't be a hero, going down in a blaze of glory. She wished for him a superficial wound, a code green, just enough to get him off the front line for a little while.

She took a deep breath of the cool night air. It struck her that there were only two routes home: failing as a nurse or winning the war. She prayed for the latter and fell into an exhausted sleep.

CHAPTER SEVEN

In early April, news filtered in through the *Stars and Stripes* and Armed Forces Radio that the British Eighth Army had won a significant skirmish at Wadi Akarit in Tunisia. Allied air strikes were hitting Axis aircraft and supply ships traveling from Sicily, putting a dent in the enemy's resupply efforts. Every positive report buoyed morale in Laura's unit.

After a third move, their convoy, traveling through the desert to keep up with the troops, the 48th Evac Hospital settled in about 12 kilometers from Tabarka, Tunisia. The work was no less horrific, but the unit fell into a rhythm of around-the-clock shifts when the casualties came in, followed by stretches of boredom and longing for home. Laura had grown more confident that she could handle the work. She'd stopped throwing up, no matter how gruesome the wounds. The list of names at the back of her journal grew with each shift. She wrote to her sister when she could, but struggled to put it all into words.

Laura and Frances emerged from the mess tent after dinner, walking with Mildred. The sky was thick with stars, the springtime air perfumed with the scent of desert flowers blooming among the sand and rocks. The faint boom of artillery sounded in the distance. They'd been in the desert for a month now, and Laura was no longer panic-stricken every time she heard the sounds of battle.

"Any word from Donny?" Mildred asked Frances. Frances's fiancé had been officially listed as missing in action in the Philippines. She'd gotten the V-mail from Donny's mother a couple of weeks back, and it shook them all up. Laura couldn't help thinking about Giovanni, somewhere in the Pacific; Rose's last letter said they hadn't heard from him in a while. The not knowing troubled her mind.

Frances lit a cigarette. "I've pretty much given up hope. It's a safe bet he's dead, and I'm not going to wait around for some official news."

"You can't know that, Frances," Mildred said. "Don't give up."

"People turn up. There's a lot of confusion over there, I'm sure," Laura said. She'd never had a fiancé, or even a boyfriend, but she couldn't imagine losing hope that easily. She knew what Frances was doing, putting Donny in a box so she wouldn't have to feel the pain of his absence. "He might be OK."

"Maybe. And if he's alive, we'll get hitched when we both get back home, and that will be that. Donny, or someone like him, I guess. I'll quit nursing and start pumping out babies."

Laura wasn't sure if Frances was being sarcastic. "Well, no sense planning that far ahead, I guess." Laura wondered if that's what she'd do too, post-war. She struggled to picture her life in the future—most days it felt like the war would last forever. The only thing she knew for sure was that she'd always be a nurse.

Frances pulled on her cigarette. "All we can do is live our lives. That's all we have."

Captain McCarthy came up behind them. "Party's over, ladies. Just got word. The ambulances are only ten kilometers away. Marino—I want you with me in surgery tonight with Doctor Pierce. Frances—triage. Tell Mavis, I need them in shock." Everyone had adopted Frances's pet name for Mildred and Avis together; they didn't seem to mind.

They watched as Captain McCarthy walked toward the surgical tent. Frances sucked the last of the smoke from her cigarette before throwing the stub to the ground. "Sounds like you've been promoted," she said to Laura.

"Or she just wants to keep an eye on me." Laura hadn't yet done a rotation in surgery. The stories she'd heard from the other nurses made it sound even more harrowing than triage.

"You'll be fine," Frances said. A bomb exploded on the horizon, sending a flash of light into the dark sky. "I'll go pass the word to Mavis. Good luck."

The ambulances began to arrive as Laura walked to her assignment, tires crunching over the rock and sand, disgorging all manner of wounded men. The litter-bearers quickly formed a grim assembly line, moving the patients into triage. Frances would have her hands full.

In the surgical tent, the generators hummed behind the clink of metal instruments and the whoosh of the ether machines starting up. Doctors and nurses murmured to each other. Laura's mind clicked through the checklist: clear the pathways, secure the blackout curtains, sterilize the equipment, wipe down the table. She touched her fingers to her wrist, willing her pulse to slow, then pulled on her mask and gloves.

Dr. Wayne Pierce stood at the far end of the tent, preparing his station. He was tall and lean, with a blond buzz cut. Frances had called him "a tough customer."

"I'm Laura Marino. Captain McCarthy sent me over," Laura said.

Pierce's icy gray eyes flashed above his mask. Before he could speak, two litter-bearers carried in their first patient and started to lift him onto the surgical table. "Hold up," Pierce said. He pushed at the patient's arm, his flesh torn but not actively bleeding. "Just needs sutures. Send him back to triage. Why didn't they just handle it?" he asked nobody in particular.

The soldier's eyes widened. "Enough to get me a ticket home, doc?"

Pierce shook his head. "Sorry, pal. Not your lucky day." He motioned for the litter-bearers to take the man.

Freddy Gomez brought in the next patient, a bloody stump where his left leg should have been. Captain McCarthy was right behind them. The man on the stretcher thrashed and shouted. "Give it back. What did you do with my leg? I can't go home to Jenny like this!"

Laura took his hand, tamping down her own terror in an effort to calm him.

"I need your hands on the instruments, nurse," Pierce barked at Laura. She knew his edge was part of what made Pierce effective—the Charity surgeons were notoriously difficult. Still, what would it cost him to be kind?

Captain McCarthy pointed at the empty surgical table. "On three."

Laura helped Freddy lift the wounded man and inhaled sharply, hoping the patient hadn't heard her gasp. "Doctor?" she said, nodding at the stretcher, soaked with dark blood where the soldier's back had been. Clearly, he had another wound, perhaps even worse than the mangled leg.

"I see it," Pierce said.

The soldier grabbed the fabric of Captain McCarthy's uniform. "Someone needs to find my leg, sister!" The Catholic boys often mistook the nurses in their white caps for nuns.

Captain McCarthy put her hand on the man's shoulder, pressing him down to the table as he squirmed. "Lie still, son. Dr. Pierce is gonna get you fixed up," she said in a firm, calm voice that Laura wished she had.

The anesthesiologist placed the mask over the patient's nose and mouth as Laura adjusted the IV, pumping saline into his arm. Within seconds, the soldier's contorted face went calm, his eyes fluttering closed.

Pierce worked quickly to cut away the damaged tissue around the bloody stump, frown lines on his forehead. "What a mess," he murmured under his breath. He worked fast, trying to stanch the bleeding, which only seemed to get worse.

The soldier's face grew pale. Pierce touched the man's throat, then threw his instruments down on the metal tray. "Fucking triage. This guy should've been black-coded." He stripped off his gloves and stalked away, rubbing the back of his neck.

Laura checked the soldier's dog tags and motioned to the chaplain, who was standing nearby. "Catholic, Father," she said. Tall and lanky, Father Bill Neenan was a comforting and familiar presence in his Roman collar and wire-rimmed glasses. The priest took rosary beads, oil, and a small, black, worn leather Bible out of his pocket. "Through this holy anointing, may the Lord in his love and mercy help you with the grace of the Holy Spirit." He made the sign of the cross with his thumb on the man's forehead. "May the Lord who frees you from sin save you and raise you up." He kissed the crucifix dangling from the rosary beads.

Laura blessed herself, whispering, "Amen." She'd spoken with Father Bill in the canteen between shifts. He'd told her about his work as a Jesuit college chaplain in St. Louis, and she told him about her family's church in the French Quarter. Laura felt for him. He spent so many hours on his feet blessing the nearly dead—or sometimes the freshly dead—witnessing the worst of what God's children did to hurt each other with no one to confide in except God Himself.

A nurse called out from across the room, her voice shrill. "Father, we need you over here! Quickly." The chaplain patted Laura's shoulder, then wound his way through the tables to the other side of the tent.

Freddy Gomez appeared at Laura's elbow. "Freddy, please take...," she said, checking the soldier's dog tags again and committing his name to memory for her journal. "...Private Horrigan to the morgue."

Freddy blessed himself. *"Dios lo bendiga,"* he said.

Laura gathered the bloody bandages, wiped down the table with alcohol, and placed the instruments into the sterilizing autoclave. She changed her gloves. There was no time to mourn. The noise level had risen—doctors barked commands, wounded men groaned, sometimes crying out above the *woosh-woosh* of the ether machines and the clatter of stretchers.

"Check his vitals," the medic told Laura out of the corner of his mouth before they hefted the man from the stretcher to the surgical table. Laura held the soldier's wrist and timed his pulse with her watch. Weak and thready, though he was still conscious, writhing in his tattered uniform, singed around a shrapnel wound to his belly. A bloody bandage covered his eyes, but she could see olive skin at his throat and dark stubble on his cheeks. A tarnished Saint Christopher medal—just like the one Giovanni wore—hung on the dog tag chain around his neck.

She felt the tent spin, losing her count on his pulse. *It can't be him,* she told herself. She took a couple of deep breaths, her chest constricting. *It can't be. Giovanni is in the Pacific, not North Africa.* Gently, she removed the bandage and exhaled—his eyes were blue.

The anesthesiologist tried to administer the ether, but the soldier pushed his hand away with surprising force. He gripped Laura's wrist. "Am I gonna die?"

"Not today, soldier," she said, her voice a little shaky. "Try to relax."

The patient closed his eyes and breathed in the ether. Laura kept her fingers on his wrist; his pulse became a little steadier. With his eyes closed, he looked so much like her brother. She willed herself not to cry. *"Santo Giovanni,* keep him safe," she said aloud, not sure if the prayer was for this soldier or her brother. Perhaps herself.

"He's under, doc," the anesthesiologist called to Pierce, who'd been consulting with another doctor nearby.

Pierce stepped over, holding up his gloved hands. "Nurse Marino, are you with us? Marino?"

Laura let go of the patient's wrist. "Yes, sir. Sorry."

"IV," Pierce ordered, shifting his weight from foot to foot like a boxer preparing to fight.

Laura hung an IV, then dabbed the back of the soldier's hand with a cotton ball soaked in alcohol, wiping away dirt and blood to find a vein. She missed the first stab. "Dammit," she whispered. She'd done this procedure hundreds of times, both at Charity and here.

"Again," Pierce said. "Focus, for Chrissake." Pierce began the incision around the gut wound.

Laura slid the IV needle in easily this time, but the flesh where she'd missed was already bruising. No doubt the least of this man's problems, but even so, she was embarrassed.

A mortar round landed close by and shook the tent so hard she had to hold onto the IV line to keep it from ripping out of the patient's hand. Pierce halted mid-incision, waiting for the rocking to stop before continuing to work on the boy's stomach. "Retractor," he barked as he cut away the damaged tissue to get to the shrapnel. Laura was there with the instrument, but it slipped, and she jabbed it in the wrong place before correcting herself.

"*Now, dammit!*" He picked pieces of shot out of the patient's wound with surgical tweezers and threw them in a metal bowl with a clang. "And do something about this mess," he gestured with his scalpel.

Laura reached in with a ball of gauze on the end of long silver tongs to dab up the blood. She couldn't stay out of the doctor's way, though, only making it worse.

Pierce pulled back from the patient and glared at Laura. "Step back."

"I've got this, Doctor," Laura stammered.

"You *don't* have this," Pierce said, so loudly that several heads turned around the room. "Step *back* before this boy bleeds out. Captain McCarthy," he yelled across the tent. "Get someone competent over here."

Laura pulled away, horrified. Captain McCarthy walked over quickly and placed a hand on her back. "Step in, Nurse Marino." Her voice was calm but urgent.

"I *said*—," Pierce started to object.

"Later," Captain McCarthy held up a hand. "Let's remember why we're here," she pointed her chin at the man on the table. "What do you need, doctor?"

"Number two," he said.

Laura already had the suture and needle ready and handed them over. She was in awe of Captain McCarthy. She'd defused the situation in seconds and refocused Pierce. If McCarthy were a man, she'd be in charge of the whole war, like Patton. And they'd already be winning.

When Pierce finished stitching the wound, he stepped away without a word. Laura checked the soldier's pulse—almost back to normal—one of the lucky ones.

CHAPTER EIGHT

When things slowed enough for a break, Laura found Frances outside the mess tent, smoking a cigarette. Bombs were still exploding, farther away now but still lighting up the sky. Soft booms echoed, a few beats behind the flashes, almost like fireworks.

"Give me one of those," Laura said.

"You smoke now?" Frances asked, one eyebrow raised. She held out the red and white pack of Lucky Strikes.

Laura put the cigarette to her lips, and Frances sparked the flame. Laura drew down the hot smoke and immediately started coughing.

"Whoa there, cowgirl," Frances said. "Take it slow."

Between puffs and coughs, Laura recapped her confrontation with Pierce, leaving out the part where she froze up and started praying audibly.

Captain McCarthy approached, silencing the story. "Ladies," she said.

Frances shook out a cigarette, lighting it for the Captain. McCarthy took a deep drag and exhaled a small ring of smoke. Lights flashed on the dark horizon.

Laura flicked the ash off as she'd seen Frances do. "Thanks for stepping in back there, ma'am. I'm sorry you had to, but he was being so unreasonable." She wondered how many times the Captain had dealt with jerks like Pierce in her long career.

Captain McCarthy took another pull. "That may be true. But he's a damn fine surgeon. Don't forget that."

Laura felt her face flush. Frances avoided her eyes.

"I can't control *him*," McCarthy said. "But I expect my nurses to be able to take a little heat. Just do your job. Understood?"

Lights flashed in the distance; Laura felt the booms in her throat. "Yes, ma'am." She pressed her lips together around the cigarette but didn't inhale. Embarrassment twisted in her guts. The Captain's words stung. She'd always been at the top of her class, a teacher's pet.

"I love you girls," McCarthy said. "But the soldiers come first. This is war. You're a good nurse, Marino. It's why I had you step in. Still, I won't hesitate to pull you off a shift if I think you can't handle it. I've sent nurses home, as you know. Nobody wants that, but I *will* do it."

Frances didn't say a word. Laura flung the rest of her cigarette to the ground, thinking of that young nurse who'd broken down their first night in triage, who'd been shipped out without so much as a goodbye. She wanted to protest, to tell McCarthy she'd been momentarily distracted by the soldier who looked so much like Giovanni, but there was no point. Excuses wouldn't matter.

"Understood?" McCarthy asked.

"Yes, ma'am," Laura managed.

"All right then. Shake it off and go get a cup of joe," McCarthy said, motioning with her cigarette toward the canteen entrance. "Then head over to post-op. Sorry, but I need you both to work another shift."

"What the hell?" Laura said once the Captain was out of earshot.

"Coffee," Frances said.

The canteen was mostly empty now, just a couple of enlisted men playing cards at a battered wooden table in the corner. Frances and Laura sat down with their tin mugs. Laura wrapped her hands around the cup, absorbing the warmth in her fingers. "I *hate* that man," she said, unable to keep her outrage inside for another minute. "Such a bully. He acts like he's king of the world."

Frances stirred some powdered milk into her coffee, turning it gray. "The Captain's right, though. When he has that scalpel in his hand, he *is* the king."

Laura sat up straight and took a sip of her black coffee. She'd have given anything for a little sugar to cut the bitterness. "You weren't there. He treated me like dirt. And the Captain gives *me* a hard time?"

Frances held up her hand like a stop sign. "Keep your cool, kid. Pick your battles. Here on the front, out there in the world. They're in charge, like it or not."

Laura shook her head. One of her teachers in nursing school used to say. *It's the surgeon who saves a man's life, but it's the nurse who helps him to live.* "It's not fair. They couldn't do this without us."

"No, they couldn't. But this isn't about what's fair. It's about survival, for the boys and for us. It's about not getting sent home. McCarthy works hard for us—you don't want to disappoint her, right?" She took her cap off and released the clasp from her hair. Her blond waves fell over her shoulders as she scratched her head. "The trick is not to let them get to you."

Laura hesitated. She wished she could let insults and injustices roll off her back as Frances did. They were not made of the same stuff.

"Pierce is all bluster," Frances continued. "They're the easiest kind."

"How so?" Laura asked.

Frances smirked and batted her eyelashes. "Just play dumb, make him think he's in charge," she drawled. "Or ask him for advice. Make him feel like a big man. He doesn't need to know if you're laughing inside."

"Does it work?" she asked.

Frances pinned her hair back up under her cap. "Most of the time."

"I'm no good at that," Laura said, finishing the dregs of her terrible coffee. Her mother's words rang in her head: *Mark my words—you'll wish you'd never left home.* "Maybe I'm not cut out for this."

"Knock it off," Frances said, putting her hand over Laura's fist. "You belong here as much as anyone. Tonight was a hiccup. It means nothing."

"I hope you're right," Laura said.

"I'm always right," Frances said, releasing her grip. "Don't you know that by now?"

They stepped outside, where two ambulances idled by the triage tent. It was quieter now, the sound of gunfire and bombs faint. Delayed flashes of light sporadically illuminated the landscape—probably positive news for them. Still, the night felt endless.

Frances smoked another cigarette as they walked. "By the way, what happened with that patient to shake you up in the first place?"

The young soldier's face flashed in Laura's head. The Saint Christopher medal around his neck. "I know it sounds crazy, but for a moment, he was my brother."

"He looked like Giovanni?"

"He *was* Giovanni. Crazy, right?"

Frances paused, then exhaled. "They're all somebody's brother, I guess, or somebody's son."

At the door to the post-op tent, Captain McCarthy waved them over. Medics rushed by her carrying stretchers bearing patients fresh from surgery who needed tending. Frances threw her cigarette butt into the sand. "Boots and saddles, kiddo."

By the time Laura and Frances finally got back to the tent after their second shift, a rosy dawn was starting to lighten up the desert sky. Frances dropped immediately onto her cot and was snoring in seconds. Mildred and Avis were asleep, too, their cots pushed close together. Mildred's arm was flung over Avis's waist. So sweet, like an old married couple. Laura felt protective of them, knowing the world could be cruel.

She was exhausted but too hopped up on caffeine and adrenaline from the double shift to sleep. McCarthy's scolding still rang in her ears. She pulled out her pen and paper to write her sister an overdue letter by the sunlight seeping through the edges of the tent. She wrote about the bombings, the constant state of wariness, how she felt like a failure because she couldn't properly take care of the endless stream of wounded men, wondering what all the suffering was really for. She told Rose how terrified she was almost all the time—not just about the bombs, but that maybe their mother was right after all, that she'd made a terrible mistake.

She read over the pages and tucked them into her journal, knowing they would never get past the censors. Besides, she didn't want to upset Rose with talk of bombs and death. And she couldn't betray the boys by admitting to her doubts and fears.

She took out a fresh sheet of paper and wrote a few benign lines about the food and the weather. She asked Rose if the family had heard from Giovanni, knowing they were all racked with constant worry about him. Before he'd left for the war, Giovanni had tried to fix Laura up with one of his buddies, a dock worker—Sicilian like them, good-looking but rough around the edges. Laura was in training at Charity at the time and wanted no part of him. Giovanni had accused her of putting on airs, and she'd told him she wanted to find someone outside the neighborhood. *Someone educated, not like you and Pa. Someone with class.* Giovanni had flinched as if she'd slapped him. As soon as the words were out of her mouth, she regretted them.

Still, she hadn't apologized. Then he was gone, off to the front. She'd started letters to him but hadn't been able to find the right words. Just like tonight with Pierce and Captain McCarthy, her pride had gotten the better of her.

She finished up her letter to Rose, then shook some desert sand into an envelope. She tore out an Ernie Pyle column from the *Stars and Stripes* and added it to the letter. Ernie said it better than she could:

There is an agony in your heart, and you almost feel ashamed to look at them. They are just guys from Broadway and Main Street, but you wouldn't remember them. They are too far away now. They are too tired. Their world can never be known to you, but if you could see them just once, just for an instant, you would know that no matter how hard people work back home, they are not keeping pace with these infantrymen in Tunisia.

She turned to the back of her journal and added the night's names to the growing list of her personal war dead. Weiner. Webber. Blackwell. Shapiro. She'd been present for other deaths, of course. At Charity, people died all the time. But their loved ones were usually there too, or just outside in the waiting room. Here, the men died thousands of miles from home in a foreign and hostile land, their bodies torn, with only a stranger's hand to hold. Her hand. She wiped the tears from her cheeks and offered up a prayer for them to a God she wasn't sure was listening.

CHAPTER NINE

In May, the 48th Evac pulled up stakes for the third time. The Allies had just taken Tunis, and it felt like the Germans and Italians would soon surrender in North Africa. Laura peeked out from behind the canvas sides of the truck as the convoy rolled along, trying to memorize the landscape. Breathtaking mountainsides bloomed with cork trees, fragrant thyme and rosemary grew wild, oleander, jasmine, and bougainvillea reminded her of home. She was glad for the drier springtime weather but felt the coming heat of summer on the sandy breeze.

Land mines kept them on cleared roads. When they stopped for bathroom breaks, the nurses held up sheets to provide each other a little privacy. In the small villages along the way, Laura summoned a few words of high school French and her family's Sicilian phrases to communicate as best she could, trading cigarettes and chewing gum for figs, olives, bread, and oranges that reminded her of home. Frances swapped some C-rations for a crude dagger one of the locals had fashioned from a German bayonet. "You never know," she said.

The convoy came to a stop at Medenine, where the unit moved into a hospital the Germans had abandoned. The partially bombed-out building, riddled with bullet holes and without doors or windows, sat on a hillside high above the Mediterranean port of Bizerte, recently captured by the Allies. After scrubbing swastikas off the walls, the nurses settled into some rooms on an upper floor, happy to be out of their dusty tents, at least temporarily.

That night in the mess hall after dinner, one of the surgical techs pulled out a guitar and started a sing-along with Avis, who had a beautiful voice. At first, the only songs she knew were Protestant hymns. She'd grown up singing in the church choir. After that, Frances made a project out of teaching her some popular music, the more scandalous, the better.

Laura sang along with Mildred and Ellen, cracking each other up with absurd, made-up lyrics when they couldn't remember the words. Among the nurses, nobody doubted that Mildred and Avis were an item now. Laura had walked in on them kissing once and was startled, but like so much about the war, it didn't bother her anymore. Mildred and Avis were good nurses and loyal friends. In the end, that's all that mattered.

A few couples danced around the tables. Frances leaned into a tall, broad-shouldered, baby-faced enlisted man. His hands roamed all over her waist and hips. Frances didn't bat them away. Then Avis whispered in the guitar player's ear. He started strumming softly while Avis broke into "Swing Low, Sweet Chariot." The chatter and the dancing stopped. Even Frances returned to their group and linked arms with Laura. Waves of emotion hit Laura with every beautiful note Avis sang, her voice soaring, clear as a bell.

Swing low, sweet chariot
Coming for to carry me home

Laura felt a catch in her throat, thinking about Rose and Giovanni, her father, and Aunt Inez—even her mother. The old spiritual reminded her of the hymns she'd heard as a girl, when she'd believed every word as God's truth. Now she wasn't so sure.

If you get there before I do
Tell all my friends I'm coming too

Coming for to carry me home

More than a few people wiped away tears. Laura noticed their hospital commander, Colonel Beaudet, standing at the entrance, his hands folded behind his back, listening to Avis sing. As the song ended, the master sergeant with him whistled through his fingers. Everyone rose to attention as the Colonel entered the room.

"What now?" Ellen said under her breath.

Laura shrugged. They didn't see much of their commanding officers, only when there was momentous news.

The Colonel stood straight and tall in his crisp khaki uniform. He took off his cap and ran a hand through his close-cropped silver hair. "Sorry for the interruption, folks. I know it's been a long day." He spoke with a faint accent Laura recognized as Cajun; his pronunciation made her all the more homesick. "Ladies and gentlemen, I have good news."

"Is it over?" someone shouted. A few whoops of celebration broke out.

"Settle down. Nothing's over, over. But I just got word that the Germans have surrendered here, and the Allies have won the battle for North Africa. Operation Torch has concluded. Victory is ours."

Cheers and applause erupted. "We're going home! Hallelujah!" Ellen cried. Avis made a beeline for Mildred, lifting her into the air. Laura hugged Frances.

The Colonel waited for the crowd to settle down. "Nobody's going home, I'm afraid," he said. "We'll be in a holding pattern here until further notice. We may move on to Sicily, southern Italy, or somewhere else. But I do want to thank you all for your tireless work these last few months. You've saved countless lives, and you should all be proud. Give yourselves a round of applause."

The crowd cheered and banged on the tables. The Colonel explained some logistics: two field hospitals would be pulled back from near the front line and folded into their operations. They'd also be processing wounded and sick German and Italian POWs, along with American and British casualties being brought in from Sicily on hospital ships.

The crowd slowly broke up as everyone drifted off into the night. "Take a walk?" Frances asked Laura, holding out a package of Lucky Strikes. Behind the building, they sat on a low wall overlooking the valley below. A searchlight swept over the port, illuminating the big white hospital ships and troop transports anchored there, along with the jagged silhouettes of sunken wrecks jutting from the water. The dim glow of scattered fires still burned in the ruins of warehouses and bombed-out buildings.

Laura appreciated the calm and quiet after so many weeks of noise and destruction at their last post, where the relentless sirens and air raids rattled them day and night, bombs and artillery firing close enough to rock their tents. She inhaled deeply, the tobacco creating a pleasant buzz in her brain. "I try not to think ahead too much. So much is out of our control," she said. "But it feels like a turning point, doesn't it?"

"Maybe," Frances said. "But I don't think the bad guys will give up that easily. Europe and the Pacific. We still have a lot of work to do."

Laura knew Frances was probably right. She felt like she was just hitting her stride. Captain McCarthy had even put her in for a promotion to First Lieutenant. Still, she wanted to savor the possibility—at least for now—of all the suffering and death ending.

"You're lucky. You have something to go back to," Frances said.

The thought of returning home to Charity, to her old life, made Laura a little queasy, but she knew she should be grateful for her family—as difficult as her mother could be—and for the hospital job waiting for her at home. She could pick up her life where she left off. "You have your mom and dad, don't you? Your brother?"

Frances just shook her head. "For whatever that's worth."

Laura knew Frances didn't like talking about her life in Texas, so she didn't press, especially now that Donny was missing. "Who was that young fella you were dancing with?"

Frances took a deep drag of her cigarette. "Nobody. His name is Jimmy. A sweet kid."

Laura didn't say that he looked about seventeen. It was possible; plenty of guys lied about their age when they enlisted. "Let's go back. I'm exhausted."

Frances stamped out her cigarette butt on the ground. Laura could only see the faint outline of her face in the dark. "Go on ahead," she said. "Jimmy's meeting me here."

After breakfast the next day, Captain McCarthy called an all-hands meeting for the nurses in the main lobby of the building. Laura stood near the back with Frances, who was groggy and quiet—she'd only gotten a couple of hours of sleep after returning from her rendezvous with Jimmy.

"Like the Colonel told us last night, playtime is over," the Captain was saying. "We're about to get slammed again. That's the bad news. The good news is we'll have more help. The field hospitals joining us today are bringing twelve more doctors, thirty nurses, and a few dozen other support staff."

A cheer went up in the crowd. They'd been short-handed for so long. "We're putting together a consolidated surgical unit. I need five volunteers to work with the new group, help them get settled in the vacant wing, and cross-pollinate so they know how we're doing things here."

Without hesitation, Laura and Frances both raised their hands, then looked at each other and laughed. Laura had made a unilateral truce with Dr. Pierce; still, she'd rather be assigned to anyone else, even a stranger.

"Marino and Harris, you're on," the Captain said, then named three other nurses who had their hands raised. "Report at 0-800 tomorrow to the east wing."

"Fresh blood—yahoo!" Frances said.

Laura cringed. "Terrible."

"Sorry," Frances said. "Poor choice of words, I guess."

The next day, Laura and Frances reported for duty to their new surgical assignment. A doctor wearing a mask and cap greeted them. "Welcome, ladies. Nicholas Bruno."

Frances gripped his offered hand. "I'm Frances Harris, and this is my partner in crime, Laura Marino."

"Nice to meet you," Laura said. She shook his hand, feeling the smooth warmth of his palm. "Bruno—Italian?"

"*Sí*. Of the Boston Brunos. You?"

"New Orleans. Sicilian, though."

He backed away in mock fear, putting his palms up. "Oh, well then—"

Frances laughed. "Don't worry. She won't have you killed as long as you play nice." Laura shot Frances a look.

"Well, I'll try to be on my best behavior then," Dr. Bruno said. "New Orleans, you said. Charity?"

"You've heard of it?"

"Best nursing school in the country."

She'd never had anything to compare it to, but his compliment made her proud.

"Here come the customers," he said. Medics and litter-bearers had begun carrying in a parade of stretchers. He pulled on his gloves, but not before Laura noted the glint of gold on his ring finger.

Throughout the morning, the three of them worked together, quickly falling into a rhythm as if they'd been colleagues for years. The cases were often gruesome and complex—penetrating injuries from shrapnel and bullet fragments, sucking chest wounds, abdominal trauma. Dr. Bruno's hands were deft, his touch with the instruments delicate, yet firm. Caring. He was just as skilled as Pierce, but patient and kind.

In between patients, he asked Frances and Laura questions and joked around with them—a little flirtatious, Laura thought. She was polite and friendly, but let Frances take the lead on flirting back—no point showing interest in someone who's off-limits. There was no shortage of affairs in their company, but Laura couldn't stomach the thought of crossing that line.

After six hours, the flow of patients finally stopped. Dr. Bruno snapped off his gloves, tossed them on the table, and removed his cap and mask for the first time. His smile disarmed Laura completely.

Frances elbowed her. "Great working with you, doc. I hope we'll get to do it again." They hadn't lost a single patient, despite some complicated cases, and a day like this made up for the others. Laura was exhausted but knew she was exactly where she was meant to be.

"I think we make a good team, and I'll put in a word with the Captain," he said. "Will I see you, ladies, at the dance?" he asked. The USO was planning an event at the Red Cross Club the following Saturday.

"Wouldn't miss it," Frances said. "Our friend Avis is singing with the band."

"Great—I'll buy you both a drink."

"Goodbye, Doctor Bruno," Laura said, suddenly flustered by her attraction to him. Working together was one thing, but socializing would mean she'd really have to keep her guard up.

"Please, call me Nicholas," he said, flashing a thousand-watt smile.

"Good night, Nicholas," Frances sang out, taking Laura by the elbow. "See you at the dance, if not before."

"He likes you," Frances said, once they were out of his earshot.

"What on earth are you talking about? You were the one flirting up a storm back there."

"Don't play coy with me. I pick up on these things. Those eyes— Doctor Dreamboat was studying you."

"Knock it off, Franny. He's married."

"So what? We're at war."

"So, he's off-limits, at least to me, same as at home. Have him yourself if you want."

Frances shook her head. "Much as I'd like to take those lips for a ride...I have my hands full with young Jimmy at the moment. Besides, I can see the good doctor only has eyes for you."

"You're wicked," Laura said, smacking Frances lightly on the arm.

"Wicked can be fun."

CHAPTER TEN

They worked nonstop during the week leading up to the Red Cross dance, but there was an air of excitement in the camp. Rumor had it that the band coming to play was straight from New York City, a real swing orchestra. The nurses unearthed long-neglected civilian dresses from their footlockers and hung them on laundry lines to shake out the wrinkles. Laura was as eager as the rest of the nurses to let loose. Regardless of what she'd told Frances, the truth was she did feel a little extra anticipation thinking about seeing Nicholas there. She and Frances had worked alongside him all week, and Laura enjoyed every minute. He was friendly and solicitous, complementing them on their skills while staying focused and unflappable. He treated the nurses with respect, like partners.

On the evening of the dance, Laura and Frances helped each other with their hair and shared the nub of a worn-down red lipstick, dabbing some of it on their cheeks for rouge. Ellen had lent them red nail polish, an unimaginable luxury, and they'd painted each other's nails. Frances finished plucking her eyebrows in front of a small mirror, rag curlers in her hair, and then held out the tweezers to Laura.

"That's OK, thanks," Laura said.

"Oh, honey. You need to do this."

She took the tweezers and reached out for the mirror. Frances was right. She didn't mind. For once, Laura got to be the little sister.

They finished styling their hair and zipped each other up. Lacking a full-length mirror, they posed for inspection.

"Tell me the truth," Frances said, hands on her hips, her chin pointed up like she was ready for a glam shot.

"You look stunning," Laura told her. It was the truth. Frances's blond hair cascaded over her shoulders, the navy blue crepe gown just clingy enough to show off her curvy figure, with a cinched waist and a sparkle of rhinestones at the decollete—just short of scandalously low-cut. More daring than anything Laura would ever wear. "You'll be beating off the dance partners like flies."

Laura smoothed the slightly flared skirt of her dress, a dusky rose, rayon gown Aunt Inez had altered for a long-ago dance at the Italian Club. Laura had lost weight, and the dress hung on her war-thin body. "It's a little out-of-date, but I don't suppose anyone here will mind."

"Trust me, they won't. It's a good color for you," Frances said. "Shows off your complexion and those pretty dark eyes. Except—" She reached over and pulled the scoop neck of Laura's gown off one shoulder. "There. Makes your neck look like a swan. And the pearl earrings are darling. What's this?" Frances lifted the gold Miraculous Medal that hung on a thin chain around Laura's neck, a gift from Rose before she shipped out.

"Catholic stuff. Divine protection," Laura joked, though she wore it and her Nonna's earrings because she had no other jewelry.

Frances pulled a small silver flask from her purse, took a swig, and handed it to Laura. "Here's my divine protection."

"Where the heck did this come from?" Laura turned the flask over in her hands and saw it was etched with a filigree design of a cowboy hat.

"One of the patients gave it to me last week. Guy was from Dallas, so I hammed up the Texas drawl. He called it the 'Good Thing'. Go on—you need a little liquid courage."

It was true. Laura was self-conscious, and they both knew it was because of Nicholas. She reached for the flask and took a sip; the whiskey burned her throat.

With no stockings to wear, they squeezed their feet into their black service-issue pumps—their toes pinched after months of wearing too-large combat boots. They tottered toward the Red Cross Club, a makeshift operation inside an old airplane hangar down the road from their hospital, both of them laughing uncontrollably as their heels sank into the sand.

"Why was it a good idea for us to walk?" Laura asked.

She clung to Frances's arm to keep from falling. "Because someone forgot to send Cinderella's carriage for us."

The strains of "Chattanooga Choo Choo" drifted from the club. Inside, the party was getting into full swing, with a few couples already jitterbugging on the floor. A seven-piece band, complete with horns, was dressed in tuxedos on the stage, their hair slicked back and shining with brilliantine. Laura smiled; she missed the live jazz she'd taken for granted back home. The room was festooned with American flags; candles on the tables twinkled, giving the cavernous room a romantic air.

Laura scanned the crowd but didn't see Nicholas. She and Frances waved to Mildred, who was serving punch over at the refreshments table. Avis was up on the stage, singing into a big silver microphone on a stand. Laura waved.

"Look at our girl!" Frances said, blowing a kiss to Avis, who wore a tight-fitting black sheath, her long legs peeking out of slits on the sides. "I think she's wearing lipstick too."

Within minutes, a tall, smiling soldier in a British uniform approached Frances. "Good evening, miss," he said, kissing her hand. "Would you do me the honor?"

"How can I say no to that accent?" Frances said.

"This is my mate," he said, pointing his thumb at a shorter, pudgier man, a shy smile on his face.

The two men escorted Frances and Laura to the dance floor. Luckily, the song was almost over, and Laura politely extracted herself from the man's sweaty embrace after a few twirls. She walked briskly to the refreshments table before anyone else could corner her. Mildred handed her a glass of punch. The band started up "Sentimental Journey," and they watched as Frances was handed from one soldier to the next.

Ellen walked up, wearing an emerald green gown that accentuated her hazel eyes. "Evening, ladies. You two sure clean up well."

"I could say the same," Laura said. "Love your dress."

Frances danced away from her current partner to stand with them. "These guys are going to wear us out!" She gave Ellen a hug and an air kiss, then pulled the Good Thing from her purse, adding a splash of whiskey to their punch glasses.

Mildred shook her head, laughing. "I see nothing."

Frances flicked her chin. "Speak of the devil. Doctor Dreamboat, two o'clock. Laura's sweet on him."

"Oooh," Ellen said. "I met him. He's a dish. Nice guy, too."

"And married," Laura insisted. "Not interested."

Mildred broke out into a knowing smile. "Methinks the lady doth protest—"

"Can it," Laura said, cutting her off. Still, her heart raced.

Nicholas made a beeline for them, just as the music stopped. He wore a crisp khaki single-breasted service coat with the gold Medical Corps insignia on the lapels, a Windsor-knotted tie tucked into the shirt.

Avis tapped the microphone. "Ladies and gentlemen, how 'bout a hand for our wonderful band tonight?" The crowd applauded; a few soldiers whistled. "And now for a slower number—it's one of my favorites, called 'We'll Meet Again.'"

Mildred stayed behind the punch bowl. "You kids have fun. I'll hold down the fort here."

A young GI took Frances's hand. Freddy Gomez, looking dapper with his dark hair combed back, led Ellen to the dance floor.

Nicholas looked at Laura and raised one eyebrow. "Shall we?"

She took his hand, a little damp, and let him pull her out into the swirl of dancers. "It's been a long time since I've seen a gal in a dress," he said into her ear. "You look lovely, if I may say so."

"Oh, thanks," Laura said. He smelled like soap and tobacco, with a hint of sage—or maybe that was just the desert. She tried to savor the moment, losing herself in the rhythm of the music, the timbre of Avis's voice, the pressure of Nicholas's hand on her waist, firm but gentle. He kept her close rather than whirling her around; she was fine with that. Another soldier tried to cut in, but he wouldn't allow it.

"Don't be greedy, doc," the GI said.

Nicholas waved his hand at the man. "Buzz off, Al. This one's mine."

The song ended, and Avis took a bow. She climbed down from the stage as the band started up a faster instrumental number. Immediately, two GIs pulled her out to the dance floor. Nicholas steered Laura toward a table in the corner. "Do you mind keeping me company while I sit for a few minutes?" he said, a little breathless.

They sat in the shadows at the edge of the room, a small white candle in a jelly jar flickering between them. Nicholas pulled a pack of cigarettes from his pocket and held it out. He lit his own from the flame, then leaned over to press the end of his ember to the tip of hers. She noticed his steady hands and clean fingernails. A surgeon's hands.

"Thanks for sitting with me," he said. "I'm kind of beat. Just coming off a double shift."

Laura inhaled the smoke deeply, trying to stay cool and casual. "I thought things were supposed to be slowing down."

"These are non-emergencies. They're trying to clear all the injured POWs to transport them out, so they've got us running ragged."

"Where will they take them?" Laura had treated some of the prisoners, too. She didn't mind, as some of the girls did. They were mostly just young boys, scared and hurt. And the Italians all looked like cousins she knew back home. She'd spoken a few words with them in the Sicilian language of her youth. She was surprised when they found it hilarious, explaining that the words she used were not "real" Italian.

Nicholas tapped his cigarette on the edge of the ashtray. "The Brits will take some to Australia and India. Ours will go to the States, believe it or not. All those empty military bases. They'll probably put them to work."

"Interesting," she said. "I guess they need the help back home." She couldn't quite picture the prisoners on American soil, though. They'd been shooting at the Allied troops just a couple of weeks ago.

Nicholas leaned forward, his elbows on the table, looking directly into Laura's eyes. "Tell me about yourself. Where are you from? Who are your people? I know you're Italian—sorry, Sicilian—and from New Orleans, but that's about all." Laura heard the exhaustion in his voice, but also a gentleness she found compelling. It was the first time any doctor had asked her anything personal about herself, beyond checking her nursing credentials.

"Well, it's not much of a story," Laura said. "My parents run a grocery store in the French Quarter, in the Sicilian neighborhood."

Nicholas followed up with more questions about her family, about New Orleans. He seemed genuinely interested, not just flirting or talking about himself, like other men she'd met. She wasn't sure how to act. She'd only ever had a smattering of dates back home; she was always studying or working. She'd attended an all-girls high school and didn't have much experience with men.

"What about *your* family?" she asked, redirecting the conversation, hungry for information about his life. She tried not to stare at his wedding ring.

"I'm the eldest of four," Nicholas said. "All boys."

"Your poor mother!"

He closed his eyes briefly, then returned them to her. "She died when I was 12. Left my father with the four of us."

"I'm so sorry." Laura thought of her own father with a pang, how he loved the three of them, how he put up with their mother's moods.

"Thanks. I was lucky, though. My mother's sister lived nearby, and my grandparents on both sides. A big Boston Italian family that raised us."

"Still. That must've been hard on your father. And you, being the big brother."

"I had to grow up pretty fast. Good training for this, I suppose."

She took a deep drag off the cigarette, stubbed out the butt in the ashtray, and pointed to Nicholas's wedding ring. "And tell me about Mrs. Doctor Bruno."

He lowered his hand to his lap. "That's...complicated. A story for another time." He tipped the remains of his punch into his mouth, then snuffed his cigarette as the band struck up again. "One more dance?"

She was a little annoyed that he'd dodged her question, but followed him to the dance floor, nonetheless. He held her close as they swayed to the music, her arm folded tight to his chest, his hand firmer on her waist this time. She pressed herself closer, allowing herself a flutter of attraction. *Harmless*, she told herself, just for tonight, to feel something other than fear and loneliness. She wouldn't let it go any further.

Suddenly, a commotion broke out on the other side of the room. A wooden folding chair flew across the floor with a clatter. The band stopped. "I said *enough*!" Laura recognized Frances's voice. She was shouting and slurring her words.

"Yikes," Laura said, pulling herself from Nicholas's grasp. He followed her to where Frances was fending off young Jimmy, who was barely remaining upright while drunkenly pawing at her.

Nicholas pulled him back by his collar. "That's enough, soldier."

Jimmy took a wild swing. "Mind your own damn business," he said, before his eyes landed on Nicholas's officer's bars. "Sorry, sir."

"Beat it. Go sober up," Nicholas said. Jimmy stumbled away, cursing to himself.

"Bring on the music!" someone shouted. The band started up again.

"Thanks, doc," Frances said, kissing Nicholas on the cheek. "I could've handled him, but I appreciate the assist."

"I think we should head home, Frances," Laura said.

To her surprise, her friend didn't argue. She looked exhausted and disheveled, her dress sleeve torn at the shoulder seam. "I'll just grab my purse."

"Let me get you a ride back," Nicholas said.

Outside, he flagged a GI in an idling jeep. Frances climbed in the back, while Laura hoisted herself into the passenger seat, trying not to rip the hem of her dress on the running board.

"To be continued," Nicholas whispered, leaning in and kissing her lightly on the cheek.

Back in their room, Laura lay on her back, her dress off, silently reviewing the conversation with Nicholas.

"I told you so," Frances mumbled across the dark.

Frances knew her too well. "He's married, remember?"

"Not for the duration. What are you afraid of—hell? Us girls have needs just like the men."

Within a few minutes, Frances was snoring. Laura told herself that what she'd felt at the dance with Nicholas was nothing. They were just two colleagues, a little homesick, enjoying the music. The flirting was innocent enough; the attention was nice and made her feel pretty for a change amidst the chaos of the past few months.

But she couldn't help thinking about the feel of his warm hand caressing her back, ever so lightly, as they danced. The intense way he asked her questions—then really listened to her answers. It all made her want to be closer to him, in a way she knew she shouldn't. Nor should he. She wasn't like Frances; certain lines were sacred, even here. She pictured that ring, and his wife, no doubt waiting patiently, praying night after night like so many others, for her man to return.

CHAPTER ELEVEN

A few weeks later, the POWs had all been shipped out, and the flow of patients slowed. They were still getting surgery cases, but mostly they saw malaria, dysentery, and heat stroke—a different flavor of stress compared to battlefield wounds, but no real relief from the grind.

Laura was headed to her room after an evening post-op shift when Frances came out of the surgical wing and bumped shoulders with her. "One and done?" she asked, pulling the silver flask from her pocket.

Laura had been greedily anticipating sleep, but nodded. Whiskey helped to take the edge off. "Just one."

They headed to the canteen. Inside, the room was fairly empty at this late hour—a couple of MPs playing dominoes, Mildred and Avis talking in the corner, their foreheads almost touching. Nobody teased them anymore. The war had changed the rules. What might have raised an eyebrow at home now felt almost normal. Living, surviving were the only things that mattered.

Frances waved the flask in the air. "Hey, Mavis. Last call?"

"Not for us, thanks," Avis answered for both of them, standing up. "We were just heading out." She hooked her arm through Mildred's, and they walked off.

Frances poured a splash into two coffee cups. "To the good guys," she said, clinking her mug against Laura's and throwing the liquor down her throat.

"*Salute!*" Laura said, sipping at hers. "Not the usual rot-gut. Where did you get good whiskey?"

"You don't want to know," Frances said with a wink.

Frances poured another drink for herself; Laura put her hand over her own mug.

"Suit yourself. I need this right now," Frances knocked back another shot and wiped her lips with the back of her hand. "We lost a guy tonight—a kid, really. Couldn't have been more than eighteen. Thought he was out of the woods, but he coded. I remembered him from triage—a southern boy. Real polite."

"Sorry," Laura said. She thought it would get easier to witness these deaths, but they all got ambushed sometimes.

"Doctor Dreamboat saved the rest, though. I was sure a couple weren't going to make it. When he gets to take his time, Bruno's beautiful to watch. It's like a ballet, the way he operates. Better than Pierce, if you ask me."

"Sounds like you have a crush on him," Laura said. During the weeks following the dance, Laura was assigned to triage and post-op. She'd seen Nicholas only across the mess hall, always surrounded by a group of other doctors. He hadn't approached her. *Just as well*, she'd told herself, even if she was disappointed. *Maybe he came to his senses.*

"Naw, too clean-cut for me. He's all yours." Frances said. "Uh-oh. Twelve o'clock."

Laura turned and saw Nicholas, his shoes spattered with blood, his shoulders hunched. He looked exhausted but flashed his perfect smile. Laura patted her hair and sat up straighter, feeling the alcohol a bit.

"The man sure has a sense of timing," Frances whispered. "Doctor Bruno," she called out, cupping her hands.

"Don't—," Laura tried to stop her.

He walked to their table. "Laura, good to see you again."

Frances smirked, then held up the flask. "Nightcap?"

"Please." He took a mug off the rack and sat down.

Frances poured him a shot. He downed it in one gulp. "Nice."

"Top shelf," Frances said.

"Hit me again, would you?"

She poured him another, along with one more for herself. She held the flask over Laura's mug; Laura nodded. They all gulped down the whiskey, then slammed their mugs on the table. Laura laughed. Never at home had she done such a thing. It was what she imagined roughnecks did in dark bars in the French Quarter. Here, it felt liberating. A little wild. She liked it.

Frances screwed the cap back on the flask. "I'm out." She stood abruptly, reaching for the edge of the table.

"Steady there," Nicholas said. "Good work tonight."

"You too, doc." Frances walked away.

Laura stood. "I'm right behind her. Long shift."

Nicholas touched her elbow. "Take a little walk with me, will you?"

She hesitated, slightly drunk and not wanting to give the wrong impression.

"I just need some air. I don't want to go back to my room alone right now."

"Sure," she said, remembering he'd lost a boy on the surgical table. Outside, they sat on the wide stone steps. The night was mild, nearly silent; a slight desert breeze ruffled her hair. Sometimes Tunisia no longer seemed like an alien land. New Orleans felt like another lifetime.

He reached into his pocket for a pack of cigarettes, handed one to her, and lit them both. They were quiet for a few moments as they smoked, pinpricks of light here and there on the dark horizon.

"We lost a boy on the table tonight," he said, breaking the silence. "Made me think of my brothers. I know we did the best we could. Still, it shakes me up."

Laura thought of her own brother, wondering where he was at this moment, whether he was safe. "It never gets easier, does it?"

"Especially when you're the one holding the scalpel."

She resisted the urge to pat his shoulder, to comfort him the way she would one of her patients. But he was a doctor and outranked her. Two MPs came tumbling outside and down the steps past them, joking around loudly with each other.

Nicholas tapped his cigarette ash. "You asked me a question that night at the dance. I didn't want to answer it."

"It's none of my business."

"I want to answer you. It's been on my mind. My marriage is..." Then he took a long drag and exhaled the smoke out of the corner of his lips. "...as I said, it's complicated."

"You're either married, or you're not, though, right?" He looked away. She'd struck a nerve. She knew he was uncomfortable, but she wanted the answer. Needed it.

"Fair enough," he said. "We got married too young. She was literally the girl next door. Everyone expected it—our families and friends—and we never questioned ourselves, or each other. We should have." He took another puff, a long pause. "I had regrets almost right away. Then the war. Since I've been over here, well, it's brought some perspective, along with the distance. I know what I have to do."

"Which is?"

"End it."

Laura took a drag from her cigarette. "But you're Catholic."

"Annulment's a long process." He shook his head. "No kids, though. That makes it a little easier."

She was relieved, though she knew she had no right to even think about that. She'd only known him for a few weeks.

"Sorry, I don't know why I'm babbling on like this," he said. "What about you? What are you running away from?"

She inhaled. "Who says I am? I'm just like everyone else, here to do my part."

He cocked his head and pointed his cigarette at her. "A nice girl like you, over here?"

She hesitated, unsure how much to share, what he might read into it. "More like getting out from under my parents, especially my mother. I wanted to be my own person, out in the world, not be put into a box. She just wants me to marry a nice boy from the neighborhood, settle down, have a bunch of kids." For a moment, she thought of Frances. On the surface, they seemed so different, and yet what had brought them here was the same.

"Would that be so bad?" Nicholas asked. "I'm sure you'd have your pick of fellas, pretty as you are. And smart, too."

She felt the blush rise in her cheeks. "I'm sure Mrs. Bruno is smart," she said, not sure why she felt the need to bring his wife back into the conversation.

He paused. "She is, but she's more of a traditional girl. Not...independent, like you and Franny. I can't even imagine her here, putting up with..." His voice trailed off, and he took another long pull on his cigarette, burning the ash down to the filter, then tossed it. "I've learned so much from you nurses. Honestly, it's a little intimidating."

"Intimidating? That's a first."

"Maybe that's the wrong word. Impressive, I mean. I told you, I grew up with just brothers, and my mom passed when I was so young. None of the women in my life is anything like you."

"What about the nurses at the hospital where you worked?"

"Nuns," he laughed. "Saint Elizabeth's. They were great, but your drive, your ambition, your ability. Maybe it sounds naive, but you've kind of thrown me for a loop."

Laura was flustered by the compliments. She told herself to steer clear, to not give in to the flattery. He was still married, no matter how "complicated" it was. She looked down at her watch. "It's late." She stood up, and he did too.

She turned to walk inside, but he touched her lightly on the arm. She remembered his hands on her back at the dance.

"Look up," he said. She tilted her face to the sky, a fuzzy blanket of light glowing in the clear desert night. "Do you see it? The Milky Way?"

She shook her head, unsure of what she was supposed to be looking for.

"It's so dark here—much easier to see the constellations than back home." He took her hand and guided it toward the sky. "Right there, that mass of stars. That's our home galaxy. And there's Sagittarius the archer, right in the middle. He's half man, half horse. See his bow and arrow?"

She squinted her eyes, trying to focus on the image he was pointing out. Then, the points of light came into alignment. "Wow. I see it now. I never noticed before."

He was still holding her hand. "It's my Zodiac sign. My cousin knows about those things. She says it means I'm adventurous and optimistic. Maybe that's why I'm here," Nicholas laughed. "I don't know about all that, but I like the science."

"It's beautiful." She asked the stars to help slow her racing heart, acutely aware of his fingers laced into hers.

"Hey, I've got a jeep for Friday. If you're off, too, maybe we could get out of this place for the day? There's a secret wadi I heard about from one of the Tunisians. An oasis. 'Like the Garden of Eden,' he told me."

"Will there be forbidden fruit?" Laura asked, surprising herself. It was the whiskey talking.

"I can only hope so." He squeezed her hand before letting go, then leaned over and kissed her quickly on the cheek. "*Buona notte,*" he whispered before turning toward his quarters.

She stood on the steps for a moment, her hand touching her face where his lips had been.

CHAPTER TWELVE

Nicholas pulled up in a borrowed open-topped jeep and hopped out. "My lady," he said, pantomiming opening the nonexistent passenger door for her.

Laura laughed. "Such a gentleman."

"I know you're used to that down South." He climbed in behind the wheel. "Are you ready for an adventure, Nurse Marino?"

"You sound like some kind of crazy nut," she said.

"I feel a little crazy around you," he said. "Let's get away from these prying eyes."

He threw the jeep into gear and headed down the dirt path out of the camp, careful to avoid the flags that marked minefields. Laura was a little frightened. What was to keep them from getting blown up? Captured? Lost in the desert? She told herself to relax, remembering his capable hands at the operating table. She wasn't sure why, but she trusted that he wouldn't let anything happen to her. She'd do as Frances suggested and live in the moment. Just for today.

They rode mostly in silence rather than shouting over the jeep motor. He drove fast, his hands firm on the wheel. She noticed a lighter band of skin on the finger where his wedding ring had been.

She tied her hair back with the white scarf against the wind. The speed was exhilarating. She closed her eyes and tilted her head back, her face catching the warmth of the sun as it climbed higher in the desert sky. Other than their convoys, this was the first time she'd been outside of camp, and the first time she'd been alone with a man since she left home.

The earthy, green fragrance of the wadi reached her before she saw the giant date palms looming on the horizon—such a stark contrast to the endless sand and earth tones beyond. Nicholas parked the jeep, and they climbed out. "It's like going from Kansas to Oz," Laura said.

"Except there's no wizard here, Dorothy."

Two Bedouin men sat in the shade by a crystal clear, turquoise pool of water. Their camel stood nearby, a red saddle blanket on its hump. The older man leaned on a long, ornately carved staff. He wore a flowing white robe, his angular, weathered face and neatly trimmed beard framed by a brown headscarf. He held up his palm in a gesture of greeting. The younger man just stared at them, seeming more curious than concerned.

Nicholas waved at them and smiled. "They don't get many tourists here, I guess," Nicholas said. The younger man lowered a leather pouch into the pool, filling it with water.

"Where does the water come from?" Laura asked.

"From deep underground. The Tunisians built an irrigation system hundreds of years ago. It's a way station on a trade route."

"How do you know these things?"

"I listen, I read. We think we're so sophisticated. These civilizations have been at it for centuries."

Laura was beginning to see there was depth to this man—intelligence and curiosity. He'd said he was intimidated, but he seemed so much more worldly than she was.

He pulled a basket from the rear of the jeep, then led her by the hand to the opposite side of the pool from the Bedouin men. He spread a rough woolen blanket on the sand, in the shade of a palm tree. She sat, and he unpacked the picnic lunch he'd somehow procured for them, placing dates, flatbread, olives, and something resembling a turnover on a tin plate he must've swiped from the mess tent.

"Sorry, I don't have any beer or wine to go with it. Just mint tea for now."

"This is miraculous," Laura said. She pointed to the turnovers. "What are these?"

"The Tunisians call them *brik*. Inside the pastry, there's egg, some sort of meat we might not want to think about, and spices. Delicious."

She was impressed by the trouble he'd gone to. Also, a little wary of what he might expect in return. "Where on earth did it all come from?"

"Dennis in the mess tent befriended some locals and trades for these delicacies."

"He just gave them to you?"

"You'd be amazed at what a carton of the right cigarettes can get you."

The Bedouin men gathered their belongings and began leading the camel away. As they passed Laura and Nicholas, they stopped, and the older man handed her a large red orb, some sort of fruit. She took it, puzzled. "Thank you," she said to the man. "*Shukran*."

They laughed, and he took the fruit back from her, quickly slicing it in two with a machete he pulled from his white robe. Blood-red juice and a river of tiny seeds ran down his arms as he handed the two halves back to her and Nicholas, gesturing that they should eat. They said something in Arabic to Nicholas, laughing, and the younger man slapped him on the back. Then they walked away.

"What was that about? What is this fruit?"

"It's a pomegranate. My Arabic's not great, but I think they said something about the red color representing the heart, and the seeds symbolizing fertility." He was blushing. The fruit did look slightly obscene.

Nicholas scooped out some of the translucent seeds with his fingers, tasted them, then offered her some. "Open your mouth. They're delicious."

She did as he said, and he gently placed the dripping mess into her mouth. The flavor exploded as the seeds slid down her throat, sweet and slightly tangy, unlike anything she'd ever eaten.

"You like it?" he asked. The juice ran down her chin. Laughing, he wiped it off with a cloth and fed her another mouthful. They ate more of the food—all of it delicious—and washed it down with the mint tea. He used the empty thermos to scoop up water and poured it over both their hands, then handed her a small towel.

It was hotter now, but bearable in the shade. He took two clean handkerchiefs from his pocket, soaked them in water, and handed one to her. "For your neck." He'd thought of everything.

She lay back on the blanket with the cool cloth around her neck. Dappled sunlight flickered through the palm leaves. The wadi looked like a scene from the movies. Magical. She wished the day could last forever, that the war would end this minute, that they could stay here and make a home for themselves in the oasis, among the friendly locals. They would eat pomegranates every day and feed each other dates. They would raise their children like wild animals. She laughed.

"What is it?" he asked.

"I'm happy."

She almost dozed off in the heat when she felt him take her hand and kiss the inside of her wrist. A shiver ran through her. She knew it was wrong, but she would've been happy if he'd kept doing that for a long time.

He squeezed her hand. "There's one more thing I want to show you before we head back, but it'll require a little drive into the mountains. The view is spectacular."

She sat up. "Doctor's orders?"

He laughed. They packed up and climbed back into the jeep. He steered as if he knew where he was going, higher and higher up the rocky mountain path until the vast plain stretched out below them.

Finally, they reached a flat shelf, and he parked under a rock outcropping. "In case there are bad guys up there," he said, pointing to the sky.

She knew he was only half kidding. The Germans had almost entirely gone, but occasionally, stray enemy planes found them. They sat on the back of the jeep. Beyond the salt flats were the looming hills. Cacti bloomed on the slope below, orange, yellow, and white flowers nestled in their thorns.

"There," he said, pointing to a red desert fox scurrying between scrub bushes. Vultures hovered overhead in the distance. "The circle of life."

She leaned into him, and he put his arm around her shoulders. "It's stunning."

"You're stunning." He touched her lightly under the chin, his kiss sweet but firm, tasting of pomegranate and mint. "I've been wanting to do that for a long time."

This is real, she told herself. She leaned back, looked at him, and saw her future.

PART THREE

New Orleans, 1951

CHAPTER THIRTEEN

Laura and Nicholas arrive at her sister Rose's house for dinner. She'd been asleep when he came home late from the VFW the night before. While he was out, she'd continued reading through her war journal, surfacing memories she thought had been safely buried. In the back of the journal, she found the list she'd kept of those who hadn't made it. She'd promised herself she wouldn't forget them, but she can no longer conjure up their faces. Maybe that's why they visit her dreams. She tucks the notebook and the letters back in her drawer. She still hasn't shared the news about Frances. She can barely function from the weight of it.

Rose's kids come tumbling out of the house. Two-year-old Marlene is blond and blue-eyed like Rose's husband. Four-year-old Gregory is a quiet, dark-haired boy. With the right expression on his face, he takes Laura's breath away with his resemblance to her brother Giovanni.

"*Zia!*" the children cry, as they mob Laura with hugs and kisses. "Did you bring lollipops?" She regularly swipes candies from the pediatrician's desk for the kids.

"I totally forgot," Laura feigns. "Did you want lollipops?"

The children frowned at her.

"I'm just kidding!" Laura pulls two cellophane-wrapped lollipops out of her pocket.

Rose appears at the door, trim and petite. Her olive skin shines with perspiration. She wears a faded floral apron over her skirt and blouse, looking more like their mother every day with her dark, curly hair cut in a chin-length, no-fuss bob. "What do you say to your aunt?"

"*Grazie,*" the children say in unison. They hug Nicholas around his thighs, and he tousles Gregory's hair.

Laura loves these kids, though there's always a bittersweet twinge, thinking of the children she and Nicholas couldn't seem to have. Meanwhile, Rose, who'd always said she could take a pass on a husband and children, had married a great guy, conceived effortlessly, and delivered two healthy babies.

Rose holds the door open. "And save those pops until after supper," she calls as the children run past her back into the house.

Nicholas kisses Rose on the cheek. "How's my favorite sister-in-law?"

"Hah! Doing fine. Nice to see you, Nick," Rose says.

Laura gives her sister a brief hug, trying to keep the children's cheerfulness in her smile. She tells herself she'll do her best not to think of Frances, to try to relax and enjoy the time with her family.

They make their way into the kitchen, a warm, cozy space with a black-and-white check linoleum floor, a big white range, and green chintz curtains framing the window over the sink. Rose worked as a bookkeeper at the Higgins Shipyard through the war and bought the two-family house with her wages. Her parents were scandalized—a single woman shouldn't live on her own. After Rose married Walter and the kids came along, they took down the wall between the units and made it into a spacious single-family house. Now, Rose manages the finances for Aunt Inez's real estate business, which means she can be home with the kids.

Rose fills three short glasses with wine and hands one to Nicholas. "Walter's out in the yard. Go say hi." Nicholas clinks glasses with her and walks out the back door. Laura takes a long drink of her wine, trying to swallow the melancholy mood descending like a fog.

Rose sets her wine down on the counter. "You look tired."

"I haven't been sleeping much lately," Laura says. "But I'm all right. Just work stuff." Laura can't say anything to Rose about Frances yet, not before she tells Nicholas. She considers talking about what's happening at work, weighing how much to share. "When you were at Higgins, did you ever feel pushed aside?"

"Only every day," Rose says, handing Laura a fistful of silverware. "Remember, I was the only woman in the office. Not like on the shop floor."

Laura begins to set the table. "Right. Well, I do get to work with a lot of women, but the men call the shots now. Not like when the nuns ran the place."

"I thought you loved your job."

"I do—or I used to." Laura takes the plates from the cabinet and sets them around the table while Rose tosses the salad.

"What happened?" her sister asks.

"I was supposed to be in line for a promotion, but it's dragging on, and I'm afraid I might get passed over again, like I did when I came back from the war." She'd lost out on seniority after leaving Charity for her three-year stint in the Army. *No good deed goes unpunished.*

Rose opens the oven door, releasing the delicious aroma of lasagna. She pulls the glass dish out of the oven, her hands wrapped in dishtowels against the heat, and places it on a trivet. "Well, think positive. Maybe you'll get the job. You've earned it, right?"

Laura takes a deep breath and exhales. She's earned it, yes, but the conversation with Phyllis left her uneasy. For as close as they are, Rose cannot understand her pain, her frustration. She's never had to fight for things, at least not lately.

"Enough about that. What about you? How are you doing?"

"Me? Oh, you know. Same as always."

"That's what I love about you, Rose. So steady. Wish I could be like that."

Rose stands on her toes to pull another bottle of wine out of the pantry. "Steady? That sounds pretty boring."

"I didn't mean it that way. Just...normal, I guess."

Rose runs her hand through her hair. "It's not like you're abnormal, Laura. I just think you take things a little too personally sometimes. As Aunt Inez says, '*It's just business*,' you know?"

Laura drains the last of the red wine into her glass. But nursing isn't just business to her. It's her only source of pride, her whole life, really. If she can't be a mother, or even a good wife, what else does she have?

The children come racing back into the kitchen. "Don't run in the house!" Rose scolds. "You'll fall and crack your head open."

"You sound just like Mama," Laura says.

"God forbid," Rose says.

They laugh. As girls, Laura and Rose had made a pact not to repeat their mother's particular brand of child-rearing, one driven by guilt, shame, and fear.

Rose cuts the lasagna into squares, then opens the back door and calls the men inside. Gregory climbs onto the phone books stacked on his chair. Laura buckles Marlene into her high chair, then kisses her on the top of her head, her silky hair smelling of baby powder, sweet and innocent.

Laura opens the second bottle of wine and starts to top off her sister's glass, but Rose puts her hand out to stop her. "I'm fine, thanks. You might want to slow down." Laura frowns at her but pours herself just half a glass.

The men come in and take their seats. Rose's husband, Walter, is an "American," which hadn't gone over well with their parents at first. Once Gregory was born, they'd lightened up. For her part, Laura liked Walter from the beginning. He's solid and dependable, and he adores Rose and the kids.

"Smells delicious, Rose," Nicholas says, settling in at the table. "Your lasagna is the best."

Laura flinches. Rose *is* a better cook than she is. Still, his words feel like a personal affront. Walter bends down to kiss Laura on the cheek. "Hey, sis."

"Walter tells me he got a promotion at the Sewerage & Water Board," Nicholas says, patting his brother-in-law on the shoulder.

Laura forces a smile through a mouthful of lasagna. At least someone's getting promoted. She's instantly irritated, though. Nicholas doesn't get the irony—praising Walter's promotion while not seeming to care about hers—at least not enough to help her.

Rose beams at her husband. "Pretty soon he'll be running the whole show over there."

Walter pats her hand, and Laura feels a pang of jealousy; they're so in love still, so easy with each other—like she and Nicholas used to be.

After dinner, the children follow Walter and Nicholas out the back door. Laura tops her wine glass off again, feeling a little self-conscious since Rose's earlier comment, but eager for another glass. She switches on the radio. "Rocket 88" is all over the airwaves that summer. A new sound out of Memphis that all the kids are crazy for.

Rose clears the table. "Hey, is everything all right at home? Feels a little tense between you and Nicholas."

"Maybe you should ask him," Laura says, the wine loosening her tongue. "All he does is work and play cards with the boys down at the VFW. It's been like this for a while now."

Rose starts washing the dishes but doesn't respond. Laura wants sympathy from her sister, instead of her judgmental silence, as if the distance between her and Nicholas is Laura's fault.

Laura lights up a cigarette. "You know it was a year in April since we lost Michael," Laura says. When the baby died, Laura's grief was overwhelming. Her mother was unavailable—the grandbaby's death dredged up too much pain over the loss of Giovanni. Rose was there for her sister back then, though she was dealing with her own little ones at the same time. Laura and Nicholas cried and held each other that first night after she came home from the hospital without the baby. They've rarely spoken of their son since. The ache in Laura's heart is permanent. "We don't talk about it. Ever."

Rose dries her hands on a dish towel, then sits down across from Laura. "There's such a long list of topics we can't talk about. Sometimes it's hard to keep track."

It's true. After Giovanni was killed in the war, the secret came out that his father was not Rose and Laura's father, but the parish priest, Father Tony. Laura didn't find out the truth until she came home—a whispered recitation from Rose, a few words from her father, and then, nothing. Father Tony moved away, and the family never spoke of it again. Like it never happened.

"I miss Giovanni every day," Laura says. "I know you do too."

"I do. It's hard to keep him alive, but I try," Rose says. "He would've been such a great uncle to the kids." She reaches for Laura's hand and holds it for a minute, both of them teary-eyed.

Laura stifles a sob. "And your kids would've been playing in the backyard with little Michael right now." She'd been so excited about sharing motherhood with Rose.

"Are you trying again? I've been afraid to ask."

Laura shakes her head. "The thought of going through that again is...overwhelming." The small kitchen is suddenly suffocating. Laura wipes her eyes and stands. "We ought to get going. Thanks for dinner. And thanks for letting me talk about things."

"Of course," Rose says.

Laura opens the back door and yells to Nicholas. "Time to go, honey." She snuffs out her half-smoked cigarette in an ashtray on the counter, gathers her purse, and heads to the front of the house, Rose on her heels. Marlene and Gregory come in with their father and Nicholas, their mouths green from the lollipops.

"I didn't even finish my cigar," Nicholas protests.

Walter hugs Laura and shakes hands with Nicholas.

"Thanks for supper, Rose," Nicholas says, fishing the car keys from his pocket.

"*Ciao,*" Rose says. "Go easy."

The children run to the front stoop. Laura squats and hugs them both tightly. "*Vi amo,*" she says, kissing their curly heads and fighting back more tears that might upset and confuse them. She presses her shaking hand to their warm little bodies. They start to squirm, and she releases them.

CHAPTER FOURTEEN

Nicholas is quiet on the ride home; Laura can tell his mind is else-where. Back at their house, she starts rinsing some dishes in the sink, and he wraps his arms around her waist from behind, kissing her neck. She stiffens, and he backs away.

"What's wrong with you?" he asks with a wounded little boy expression.

"I'm fine," she says, turning back to the sink. "Just tired."

He sits at the table. "I noticed your hand's started shaking again."

"It's nothing. It comes and goes."

He drums his fingers on the table lightly. "Hey, I need to talk to you about something. I didn't want to bring it up when we were in a rush to get to your sister's."

She rinses a few cups and puts them in the dish strainer. "Oh?" Soapy water swirls down the drain.

"I got a letter with an interesting offer," he said. She'd almost for-gotten about the mysterious envelope. "A special assignment. Korea."

She turns around, her hands dripping, not sure she's heard him correctly. "Korea? Back to a war zone?"

"It's a humanitarian organization, running a refugee camp," he says. "They came to Charity looking for trauma surgeons."

She dries her hands on a dish towel and sits down across from him; she's craving a cigarette. "Maybe I could go with you? They must need nurses too." Perhaps that's just what she and Nicholas need—a new adventure together.

He holds up his hand to cut her off. "The team's complete, and they already have enough nurses. I'm only considering it because one of the surgeons had to back out at the last minute."

"So, you'll be gone for a couple of weeks?"

"Three months."

She sits back. "What?"

"They're on three-month rotations. I'll be back before Christmas," he says. "Besides, maybe we could both use a little time apart."

The anger wells up inside her now. He's been planning to leave and never told her. She's keeping the news about Frances from him, too, but this is different. This is their life.

He takes his car keys from the counter.

"Where are you going?" Laura asks. "We need to talk about this."

"I'm going to the Post for a bit," he says.

She blocks his path to the door, arms folded across her chest. "Why would you want to go back to that craziness, after all we went through?"

"We're different like that," Nicholas says. "I'm proud of what we did over there. I've put the bad stuff behind me. Sometimes I worry you haven't, like you want to...wallow in it."

Laura hides her shaking hand in her pocket. "That's not fair."

"Look, I haven't said yes yet," he says. "We'll talk about it tomorrow. Don't wait up."

"Sure. Go on, then." She steps aside. "I'll start getting used to living alone, I guess."

Laura watches him drive off, then slams the front door shut. She leaves the half-washed dishes in the sink and uncorks a bottle of

Chianti—just a short pour, to help her calm down. Nicholas has the VFW; this is what she has.

Maybe it's true that she chooses to wallow in the sadness. She had a hard time adjusting when she got home from the war. The pills the doctor gave her to sleep helped a little, but after she lost the baby, the darkness returned. Now the news about Frances has pushed her to the edge of the abyss again. The idea of losing Nicholas, even for a few months, is unbearable.

She envies Nicholas's ability to put what they'd been through behind him. The more she tries to forget, the more she aches to remember. She takes her wine glass to the bedroom and pulls her war journal from the drawer.

The next morning, Laura rides the streetcar to work. Usually, she loves the gentle rocking, but it's not helping with her hangover or queasy stomach. The bell clangs as they cross an intersection. Out the window, she watches a shopkeeper sweeping the sidewalk on Canal Street, a newsboy hawking his papers on the corner. The shoe store windows feature a back-to-school display.

She'd left the house while Nicholas was asleep, grateful for her early shift. She thinks about what she'd read in her journal the night before. She's surprised by how much she enjoyed reading those entries, seeing Frances's name on the page, even Nicholas's, as they'd been back then. She sees how unsure she'd been in those early days—never about the mission or the work, but about herself. Hunkered down in the North African desert, she'd longed for these familiar streets, for home. She should be happy. But a part of her misses the excitement and danger, the adrenaline rush of the war. The camaraderie. Frances and the other nurses—the McCarthy girls. She misses Nicholas, as he was then, when they made decisions as though every day could be their last. Maybe Frances felt the same, maybe she just couldn't find her way back to normal life, whatever that meant.

As soon as Laura clocks in, Phyllis asks her to come to the courtyard. Her boss is all smiles. Perhaps it's good news about the promotion.

They walk across the grand lobby and through the big brass doors that lead outside. Laura's always loved this graceful space in the center of the hospital complex, with its tidy pebbled walkways framed by pink and yellow flowering hibiscus, palm trees shading the stone benches. In the middle, a fountain shaped like a giant fish spurts water into a pool; small children splash their hands at the edge. The Colored wing of the hospital is on the other side, and the courtyard is the one place where the more ambulatory patients, families, and staff from both sides mingle. Laura never understood why things had to be separate.

"Let's sit here," Phyllis says, waving her hand toward an empty bench. Laura straightens her uniform and her spine. "Beautiful day. Glad it's finally cooled off a bit." Phyllis sits side-saddle and adjusts her skirt. Jesus hangs from a tiny gold crucifix at her throat. Gone is the friendly face from just a few minutes before. "Well, I'd hoped to have better news to share with you."

Laura feels her pulse race. She clasps her left hand to keep it still. "What's up?"

"No sense beating around the bush. It's official: they're giving the supervisor job to someone from the outside. I just found out this morning."

Laura takes a deep breath, afraid she'll burst into tears. Or worse: snap. Phyllis was smart to choose a public place to have this conversation. "That's a bit of a surprise, frankly," Laura says. She craves a cigarette, but Phyllis doesn't smoke. Now she wonders why she even cares. "My interview went pretty well. I thought you were going to bat for me. I meet all the qualifications."

"Nobody's questioning your nursing skills."

"I have more than enough experience, especially counting my time in the service. What happened?"

"Apparently, they did some interviews with the other nurses and with the doctors to get feedback on the internal candidates." Phyllis stops talking. Laura can tell she's choosing her words carefully.

Laura waits a moment, trying to control her tone. "And?"

"And to be honest, nobody felt like they knew you very well."

"So, it's what? A popularity contest? I thought we were talking about a professional nursing position, not Miss Congeniality." Phyllis's words strike a nerve, though. Laura hasn't made any real friends at work, not since the war. Her few nurse friends at Charity who'd served were forced to quit work when they started having babies. That's what was expected—to just go back to "normal." To forget.

"They thought it best to get 'fresh blood.' She's coming from up north somewhere, Cleveland, I think." Phyllis vaguely waves her hand around. "She's a veteran too—maybe you'll have something in common."

Laura scoffs. Another Army nurse. They already have one of those—one who knows Charity like the back of her hand. "Fresh blood? What does that even mean? I'm only 31 years old." Laura swallows the bile in the back of her throat. She glares at another nurse who's staring at them, clearly trying to overhear the conversation. Laura wants to tell her to get lost, but bites her tongue.

Phyllis holds up her hand. "I'm just the messenger. Bottom line is you'll be moving over to the new ward, but you'll be working for someone else. I hate to lose you here, but—"

"Didn't you have a say?" Laura interrupts. She lights a cigarette; what does it matter now?

"I'm sorry, I did what I could."

Laura shakes her head, too furious to respond. Betrayed.

Phyllis's face flushes as she waves away the smoke. "Please don't say anything to the others yet. They'll make an official announcement tomorrow. I wanted you to hear it from me first."

"Right. Thanks for telling me." Laura grits her teeth, trying to keep from saying something that will threaten her job altogether.

Phyllis puts her hand on Laura's arm. "Maybe it'll be a good thing, you'll have more time to yourself. You've earned a vacation. Why not take a break from all the stress?"

Laura stands up abruptly, pulling her arm out of Phyllis's grasp. "I don't need a break," she says, more loudly than she intends. The nosy nurse is openly gaping at them now. Laura straightens her uniform, tucking her fallen bra strap back into place.

In the public ladies' room on the lobby floor, Laura locks herself into a stall. She cries as silently as she can, hearing others come and go. She's always been the reliable one, no matter the situation. Stuff it down, don't complain. Eventually, she'd get her due. Or so she'd thought.

She wipes her eyes. Her watch says it's only one o'clock, and she's already anticipating the drink she'll have at the end of her shift. But that's four hours away. She takes Frances's silver flask from her purse, unscrews the cap, and takes a swig—just enough, like they used to do. Just to calm her nerves before she goes back to work.

CHAPTER FIFTEEN

That evening, Laura's footsteps echo through the quiet house. She pours the last of a bottle of wine into a glass, then pulls some leftover macaroni out of the refrigerator. She eats it cold, standing up, staring out the window over the kitchen sink. She feels numb, angry about losing the promotion, and still sad about Frances. Outside, her neighbor's children play hide and seek in the dusky light, but the family's collie keeps ruining it for them, barking at one of the kids crouching in the bushes.

Nicholas walks in the door, startling her. The streetlights flicker on, and for a moment, he's framed in the doorway by the glow.

"You're home," he says, hanging his jacket on the back of a kitchen chair.

"Where else would I be?" she snaps, immediately regretting her tone. "I was just eating some leftover macaroni. I didn't think you'd be home so early. There's plenty left, though. Let me heat it up for you."

Nicholas hesitates, like he's gauging her mood. "No, thanks. I had a late lunch." He glances at the empty wine bottle on the table. "Looks like you started cocktail hour without me," Nicholas says.

"Not really. Just a half glass of wine to wash the macaroni down," she says. "I only got home from work a little bit ago." She gestures to the uniform she still wears. "But I'll have a drink with you now if you want." She sits at the kitchen table, kicks off her shoes, and wiggles her stockinged toes.

Nicholas takes a bottle of Canadian Club from the credenza and pours them both a small glass of whiskey, neat. He hands one to her, clinking glasses. "*Salute*," he says, sitting down across from her.

"*Salute.*" Laura sips at the drink. The thick glass feels solid in her hand, and she swirls the whiskey, savoring the smoky smell of it.

"I heard about the nursing supervisor position," he says. He takes a sip. "Are you OK about it? I know you had your hopes up."

She was pretty far from OK about it. "They went and hired someone from the outside when I'm perfectly qualified."

"What is it Frances used to say?" A faint smile on his face. "Don't let the bastards drag you down."

"Frances is dead," she blurts out.

"What?" He shakes his head as if he hasn't heard her right. He stands up and claps a hand over his mouth.

"I meant to tell you, but I haven't had a chance. I got a letter from her mother, and a note from Frances with it."

"When?"

"A few days ago."

"A few *days* ago? And you're just now telling me?" Nicholas says, tears welling in his eyes. "What happened?"

She wishes she could climb into her whiskey glass. "Killed herself. I don't know how."

"Oh my God," he whispers. He puts his hands over his eyes. "What did her mother say?" he asks. "I mean, why?"

Laura gets up, retrieves the letters from her dresser drawer, and hands them to him. "Read this one first." Mrs. Harris's letter is on top. Laura downs the rest of her whiskey. "I'm going to change clothes."

She comes back into the kitchen, wearing only her slip. The letters are scattered on the table in front of him, and he's weeping, his head in his hands. She hasn't seen him cry since they lost Michael.

Nicholas presses his lips into a grim line and shakes his head. "Poor Frances," he says. "We should've reached out."

His voice is tender, softening her anger. He doesn't know about the apology letters Frances had written after the disastrous Mardi Gras visit, the letters Laura never answered. She puts her hands on his shoulders, rubbing them from behind. He pulls her hands down, and her body curves over his back. He smells of the hospital: antiseptic, other people, sadness.

She buries her face in his neck. "We didn't know." It's true, but perhaps she didn't want to know. She was facing her own demons after the war, trying to find her place again, desperately looking for normalcy. She didn't have room for Frances's drama.

He sobs again. "Her poor parents. To lose a child...at any age."

"Don't," she says.

Nicholas stands and takes Laura's face in his hands, looking into her eyes, as if he's searching for something there, something she no longer has. After the baby died, she shut down. Nobody wanted to talk about it. The old Sicilians believed in curses. She used to think it was superstitious nonsense, but now she wonders. Her brother Giovanni's life—stolen by enemy fire—wasn't enough. Little Michael, stuck in Limbo for eternity. And now Frances. All part of some twisted reckoning. But for what?

"I lost him, too, you know," Nicholas says.

She presses her forehead into his chest, crying now. He lifts her chin with a finger, then kisses her hard on the mouth, salty tears and all. She lets him lead her into the bedroom, pulls down the window shade against the waning early evening light and the neighbors. He sheds his clothes while she watches him, wary but eager. Starving for him, all of a sudden. He pulls the straps of her slip down, and she steps out of it, then unhooks her bra and removes her panties. They fall onto the bed, not bothering to turn down the covers.

They make frantic, desperate love. She pulls him into herself as hard as she can, wishing she could fuse herself to him, as if his life force could drag her soul out of the dark cave she's dwelt in for so long. She squeezes her eyes shut, willing herself back to that rough woolen blanket they'd spread on the hot sand in Tunisia, his hands on her, gentle and strong, loving her, seeing her, wanting her.

After, she rests her head on his chest, breathing him in. Neither of them speaks for a few long minutes. Maybe he's trying to hold onto the moment, too. She feels a glimmer of hope that this will be the beginning of something new—maybe she'll even conceive again.

"I need to tell you something," he says, his tone somber. He brushes his fingertips lightly on her back. "I took the assignment to Korea."

Laura pulls back from his warmth, props herself up on one elbow, and tugs the blanket over her nakedness. "Without talking to me?"

"I told you I was thinking about it," he says.

The glow from a few minutes ago has evaporated. "When do you leave?"

"Next week."

She stands and walks toward the bathroom.

"I'll be back before Christmas," he says. "The time will fly by."

"Go to hell, Nicholas." She slams the door behind her.

The next morning, she and Nicholas barely speak at breakfast. She takes the streetcar rather than ride with him, even though it makes her a little late. The hospital is bustling, and Laura is determined not to let the news about the promotion get to her. Maybe the new supervisor won't do well—so many transplants to New Orleans never figure out the city. Then they'd come crawling back to her. It's a slim reed to grasp, but she can't think of what else she can do.

In the break room, Laura pours a splash of vodka from Frances's flask into her coffee and swirls it around with a spoon. She tucks the flask back into her purse just as Phyllis comes in with an armful of charts. Laura takes a swig of the coffee and plasters a smile on her face. "Good morning," she says, getting up to leave as though she has somewhere to be.

"Hold up," Phyllis says before she can escape. "Can you please follow me to my office? I need to talk to you." Phyllis asks, though it doesn't sound like a request.

She follows Phyllis down the hall to her office. "Have a seat." She directs Laura to the guest chair and sits behind her desk. There are no mementos, nothing on the wall except her nursing school diploma, not even a family photo. Laura realizes she knows almost nothing about her boss's personal life, though they've worked together for years.

Phyllis points to a stack of records on her desk. "I've been checking these charts, and I've noticed not all the rounds are recorded. It's hard to make sense of some of them, and I can't read the handwriting." She points to the topmost chart. "Is this you?"

Laura stiffens, willing herself not to get defensive. Her pulse quickens as she examines the paperwork. "This is my signature, but I don't know why that line isn't filled in. You know I take pride in my charts."

"How about this one?" Phyllis asks, showing her another chart.

"Mine too," Laura says.

Phyllis pulls another one off the pile. "And this one." Now Laura breaks into a cold sweat, her left hand trembles as she checks the charts for the five other patients on the ward. All the same: missing data, and her penmanship—usually Catholic school perfect—is illegible. She has no memory of making these notations the day before.

"I'm sorry, I don't understand what happened. I guess there was a lot going on yesterday. I can update these right now." She pulls a pen from her pocket and starts updating the charts while Phyllis watches her, arms folded, silent. Laura fills in the details as best she can with current knowledge about each patient, back-dates the notes, and re-stacks them neatly on Phyllis's desk. "Should be fine now."

"It's not fine, though, is it?" Phyllis says.

Laura's dread rises in the closet-like space, her brain foggy. She wishes she hadn't added that booze to her coffee. She's never messed up like this at work before. "I'm not sure what you mean. Would you like me to review each patient with you? I know their status, the doctors are in the loop, they're—"

Phyllis holds up her hand. "That won't be necessary. Look, I know you're going through...something. If you don't want to talk to me about it, that's fine. But I have a department to run. Nothing personal, Laura. You know I'm fond of you, but..."

"But what? What are you talking about?" *Is she about to get fired?*

"I know you're unhappy with the decision to bring in someone from the outside for the supervisor job, but we don't have time for this. The patients come first at Charity." She sounds like she's reading from a script.

"I know that," Laura snaps. "Nobody cares more about these patients than I do."

"You care so much more than the rest of us? You care enough that you haphazardly fill out charts, and disappear for long stretches of time?"

"Wait, who told you that? I would never abandon my patients." A few smoke breaks on the roof, a couple of lunches at Joe's—everybody does it. But she knows Phyllis chose those words deliberately, straight out of the Nursing Board's rulebook.

Phyllis leans forward, looking Laura directly in the eyes. "Never mind, I have my sources. I'm starting to question your fitness for duty."

Laura flinches at the military term. "I'm not perfect, I know that, but nobody is. I work my behind off here, Phyllis." Laura tries to keep the tears out of her voice. Her left hand is trembling violently now.

"There's another thing I don't get," Phyllis points to Laura's hand.

"I told you, it's nothing," Laura says. "I have it under control."

"I don't think you have anything under control," Phyllis says.

Laura's face is hot, her palms sweating. She needs to get out of that room before she explodes. "Will that be all?"

"Pull yourself together, Laura," Phyllis says. "We need this place ship-shape before your new boss gets here."

A week later, Laura stands outside Lakefront Airport with her arms folded, watching a small plane lift itself into the sky. Doctors and nurses board the hospital charter plane waiting on the tarmac. Nicholas takes his duffel out of the car and closes the trunk. Other than making him dinner at home last night, she's maintained a frosty distance since he announced he was leaving for Korea. She doesn't want him flying halfway around the world with this bitterness between them, but she doesn't know how to break through it. If he'd been paying attention—or cared to—he wouldn't be leaving her alone right now.

He puts his bag on the ground and draws her into a hug. "I'll be home before you even have a chance to miss me," he says.

It's a concession she'll accept, and she holds onto him tightly. She hasn't been apart from him longer than a night or two since the war. Despite her anger and sadness, she wishes he'd change his mind right now and stay.

"Look at me," he says, tilting her chin up with his fingertip. "I love you. Don't forget that. We've been through so much. We'll get through this. Together, OK?"

She wipes at her tears. "I love you too," she says.

Then he kisses her and picks up his duffel. "*Arrivederci,*" he says.

"Write to me," she calls as he walks away. He waves his hand, but his back is turned.

CHAPTER SIXTEEN

The next day, Laura arrives at work early. She's been in a sullen mood since Nicholas left, angry and hurt, but the bright sunshine pouring through the tall windows onto the new green-speckled linoleum floor cheers her up a little. They've begun moving patients into the new ward, where the equipment and furnishings are clean and modern. And at least her left hand has stopped shaking.

She resolves to make a positive first impression on the new boss, to put her frustrations away, to start fresh. No more drinking until after her shift. At least she'll be out from under Phyllis. Maybe it's good that the new boss is a veteran. Nobody else here understands what the women went through over there.

Laura starts her rounds, greeting patients, checking IVs, and making meticulous notes on charts. She's absorbed in these simple but satisfying tasks when she hears the click-clack of heels heading her way. She makes a final note on the chart she's holding.

"You're doing GREAT, Mrs. Devlin. We'll have you out of here in no time," she says, perhaps a little too loudly and cheerfully. She forces a smile and turns to see Phyllis standing with another nurse—

the new boss, Laura presumes. She looks about Laura's age, maybe a little younger.

"Good morning, Laura," Phyllis grins with a crocodile smile.

"Good morning," Laura replies, nice as you please.

"Meet Ann Tibbetts, our new director. Nurse Tibbetts, this is Laura Bruno, one of our superstars."

Laura is taken aback by Phyllis's compliment. "Well, I don't know about that," she laughs. "So nice to meet you, Nurse Tibbetts. Welcome to Charity."

"Please, call me Annie," the new boss says, shaking Laura's hand firmly, as Captain McCarthy used to. She's a petite blond with a flawless peaches-and-cream complexion, except for a small scar above her right eyebrow.

"Laura's a veteran, too," Phyllis adds.

"North Africa, then Europe." Laura puts her left hand in her pocket, feeling a slight tremor.

"Pacific," Annie says. She has excellent posture, Laura notes, straightening her own.

Phyllis bounces on the balls of her feet. "I'm sure you two have a lot in common. Maybe you could finish giving Annie the tour, Laura? I need to get to a meeting."

"Of course," Laura says as Phyllis heads off.

Laura points out the lab, the entrance to the surgical ward, and the supply closet. "The public ladies' room is down that hall, but we mostly use the lav in the nurses' locker room." Then they circle back to the main ward.

"How long have you worked at Charity?" Annie asks as they walk along the row of beds. Her accent is flat, vaguely midwestern. Laura can't remember where she's from. Chicago? Cleveland? Someplace where it snows.

"Seven years altogether. I went into Charity's nursing program right out of high school. Then, I worked here for a year before the war. Luckily, they had a job waiting for me when I came back."

"You saw front-line action over there, I guess."

"We were right in the middle of the shit show." *Why does she feel the need to curse? What if Annie is one of those religious types?* "Pardon my French."

Annie waves her hand. "Your French is no worse than mine, I assure you."

Laura relaxes a bit, and they walk into the break room, which is empty. "The soda machine will try to eat your nickel, but just give it a smack on the side, and you'll get your Coke."

Annie's eyes are gray, unreadable. "Thanks for the tour," she says. "Look, I'm not known for beating around the bush, so I want to be straight with you. I know you wanted this job, and they didn't give it to you. For whatever reason."

Laura wonders how much Annie knows. "I'm not sure what they told you, but—"

Annie holds up a hand. "They didn't, and it's none of my business. But those patients out there are," she points to the ward. "You do your job, I do mine, and they get taken care of. Then we'll have no problems, understood?"

"Yes, ma'am," Laura says, as if she wouldn't put the patients first. As if she hasn't been doing that since day one. "I'd better get back on the floor."

Throughout the day, Annie asks many questions about why they do things the way they do, like why they call their emergency department the "accident room," which Annie finds hilarious. The Cleveland Clinic, where she came from, is apparently much more advanced, and Laura feels defensive of Charity. She's also on guard, wondering what Phyllis has told Annie about her, irritated and exhausted from trying to maintain a cheerful and professional attitude all afternoon.

She's relieved when her shift ends. Outside, the fine day mocks her sour mood. It's sunny and dry, less humid than it's been lately, but the bluebird September sky feels oppressively happy. She'll stop at Joe's for a beer before she heads home, then grab a po-boy from Campo's next door for supper. She hates cooking just for herself.

In the cool, dark tomb of the bar, Joe is polishing glasses, the air conditioning unit on low. "Afternoon, cousin."

"Joe." She sits in a back booth, then leans her head against the red vinyl, pressing her palms into her eye sockets. On the jukebox, Mary Ford sings "How High The Moon," and, like the oblivious sunshine outside, the jaunty tune somehow makes Laura even sadder. Her hand trembles, and she presses it into her lap.

"What are you having, hon?" Joe calls over to her.

"Vodka and tonic, thanks," Laura says.

"You want something to eat too? I can get Agnes to bring you a sandwich from next door."

"Maybe later. My stomach's a little upset. Thanks, though."

"You're the nurse."

Joe brings her drink, setting it down on a coaster in front of her, and pats her shoulder lightly. She takes a sip and lights a cigarette, glad to be alone. Two old men play cards at the front table. A couple of doctors she doesn't know, still in scrubs, stand by the jukebox.

At the bar, the silhouette of a man is backlit by the glow from the front window, his left sleeve pinned up. It's the one-armed veteran she'd treated the week before. She must've walked right past him. In the mirror behind the bar, he catches her staring. She looks away too late. He stands and approaches her booth, a beer in one hand, a paperback tucked under his truncated arm.

"Of all the gin joints in all the towns...Nurse Bruno. Nice to see you again. Arthur Boyer, you took care of me the other day."

"I remember," Laura says.

He shifts his weight from foot to foot. He's cleaner today than when she'd seen him in the hospital, more put-together. "Waiting for someone?" he asks, gesturing at the empty seat across from her.

She sips at her drink, fighting the urge to down it in one gulp. She shakes her head.

"May I join you?"

"Sure," she says, removing her nurse's cap and running a hand through her hair. Joe is watching them, but she ignores him. She feels his judgment, but she's doing nothing wrong.

Boyer puts down his beer and lays the book on the table—the same Carson McCullers's novel he'd had with him at the hospital. She reaches for it and studies the cover.

"I can't believe she was only twenty-three when she wrote it," he says. "It's brilliant and heartbreaking. Have you read it?"

"I have. Probably when I was twenty-three myself." Mildred had lent her the book. Laura had found it unspeakably sad—all those lost souls, searching for love. "I liked *Member of the Wedding* a little more, though. How's the wound?" The sleeve is neatly rolled up to the elbow of his good arm, the bottom of the tattoo peeking out. How does he manage that? How does he manage anything? Maybe he has help, a wife perhaps.

"Better, thanks to you. You weren't phased by it at all. You've seen injuries like this before." He rubs at the stump of his arm lightly.

"Army Nurse Corps," she says. "North Africa. Anzio. A few other places."

"I thought so," he says. His blue eyes are bright despite the dim light. Intelligent, but something else too. Haunted. Like her.

"How's that?"

"I recognized that look." She wonders what he means, but isn't sure she wants the honest answer.

"Where did you fight?"

"France mostly. 90th Division. A few of the boys made it all the way from Normandy into Germany and even Czechoslovakia. But I got hit right after we crossed into Germany. We were just kids, wet behind the ears; no idea what we were getting into..." His voice trails off.

She won't ask what happened next, knowing he'll tell her if he wants to—soldiers' protocol.

"Mortar round, in case you were wondering," he says, lifting the remains of his left arm. "Sometimes I wake up and for a split second forget my arm is gone until it starts hurting, like today. Well, like just about every day."

"I'm so sorry that happened to you," she says, swallowing the tears welling in her throat. She thinks of her lost brother, Giovanni. Of all the boys she saw over there who didn't make it back, or if they did, not in one piece. She reaches for her nearly-empty drink, but her hand starts to shake, and she knocks the glass over. "Shit," she says. "I'll get some napkins."

"Oh, don't worry about it." He sets it right, the melted ice sliding off the table and dripping onto the floor, then flashes two fingers at Joe.

Joe brings her another drink and a can of Jax for Boyer. He mops up the spill with a bar rag, then gives Laura a stern look before walking away. She knows he's only watching out for her, but she's a grown woman.

"What's that about?" Boyer asks.

"He's my cousin...well, not my real cousin, but we grew up together. Protective. It's how Sicilian men are."

Boyer reaches into his shirt pocket and takes out a pack of cigarettes, deftly shaking one out for her. "But you're a big girl now. You've seen things, been places."

"That's right." She reaches for a red Joe's matchbook on the table and lights her cigarette. Then Boyer leans over, and she lights his, her hand still trembling.

"From back then?" he asks.

She rests her hand on the table, palm up. It dawns on her that she doesn't feel ashamed to talk to him about it. His own wound is so much greater. "I thought I had it beat, but now it's back. We called it the Anzio Shakes. I wasn't the only one."

"I'm sure not," he says, tapping his ash. "I heard Anzio was a hellscape."

"Accurate." She sees the beachhead in her mind's eye. The silver barrage balloons floating over the harbor, the bombs exploding the night the Germans shelled their hospital. She pushes the images from her mind before they can take hold. "Pinned down for months with them shooting at us from the hills. Sitting ducks."

"We always talked about 'for the duration,' no one ever expected the duration to last forever," he says. They lock eyes for a long moment. "Some things never seem to go away, do they?"

She holds his gaze and takes a long drag from her cigarette. "They don't. But we had a job to do, and…some of it wasn't that bad." Tears spring to her eyes, and she has to look away. "Sorry, I'm babbling. I miss the people…well…"

"Some of them, right?" he says, with a grim chuckle.

A sharp pain squeezes her heart. Frances. "Sorry," she says. He hands her a handkerchief from his pocket, and she dabs the tears from her cheeks, hoping her mascara doesn't stain it. "I'm sure you've got your own memories that won't quit. You don't need to hear mine."

Boyer presses his warm palm, damp from the beer bottle, on her shaking hand. A wave of grief passes through her body, as though he's transmitting his own anguish through her. And something more. Desire.

"I'm married," she blurts out, pulling her hand from under his and wiggling her wedding-ringed finger, though she's sure he noticed it. "That's why Joe is giving me the stink-eye."

"No apologies necessary. I haven't held a pretty girl's hand in a long time. Nobody wants me like this."

Laura meets his gaze, searching for words that would be honest and comforting, but won't mislead him. "I'm sure that's not true…" she starts to say, but she isn't. She doesn't know anything about his world, only that he's broken, physically scarred. She doesn't feel any more whole, she wants to tell him, even with all her limbs intact.

Boyer glances over at Joe, who's openly staring at them now, two hands resting on the bar as if ready to spring into action. Laura is irritated—Phyllis, Annie, now Joe—treating her as if she's not to be trusted. As if she hadn't survived a war.

"I'd better go," Boyer says. "Enjoy your drink." He chugs down the last of his beer, then fishes two dollars out of his pants pocket, leaving them on the table, and walks away. From the back, he appears as a whole man, tall and broad-shouldered, nothing missing.

That evening, Laura eats half the sandwich she brought home. She makes herself a highball, still thinking about her encounter with Boyer. When he'd gripped her hand so tenderly, she felt something stir inside her. Boyer made her feel seen, understood, even desired— the way Nicholas used to make her feel.

She refreshes her drink, then lights a cigarette and curls up on the sofa with her journal. The letters from Frances and her mother are tucked inside the cover now, along with the photo of Frances and her that she'd found in the footlocker. She puts the picture aside, making a note to find a frame for it. Maybe she'll have a copy made and send it to Frances's mother, whose unanswered letter hangs over her head. What could she say that would make any difference now?

She thumbs through the notebook, remembering the boring stretches of days as they wound up their time in North Africa, then the grueling march up the boot of Italy. She stops when she gets to Anzio. Her penmanship there is ragged, the paper stained and torn in places. A cigarette burn obliterates part of a sentence. All she can make out from that entry is: *Decisions we make every day—who to save? Who to let go?* Boyer understands: Anzio was a hellscape. Suddenly, Laura feels her throat constrict. She's furious at Frances for giving up. To have survived all they went through, only to end up dead six years later—the waste of it.

CHAPTER SEVENTEEN

The next morning, Laura lies low at work, shuffling papers while she waits for her head to clear. She woke up at three a.m. with another nightmare and tossed and turned after that. During her afternoon rounds, as a late-summer tropical storm lashes at the windows with rain and wind, she checks on patients, adjusts IV lines, and administers medications. Then: BOOM BOOM BOOM. A loud explosion comes from somewhere near the hospital. Laura drops to the floor and covers her head with her hands. The lights go out.

"What happened?" the patient closest to her yells.

She stands and shakes it off. *Not a bomb*, she tells herself. "Just a power outage," she reassures the patient. "The generators will kick in shortly. Nothing to worry about." It's the third time that month they've lost power in a windstorm. The wiring in the new ward is modern, but the local electric utility is barely functional. Sideways rain begins pelting the windows, now their only source of light. The generator doesn't kick in, and she's concerned about patients connected to vital-sign monitors and other critical machines. She sees shadowy forms moving through the ward, other nurses checking on patients, calming them.

Cursing and a commotion erupt from down the hall, near the surgical suite. She peers in through the glass door. A doctor is prepping a patient for surgery in the dim light filtering in through the windows, Annie by his side. "Someone get in here with a flashlight, stat. This boy's got a burst appendix."

"I've got it," Laura shouts. She grabs a flashlight from the supply closet, rubs it quickly with an alcohol swab, then pulls on a pair of latex gloves, fastening a mask around her nose and mouth before running into the pre-op room.

"Mask and gloves," Annie says, her back to Laura.

"Already on," Laura says, trying to block out her irritation, focusing the flashlight on the patient's belly. The teenage boy squirms on the bed, writhing in pain.

"Keep that beam right there. We're going to have to do this now," the doctor says.

The anesthetist is monitoring a pressurized tank, which is thankfully still working on battery backup power. "He's out, doctor," the anesthetist says. The boy lies still.

"Annie, apply the topical and hand me a scalpel," the doctor says.

Annie fumbles with the instrument tray. "Laura, give me that light for a second, will you?"

Laura trains the light on the tray of metal instruments long enough for Annie to take a scalpel, then returns it to the patient. The doctor cuts into the boy's abdomen, and immediately, they are hit with an overwhelming stench. In an instant, Laura is back in Italy during the war—the last time she had to hold a light on a patient during a blackout, the bombs exploding nearby as she tried to steady her hand.

"Dammit," the doctor says, backing away from the patient. "Septic."

"I'll get penicillin," Laura says, handing off the flashlight to Annie.

Laura gropes her way in the darkness to the refrigerator in the lab, where they keep the antibiotics and other chilled medicines. She finds a vial of penicillin, still cool, and a syringe. Back in the trauma room, Laura asks Annie to shine the light for her while she injects the penicillin into the boy's IV.

Suddenly, the generator kicks in, and the lights flicker back on. "Thank Christ," the doctor says.

"I've got it from here," Annie says.

Laura switches off the flashlight. *You're welcome.* She turns and walks away. At least Annie's seen what she's capable of. *You're still a good nurse,* Laura tells herself—*a good nurse.*

After her shift, she finds Boyer smoking a cigarette in front of the hospital. She stops on the wide granite steps and puts her hands on her hips. "Mr. Boyer. What are you doing here?" She stifles a smile.

He looks up, a sly smirk on his face.

"Nurse Bruno," he tips his Army cap. "I was in the neighborhood. And please call me Arthur. It's Laura, right?"

Her heart races, certain he's been waiting for her. The thought both irritates and intrigues her. "We have to stop meeting like this."

"Walk with me, Laura," he says, throwing his cigarette butt to the ground.

She shakes her head. "I need to get home."

"Oh, sorry. Of course. To your husband? Your kids?"

"No," she says, immediately regretting it. "I mean...he's away. No kids, but—"

"Please. Just a walk. It's such a nice day now that the storm's cleared out." It is. Puffy fair-weather clouds blow through a pale blue late afternoon sky, and the air smells clean and fresh, a summer rarity. "Just to the river. If that's not too far."

It was only a mile walk to the river; she could ride the streetcar back home from there. "OK," she says, telling herself she can use the exercise. "Against my better judgment."

"Better judgment is overrated."

She laughs. It's the sort of quip Frances used to make. She looks around, hoping nobody she knows will see her walking off in her uniform with a one-armed stranger. They walk down LaSalle and take a right on Canal Street. Shoppers and tourists buzz around the stores and bars along the wide thoroughfare. At the newsstand on the corner, the headlines are about the breakdown of the armistice talks in Korea. Nicholas is over there helping people; meanwhile, she's dallying with this man. She brushes the thought away, accepting a cigarette from Boyer. She can't remember the last time she just strolled. It's a relief to simply look around and enjoy the city.

Boyer points to the Joy Theater marquee, Marlon Brando and Vivien Leigh in *A Streetcar Named Desire*. "Have you seen it yet?"

"No, but I want to. I loved the play. Poor Stella." On cue, a streetcar clangs and rattles its way past on the neutral ground. Laura loves her city fiercely on days like this.

"Tennessee Williams does broken people so well," Boyer says.

We're all broken, Laura thinks.

"Look, there's a bar up ahead," Boyer says, touching her arm. "It's nothing fancy, but I know the owner. We could have a drink before you head home."

He makes it sound so reasonable, even responsible. And she is a little thirsty. "Why not?" she says.

The bartender greets Boyer by his first name. She's middle-aged, pear-shaped, with gray hair in a scraggly bun and a toothpick affixed to the corner of her mouth. Laura has walked by this place in the past, but she'd always thought it was for rough customers. The big mahogany bar is beautifully carved, and crimson velvet drapes—a little threadbare but once luxurious—shut out the sun and the street noise, creating a hush.

"Afternoon, Gerri," Boyer says. "My friend Laura." Laura waves. "Beer for you?" he asks. "Or something else?"

"Beer is fine," Laura says. She really wants something stronger, but needs to stay alert.

"Couple of Jax, please, Gerri." They head to a booth against the far wall. He lights two cigarettes and passes one to Laura. She marvels at how dexterous he is with one hand.

She takes a deep drag of the cigarette, his Chesterfields a little harsher than the Luckies she usually smokes. "So, this is the Chart Room," she says. "Cozy place."

"Sometimes I come in here to write," he says over the strains of a blues song she can't identify. "People leave me alone. And the jukebox is great."

"What do you write?" she asks. "Novels?"

"Nothing, really. A little poetry—don't laugh. Mostly just my journal."

"Why would I laugh? That sounds lovely." The lines she wrote from Anzio spring into her head. *Who to save? Who to let go?* "I kept a journal during the war but haven't written anything since."

"I did too," he says. "But I threw it all in the incinerator. I didn't want anyone reading that after I'm gone. Too raw."

"I get it," she says. The few other customers—dock workers or maybe construction men—pay them no mind. There are no doctors or nurses here, and nobody she recognizes from the other end of the Quarter, the Sicilian end. Gerri brings their beers over, foamy mugs sweating condensation onto the cardboard coasters.

Boyer clinks his mug with hers, and they both take a generous sip. She savors the cool liquid sliding down her throat, smooth and easy. Boyer was right: just what she needed. "You never got to finish your story the other day after Joe chased you away. About..." she gestures to his truncated arm, hoping she's not overstepping. "If you're comfortable talking about it, that is."

"Not much to tell." He leans toward her. "After the explosion, I woke up in a field hospital, no idea how I got there. Somebody had pulled me out, saved me. I never found out who." He takes another long sip of his beer and wipes his mouth with the back of his hand. "I have only hazy memories...When I came to, the arm was gone. No choice, they told me."

"So awful. You must've been shocked." She'd seen men wake up with missing limbs in post-op. Some lost their minds and started screaming; others just went silent.

"Something like that," he says. "They sent me home a week before VE Day. Said I had 'battle fatigue' on top of the lost arm."

She taps her cigarette into an amber glass ashtray with a sailboat etched into it. "They told me nurses don't get battle fatigue. That we weren't in combat."

"What? Weren't you in Anzio?" He remembers.

"Even the men didn't get battle points for Anzio. A 'strategic failure,' the Army called it."

"Bullshit."

"Exactly. They told the women to get over it. That women were strong, blah blah blah."

He shakes his head. "But you didn't get over it."

"No." She wants to cry, all of a sudden, but washes the tears down with beer.

He pulls on his cigarette, then turns his head to exhale the plume of smoke away from her. She's struck by the small, thoughtful gesture. "What about now?" he asks.

She wants to tell him about Frances, the nightmares, and all the rest—the lost promotion at work, her dead child, the distance with Nicholas. To pour out her heart right on the scratched wooden table marred with cigarette burns and graffiti carvings. She fights the urge to lay all her burdens before this man who is not her husband. "Good days and bad," she says.

Boyer's eyes narrow, holding hers a little too long. He finishes his beer. "Let's go down to the river before the sun sets."

"Sure," she says, relieved that he's deciding what's next, so she doesn't have to.

He places a dollar on the bar. "Thanks, Gerri."

"See you soon, Arty," Gerri says. "Nice to meet you, hon."

They walk the two short blocks to the river. Laura feels self-conscious in her white uniform; she hopes she won't be recognized. He lays his jacket down for her to sit on a damp wooden bench outside an abandoned warehouse. The port is bustling, even at this hour. Men in overalls unload crates of bananas from a steamship, shouting to each other in Spanish over the noise of giant chains and winches. Boyer keeps his eyes on the men.

"The dock workers eat their lunch on these benches," he tells her. "Sometimes I watch them from my balcony. And the river. I never get tired of it. Different every day."

"You live nearby?" she asks.

"Right over there," he points to a three-story red brick building with wrought iron balconies, purple bougainvillea spilling over the railings. "On the third floor. One of the few buildings that survived the big fire back in 1794."

Long before her family arrived, Laura wanted to say, but she's wary of sharing too many personal details with him—a slippery slope. She pictures the inside of his apartment, a lonely bachelor pad, the rent cheap. She wonders what money he lives on, perhaps a GI pension. He hasn't mentioned a job.

A slight breeze picks up, and she catches a whiff of coal from the nearby steamship dock, mixed with the ancient funk of the river. A paddle-wheeler bobs at its berth, waiting for a group of tourists to board for a sunset ride. Gulls swoop and dive for scraps of food and trash. She wonders why they're here, so far from the sea.

"There goes the sun," Boyer says. A tugboat blows its mournful horn as if to mark the day's end, nosing a barge upriver through the swirling, muddy currents of the Mississippi. They sit quietly, watching the sky turn from blue to purple, the undersides of the clouds tinged with pink. He cradles his damaged arm, hugging himself. "Hey, a crazy question," he says. "Would you want to have supper with me sometime? It's no fun cooking for one."

She's startled. Never once has Nicholas made her a meal, not that it's the point at the moment. "Oh, no, thank you, but...I can't."

"You'd be surprised how handy a one-armed man can be in the kitchen. I don't want to be too forward, but if your husband is away for a while—"

"He's in Korea. A humanitarian mission. A doctor in a refugee camp." She stops short of telling him she'll be alone for three months.

"I know you have family, probably a lot of friends too, so I'm sure you won't lack for dinner companions while he's gone."

"I grew up right down there." She points to the other end of the Quarter, the spires of St. Louis Cathedral just visible, unsure of why she's telling him all this. "My folks own a grocery store on Dauphine, and my sister lives in the Marigny with her family."

"Right. Sicilian," he says. "I'd better watch myself."

"Not like that," Laura says, laughing. Her father knows people in *la cosa nostra*, but steers clear of them. The thought of him being involved in that kind of crime is absurd.

"Just kidding," he says. "It's obvious you come from a good family. Still, it would mean a lot to me if you'd let me cook for you to repay you for being so kind and for helping me. And I enjoy your company. Just dinner. That's all, I promise."

Of course, that isn't all, she knows. Still, she can't bring herself to refuse him outright. "I'll think about it."

CHAPTER EIGHTEEN

Two days later, the duty nurse hands Laura a slip of paper with a name and phone number written on it. "This patient called, asking for you. Said his name was John Singer, but I couldn't find a record of him, and he didn't want to talk to me." She pauses, clearly expecting Laura to offer an explanation. It's highly unusual for a patient to call for a nurse.

Laura takes the note from her and tries to keep from laughing at Boyer's pseudonym. Carson McCullers's hero: John Singer. "I'll handle it, thanks."

All afternoon as she works, Laura rehearses what she'll say to him. She's flattered, but she can't let the attention go to her head. She doesn't really know this man, after all. And she's had so little experience with men in general. Nicholas was her first serious boyfriend, and that courtship was hardly under normal circumstances. She reminds herself of the dangers: Boyer is a lonely man, she's feeling neglected, and it's clear they're physically attracted to each other. It's bad enough she's having thoughts about him, wondering what it would be like to kiss him, and more. No—she can't let him blow up her whole life. She'll tell him he can't call her like that, it's not right. She's married, after all. Whatever he has in mind is not going to happen.

At the end of her shift, she dials his number from the pay phone in the hospital lobby. He picks up on the first ring.

"Arthur," she starts.

"Thanks for getting back to me," he says.

"You shouldn't be calling me here."

"Sorry, I didn't know how else to reach you, other than hanging around outside again. That felt a little creepy. And I didn't think your cousin would welcome me back over at Joe's."

"For good reason."

He laughs. "I'm calling about that dinner I owe you." His voice is raspy, as if he's smoked a million cigarettes. She wonders if he would taste like tobacco.

"You don't owe me anything. Thanks for the invitation, but it doesn't sound like a good idea to me."

"It sounds like an excellent idea to me, though. I really enjoy talking with you. I think we have...a connection. But if it's just me, I'll leave you alone. I don't want to be a pest."

"You're not a pest," she says. He's right. They understand each other, and there's so much they don't yet know. She feels her resolve wavering. "It's just that...well, a married woman doesn't go to a single man's apartment for dinner. Not in my world."

He's quiet on the other end of the line. A man paces outside the phone booth, glaring at her. She turns her back to him.

"You're right, of course." Boyer's voice sounds choked, as if he's swallowing his words. Anguished. His hunger is the same as hers. "I let my imagination get away from me. When you spend as much time alone as I do, finding that human connection is so rare. I guess I just wanted a little more, if that makes sense."

"I'm sorry. I really can't."

"Just one dinner, then I'll leave you alone? Promise."

She takes a deep breath. The truth is she does want to see him again, to know him more. For him to know her. "Just one dinner."

"That's great. Tomorrow night? What time do you get off work?"

"I'm done at six," she says. Her head is spinning. Can she really do this? "Someone's waiting for the phone—I have to go."

"I'll see you then. You remember where the place is?"

"Yes."

"I'll look forward to it, Laura."

She leaves the phone booth, holding the door for the scowling man. She smiles at him in spite of herself, excitement battling trepidation. *What have I done?*

The next day, she wakes up nervous and excited. She takes care with her hair and makeup, then folds a skirt and blouse into a bag with her sandals. She isn't even sure she'll go through with it—the dinner with Boyer—but if she does, she can't show up there in her uniform.

During her shift, she battles thoughts of the many ways things could go wrong. Someone she knows could see her walking to his house and ask where she's headed. Unlikely—her people are all on the opposite end of the Quarter—but she'd have to come up with a plausible lie, just in case. She could be leading Boyer on, which would be cruel. But he's a grown man; he knows what he's doing, and she's been honest with him. It's just dinner, she tells herself. She thinks of Nicholas, too, of course, though he's gone off for three months without even consulting her. He'd accused her of wallowing in her pain. Maybe he was right. But maybe wallowing with someone else, someone who understands, is exactly what she needs.

After she clocks out, Laura changes out of her uniform in the nurse's locker room. She freshens up her makeup, reapplying red lipstick. After smoothing her hair into place, she spritzes her wrists and throat from the atomizer of cologne in her purse. In the mirror, she tries to see herself as Boyer might. Other than Nicholas, she's never had dinner alone with a man she wasn't related to. She can't deny Boyer has stirred feelings in her. Maybe she should call and cancel. But then, another nurse comes in and tells her she looks nice. Laura says thanks, then pulls away from the mirror, and her doubts.

The walk into the Quarter is warm and sticky; she hopes she's not too disheveled by the time she arrives at Boyer's building. She hesitates on the sidewalk outside, her last chance to back out of this probably foolish idea.

"Laura," Boyer calls from the balcony above, beaming over the purple bougainvillea as if her being there is the most natural thing in the world. "I'll be right down."

Her pulse quickens at his footsteps on the staircase inside. He opens the door wide to let her in. "You made it." His bright blue eyes sparkle. He's had a haircut since she'd seen him last.

"I'm a little worse for this heat, I'm afraid." He closes the door behind them. It's cooler in the narrow, dark foyer, with its decorative antique tile floor. The stucco walls are patched in some places, exposing the brick beneath in others. "Ladies first. Mind your step."

She walks up two flights ahead of him on the old marble stairs, worn smooth in the middle of the treads. The hallway smells of mildew, dust, and the ghosts of the people who'd lived here a hundred years ago and longer. Somehow, the scent is comforting, like the apartment where she grew up, above her parents' corner grocery store—nothing like the newer house in Mid City she and Nicholas live in now.

"Here we are," he says, reaching around her to open his apartment door. "It's not fancy, but it suits me fine."

The apartment isn't the dingy bachelor pad she'd envisioned. The ceilings are high; light streams in through a pair of tall windows facing the street. It's modestly furnished but tasteful, with eclectic lamps, a deep blue cushioned settee, and original paintings on the walls. A ceiling fan spins lazily overhead, stirring a warm breeze. Bookshelves overflow on either side of a small fireplace. A jazz album plays on a phonograph. A small kitchen has been outfitted along one wall, and a delicious aroma wafts from the oven. The apartment is just one big room, tactfully divided. She spies his bed behind a fabric screen.

A tiny tiger kitten emerges from behind the divider. It stops mid-step and stares at Laura, its green eyes widening. "Oh, and who's this?" Laura asks.

"That's Brett. She followed me home last week and decided to stay." The cat starts washing itself, its miniature pink tongue wetting down the fur of its paws. "She's not exactly cuddly, but she keeps me company."

"Brett's an odd name for a cat."

"And here I thought you were a literary type," he says.

She's puzzled for a moment, then gets it and laughs. Hemingway. "Ah, yes. *The Sun Also Rises*," she says, vaguely remembering Brett Ashley as a troubled and frustrating character.

"You got it." Boyer takes a bottle of white wine from the small refrigerator. "Dinner's almost ready. Sorry, it's so stifling in here. We can sit outside."

They climb through the floor-to-ceiling window onto a tiny balcony, shaded this time of day, where he's set a small wrought iron table for two. A votive candle flickers in a glass jelly jar, next to a single pink rose in a ceramic bud vase. She has a hard time imagining him at war; he has an artist's eye.

"Oh my," she says. "This...this is lovely."

She sits, and he fills her wine glass. "Relax. I'll be back with dinner in a flash."

She takes a small sip of the white wine. Crisp and delicious. *Keep your wits about you*, she tells herself.

A slight cooling breeze off the river riffles her hair. On the adjacent rooftops, laundry hangs on clotheslines. Pigeon coops and water tanks remind her of the view from the childhood bedroom she shared with Rose. Her parents are probably eating supper in their kitchen about now, as they have almost every night for decades. They're less than a mile down the street, but a world away.

Boyer comes back with her plate, setting it down with a flourish. Chicken cutlets with lemon and capers, on top of spaghetti. Sautéed zucchini on the side.

"Smells delicious," she says. "Thanks for going to all this trouble."

"No trouble at all. Be right back." With his one arm, he can only carry a single plate at a time. She doesn't want to offend him by offering to help.

They dig into the food, making small talk over the hum of traffic on the street below. He asks her questions about the hospital and her family. She's relaxing now, comfortable with him. He listens intently, just as Nicholas used to, back when their love was new.

Boyer points to a large gray troop transport, headed downriver. "There's another Navy ship. They loaded up with troops earlier today. Off to Korea."

Korea. Where her husband is. She pushes the thought away. "Godspeed to them." She remembers the day she shipped out of this port herself, waving to her father and Rose on the shore, so unaware of all that would come next.

After they finish eating, they climb back inside. She brings the plates to the sink before he can object, as he changes out the record on the phonograph. "Please make yourself comfortable," he says. "I'll just be a minute. There's chocolate on the coffee table. Help yourself." Before she can offer to help, he starts washing the dishes, expertly scrubbing them with one hand, then placing them gently in the dish strainer.

She takes a chocolate from a small porcelain dish and unwraps it—from Elmer's, the best candymaker in town. He's thought of every detail. The candy is decadently delicious. "Who are we listening to?" The melancholy clarinet notes are delicate, almost wistful.

"Sidney Bechet," he says over his shoulder. "Petite Fleur."

"Beautiful. I thought it sounded familiar." She'd heard Bechet before—he grew up just across Rampart Street from the French Quarter, in Tremé—but this piece somehow captures what she's feeling—a nostalgia for something that hasn't happened yet.

"He moved to France, I hear," Boyer says. "Wish I'd gotten to see him."

She wanders around the small apartment, impressed with his taste. It's soulful, personal. Brett is curled up in an adorable ball of fur on an antique upholstered chair. Photographs line the mantel—his parents, presumably, a baseball team, a younger Boyer in the front row. "Did you play?"

"I did," he says. "I was being scouted for the pros when the Japs hit Pearl Harbor. I signed up—figured I could play when I came home." He shakes his head.

She picks up a picture of him with another man. Boyer in uniform, two arms folded across his chest, a strong chin, and a mischievous smile. The other soldier is making a goofy face next to him, a rifle slung over his shoulder. "Look at you. So handsome. Who's your friend?"

"My buddy James. Everyone called him Ace. He was a card shark, a real larger-than-life character." He pours two glasses of bourbon over ice. He hands one to her. "Blown up right next to me. A split second earlier or later, and it would've been me. Sometimes I wish it had been."

"I'm so sorry." Tears lodge in her throat, and she carefully returns the photo to the mantel.

"There was no time to stop, even to take it in. He was gone in an instant, and I had to save myself and the others in my unit. But I've never quite been able to shake the sense that I was wrong to leave Ace behind, that I failed him. You know what I mean?"

She swipes a tear from under her eye, blinking back an image of Frances as she was in the war. "I do."

He leads her to the small sofa, and they sit. "Sorry, I didn't mean to make you sad." He sips at his whiskey, then shakes two cigarettes out of a pack on the coffee table.

She lights them both up. "So many men made it out of our tents only to return to the front," she says. "We'd get reports later, when some of them didn't make it."

Boyer takes a deep drag off his cigarette. He's sitting so close, the heat from his body makes her lightheaded. She presses the icy glass against the inside of her wrist. She holds it there, despite the almost unbearable cold. "I got a letter a couple of weeks ago. My best friend from the war. Frances. She...she took her own life." Her left hand trembles. She hasn't said those words out loud, except to Nicholas.

He puts his cigarette down in the ashtray and takes her shaking hand in his, rubbing her palm with his thumb. "Tell me about her."

"She was a pistol." She laughs. "Always the life of the party. Loud, from Texas. A big, blowsy blond—you know the type. She and your friend Ace would've been thick as thieves."

"I do," he says with a chuckle. "God bless 'em. You were in Anzio together?"

"And North Africa before that. We met on the first day of training. Instant friends."

"But it sounds like you were very different."

"You can say that again. Maybe we're drawn to people who have something we want for ourselves. She brought me out of my shell, and I reeled her back in when she got too close to the edge. Sometimes, anyway." A wave of sadness breaks across her chest. She could've reeled Frances back from the edge one more time. "I'm...I'm sorry."

"Don't apologize." He drops her hand and fishes a white handkerchief from his pocket. "I understand."

She blows her nose.

"She was important to you, and now she's gone," he says. "She was with you on some of the most difficult days of your life. She saw you through."

She did. "It's like what you said about Ace—I feel like I failed her, you know?" She takes a big sip of the liquor, savoring its burn.

Boyer's bourbon is gone. He fishes an ice cube from the bottom of his glass and presses it to the hollow of her throat. She shivers, then leans toward him, touching her lips to his. He tastes like alcohol and cigarettes. He puts the ice cube back in his glass and looks at her, his electric-blue eyes now a watery ocean. He kisses her throat where the ice cube had been, then hugs her to himself, burying his face in her chest. She strokes the back of his arm, holding him for a few quiet moments, then gently pushes him away. "I can't...I'm sorry. I should go."

He looks at her and nods once. "I understand. I don't like it, but I understand." He stands up and gets the whiskey bottle. He refills both their glasses.

"I shouldn't," she says.

"Just one more. For Ace and Frances."

She clinks her glass with his. "To good friends. The best."

Then he leans over and kisses her again, lightly this time, almost chaste. "Laura, I—"

"Shhh." The whiskey courses through her bloodstream. She kisses him back. He unfastens the top button of her blouse and kisses her shoulder. She's anxious for whatever will come next, knowing there is no going back to a few minutes ago, when she knew she had to leave. But she didn't, and now she wants him more than she's ever wanted anything in her life.

Then he takes her by the hand, leading her behind the screen and sitting her down on the edge of his bed. He kneels in front of her and kisses her again, his whiskey tongue finding hers. He lets her help him undress, and she's tender with him, knowing he must be self-conscious about the missing arm. He's disfigured, but she's seen it before. The rest of his body is perfect, and she allows herself a moment to appreciate his muscled torso, glistening in the heat, before sliding off her own clothes and shoes. He watches, motionless, his eyes devouring her. Then she climbs onto the bed next to him.

Laura closes her eyes and surrenders to what's happening. She wants him to know her, not the version she puts on at work or with her family. But this, her real self. He kisses her so deeply she wants to inhale him. His fingers find soft places that haven't been touched in so long. Then, he eases himself on top of her, his weight like a comforting blanket. She pulls him inside her, his movements slow, patient, skillful, until she cries out as explosive, unmitigated pleasure rolls through her body. They collapse in a sweaty embrace, clinging to each other and sobbing.

CHAPTER NINETEEN

Early the next morning, Laura wakes up disoriented when the bells of the cathedral chime six times. The soft light of dawn streams through the open window. Next to her, Boyer breathes deeply, sound asleep. From this angle, he looks whole, his good arm resting on the pillow, the Rose of No Man's Land tattoo on his muscled bicep. She's almost overcome with an urge to burrow back under the sheets and never leave. To wake him with her mouth, to touch him and make him moan again, the way he had last night. To accept his tenderness, his caresses, his desperation. His gratitude mingled with hers. He'd wept on her shoulder after he climaxed. She didn't ask how long it had been since he'd been with a woman.

But in the cold light of day, she also feels a reckoning coming on. She's crossed a line. She needs to get out before he wakes up, to put some distance between herself and this apartment. At the kitchen sink, she splashes water on her face and chest, which does little to help the throbbing in her head. The kitten rubs against her leg, and Laura puts a small dish of milk on the floor, then pulls her rumpled uniform from her bag and quickly dresses. She'll have to sneak into the ladies' room at the hospital to slap on some makeup and brush her teeth. One more glance at Boyer, still asleep, then she quietly closes the door behind her and heads downstairs.

She hurries through the streets of the Quarter, certain everyone can see her shame, can smell him on her. She scolds herself—this was not what she'd planned at all—but then finds the rationale. It was just one night, she tells herself. A reaction to all she's been going through. A fellow veteran who eased her grief with his own. A mistake she can get over. Nobody has to know.

At work, Laura hopes the smells on her unwashed body are masked by the usual hospital odors of antiseptic and humans in various states of distress. A cup of strong coffee perks her up a little, and she works hard to focus on her nursing tasks. But her mind wanders back to Boyer's apartment, his bed, the feel of him still on her skin.

At lunchtime, she unearths a bowl of cold leftover macaroni she'd stashed in the break room fridge a few days ago. It still smells viable, and she needs something in her stomach. She finds a discarded *Life* magazine on the table and takes it and the pasta outside. She finds a bench and leafs through the magazine while she eats. General Eisenhower is campaigning for president. Ronald Reagan poses in an ad for Chesterfield cigarettes, making her wish she had brought a pack. She can still taste Boyer, and shudders thinking about the way he made her feel. His hands, his lips, his body on hers, letting her unconstrained grief flow into his as he held her. His hunger for connection made her feel valued, understood, and seen. Her husband wouldn't give her that. Or couldn't. If only Frances were here—surely, she would grant Laura grace, undoubtedly with a salty comment or two, but without judgment.

She finishes her macaroni and wraps the bowl back up in its dish towel. Palm trees sway in the slight breeze, reminding her of that oasis in Tunisia with Nicholas—another lifetime. A few more weeks and Nicholas will be back. Then what? Her real life will have to resume; there's no way around that. She resolves to call Boyer tonight, to thank him for the lovely evening and to tell him it has to be left at that. It will be easier over the phone; she won't be able to see his eyes, his disappointment, his heartache. She'll do it gently, respectfully, so he doesn't think it has anything to do with his missing arm, only with her situation.

Suddenly, Annie appears, startling Laura out of her reverie. She's holding a brown paper bag and a red plaid thermos. "May I join you?"

"Of course," Laura says. "I was just finishing up."

Annie sits next to her and unpacks her sandwich. "Looks like the East Coast is getting that hurricane," she says. "I'm glad it didn't hit us."

Laura laughs. "Now you sound like a local. Hey, I was thinking—I know you and I haven't had much of a chance to get to know each other. How about we grab a drink after work? Across the street at Joe's. Everyone goes there."

Annie shakes her head. "Not for me, thanks. I don't go to bars anymore."

"Sorry," Laura stammers. "I didn't know."

Annie clears her throat and looks down at her sandwich, then takes a deep breath and looks directly at Laura, the scar above her right brow pulsing a little, her gray eyes and fine blond hair almost translucent in the sunlight. "I'm going to share something with you that I don't normally talk about. I'm a private person, for a bunch of reasons, but I think you need to hear this story."

Laura sits up straighter, feeling the remnants of last night's pleasure dissipate.

"In the war..." She looks over Laura's shoulder into the courtyard. "Well, I don't have to tell you about the things we saw, the night-mares we brought home with us. Where I was stationed for most of it—Corregidor—we had our share of horrors on a daily basis. Good times, too, to be sure. Too much drinking, of course. Close pals, some of them lost."

Laura takes a deep breath, a pang in her heart, thinking of Frances, dead at thirty-three. She wonders where this conversation is going.

"I'm a good nurse, I had no doubt of that going in," Annie says. "But over there—so many fucked up situations, guys dying for stupid reasons. Patching people up only to see them back on a stretcher the next week...." Her voice trails off. Laura remembers the gut punch every time word reached them about a man who'd died in the field after leaving her post-op tent.

"I almost didn't come to New Orleans. The weather reminds me too much of the jungle over there." Annie laughs a little. "It was just dumb luck I didn't end up taken prisoner when the Japs took Corregidor. Some of my friends weren't as lucky."

"I remember when we heard those nurses got captured," Laura says. "Terrifying."

"Anyway," Annie continues. "When I came home, I was exhausted, but figured life would return to normal. It's what we all told ourselves, right? I got my old job back at the hospital and returned to work as before the war, like you. But something was off right from the get-go. Nobody I worked with—and certainly not my friends who hadn't served—had any concept of what we went through. Even after I pointed out that the VFW rules didn't expressly exclude women, they tried to steer me to the Ladies Auxiliary. I said no thanks."

Laura nods: she'd tried to join as well. "My husband spends half his life over there."

Annie chews a mouthful of her sandwich and washes it down with a swig from her thermos. "I drank at home, alone. I drank to forget. But of course, it didn't work. The nightmares came anyway, so I drank some more. Then I started to drink during the day, sometimes at work."

Laura tenses up, wondering if Annie has heard or seen something, thinking of the empty flask in her purse, the bar over at Joe's, and the drink she's craving this very minute.

"Eventually, I tapped out. Quit the hospital before they fired me. Got a job tending bar. The employee discount was great. The results were not. I won't go into the whole fiasco, but a few months into it, I could scarcely get through a shift. One day, a doctor from the hospital spotted me on the street. I'm pretty sure I looked…rough. He bought me a cup of coffee and told me about his own journey, and about a group he'd joined when his drinking got out of hand."

"What, like AA?" Laura scoffs.

Annie flinches. "Yes."

Laura looks across the courtyard, fixing her gaze on a pale-skinned, elderly man shuffling by in loose pants and a hospital johnny, holding onto a younger woman's arm—his daughter, perhaps. "With all due respect, Annie. Why are you telling me all this? Are you saying you're an alcoholic?"

"Yes. Even if I don't drink, I'm still an alcoholic. That's what I'm saying."

She shakes her head. Annie doesn't look like a drunk. Alcoholics are those day drinkers at Joe's, the panhandlers on the street, disheveled and alone. "I'm sorry to hear that. I didn't know, obviously, and I'm sorry I invited you over to Joe's."

"I just can't be around it," Annie says.

Laura glances at her watch. "I'd better get back."

"I just wanted you to know," Annie says again. "And if you ever need to talk to someone yourself, you can come to me. Confidentially."

Laura forces a smile and tucks a lock of hair back under her cap. Annie's trying to make a connection where none exists; she won't take the bait. She gathers her purse and her lunch things and stands up. "I appreciate it, and thanks for telling me your story. I'm glad you found some help."

Annie looks up at her. "I mean it."

At home after her shift, Laura drops the mail on the kitchen counter and heads straight to the bathroom, stripping off her uniform and turning the shower on as hot as she can stand it. She scrubs off the last twenty-four hours as best she can, then wraps herself in a terry-cloth robe, feeling a little more human. It's only four o'clock—too early to go to bed, as exhausted as she is. She heads to the kitchen, where she leafs through the stack of mail on the counter—a couple of bills, a medical journal—then stops with a jolt: a postcard from Nicholas. On the front is a picture of a sunset over the mountains outside Seoul, on the flip side, his scratchy handwriting:

"Korea is beautiful, but the work is tough. Long days, too many sick kids. Great team, working well together. Feels good to be helping people. Hope all's well on the home front. Miss you. XO —Nicholas."

She reads the short note again, parsing every phrase, then pins the postcard to the refrigerator with a magnet, picture side facing out. Why couldn't he spare the time to write a whole letter? She stands at the front window, smoking. The sun is down, and the neighborhood glows with the remaining light. The little lawn out front needs to be mowed. She'll have to ask her brother-in-law to do that for her. She pours herself a short glass of whiskey, drinks it in two gulps, and refills it from the nearly-empty bottle. She's glad that she can handle her liquor, that she doesn't have to give up drinking as Annie did.

She opens the refrigerator, but she's forgotten to shop for groceries, and all that's left are condiments and a head of wilted lettuce. She thinks about the sumptuous dinner Boyer cooked for her the night before. No good can come of this infatuation, she tells herself. She needs to end it with him, now, before she gets in too deep. She takes the message slip out of her purse. John Singer. McCullers's lonely protagonist. She picks up the phone and dials Boyer's number, half-hoping he won't be there. He picks up on the second ring.

"Hello?"

She doesn't answer right away, not sure she can go through with it.

"I can still taste you," he says.

She breathes into the receiver, tears forming in her eyes.

"I have leftovers if you're hungry."

"I'm starving," she says, wiping her eyes with the heel of her hand.

PART FOUR

Anzio, Italy, February 1944

CHAPTER TWENTY

Frances was still sound asleep, so Laura tiptoed out of the tent. More than a half-foot of snow had fallen overnight. Under the blanket of white, the camp looked almost serene, but the bone-chilling cold made her long for the dry heat she'd cursed in Tunisia. And the weather wasn't the only stark difference. As bad as North Africa had been, at least they weren't cut off from the world, short on supplies, with no place to go except back to sea.

Since they landed on the beach a few weeks prior, they'd been trapped in the valley, pummeled day and night from the surrounding hills, where the Nazi troops were dug in. The area was so dangerous that the Corps of Engineers had moved the Army command center into ancient underground catacombs. The hospital units weren't so lucky.

Inside the mess tent, a small kerosene heater in the corner puffed out more smoke than warmth. Laura scanned the tent for Nicholas, but he must've still been asleep. She was grateful nobody made eye contact; she wasn't ready for chit-chat, groggy and hungover as she was. The flow of wounded had finally slowed to a trickle. She and Frances had celebrated the lull a little too hard the night before.

Someone had blessedly made a fresh pot of coffee. She sat down and warmed her hands around the steaming mug. From the corner radio, the news announcer's shrill voice droned on like a hot poker to the side of her throbbing head.

"British casualties from the ambush at Monte Cassino are climbing into the hundreds, and the Germans have boasted they will make Anzio another Dunkirk," the announcer read from the *Stars and Stripes*. "President Franklin Roosevelt is conferring with high military officials about the gravity of the situation. One of the generals we interviewed referred to Anzio as 'a half-acre of hell.'"

Laura felt the bile of panic in her stomach. The constant threat hung like a storm cloud over the blood-soaked beachhead as they waited endlessly for the Allies to break through enemy lines at Cassino in the Liri Valley. The Axis still held the Gustav Line to the south, which had forced them to Anzio by sea in the first place. It was supposed to have been a quick assault, then on to Rome. But the Nazis had other plans. The relentless bombings and the freight train sound of the big German K-5 guns, which the GIs had nicknamed the "Anzio Express," had everyone on edge. Her nerves were frayed, and she doubted once again whether she had what it took to stick it out.

Captain McCarthy lowered herself onto the bench next to her. "Morning," she grunted, sipping from her coffee. On the radio, the news was blessedly over. The Andrews Sisters sang "Don't Sit Under the Apple Tree," the lyrics somehow menacing in light of the German threat.

"Morning, ma'am," Laura said. "You missed the *Stars and Stripes*."

"Good," McCarthy waved her hand. "It's all rubbish. Don't listen to it." Laura wasn't sure what was true and what wasn't. She wished she could ignore the news, but it was hard not to worry.

Avis and Mildred stomped into the canteen, their boots covered in mud and snow. Mildred sat at the table while Avis went to get coffee. "You were up early," Laura said. Their bunks had been empty and neatly made when Laura woke up. Mildred and Avis didn't drink like Frances and she had the night before. They looked rosy-cheeked and healthy.

"You know us farm girls," Mildred laughed.

Avis sat down. "Out with the Corps," she said, handing a mug to Mildred. The Army Corps of Engineers had arrived a few days earlier to build protective mud walls to serve as bunkers around the hospital tents. Some of the nurses had volunteered to help fill sandbags as additional protection.

"Reminds me of hiding in the root cellar back home during tornadoes," Avis said. "Only without the jars of grandma's pickles."

"You girls are good to help," McCarthy said.

Mildred sipped her coffee. "Makes me feel useful," she said. "I hate just sitting around when it's quiet like this. Too much time to dwell. The GIs are going to dig slit trenches in the sleeping tents, too." Laura couldn't quite picture how a muddy foxhole would protect them from German bombs.

"We ought to get one of those photographers to document it," McCarthy said. Some news people had been wandering through the camp with the Army Signal Corps for a couple of days. "People need to know what my nurses are made of."

Laura looked at her hands, fingernails ragged and dirty. She wasn't made of the same sturdy stuff as Mildred and Avis.

Ellen appeared and sat down. "They dropped these on the beach again." She handed a leaflet to Laura. "In case you want to switch sides."

The flyer featured a drawing of a scantily-clad nurse. The English was crude, but the message was clear enough: *Your situation is hopeless.* Laura crumpled it up and threw the ball of paper, missing the trash barrel. She felt like refusing to let the Germans get under her skin was an act of defiance, but she wasn't sure it was working.

"What'll happen to us if they can't hold the bad guys off?" Mildred asked. "Feels like we're sitting ducks." It was the question they all had on their minds. A few days prior, the Germans had shelled another nearby evacuation hospital despite the big red crosses on its tents. Nurses had been among the wounded.

Avis took a sip of her coffee, her forehead creased. "We would never surrender, would we?"

"Hopefully, it won't come to that. They'll probably evacuate us to ships in the harbor," Captain McCarthy said, sidestepping Avis's question. "I'm sure they're working on a plan."

"They didn't evacuate those nurses when Bataan fell," Ellen said. They'd all been terrified to hear about American and Filipina nurses taken as Japanese prisoners of war in the Pacific. "Something about the women being a morale factor for the wounded."

What about our morale? Laura wondered. It made her sick to think about being captured and sent to a Nazi POW camp. More than once, the thought had kept her awake. She'd never even considered the possibility when she'd joined the Army. Now it was all too real. Laura wasn't sure the Captain even knew what the plan was, or if she was just passing along more propaganda, but she kept that to herself.

"That was a different situation," McCarthy said. "It does nobody any good to start imagining worst-case scenarios. Stay focused on the mission at hand. Do our jobs. Speaking of which, I'm off to do mine."

"I guess she's right," Ellen said.

"Same as my granny always says: 'Don't borrow trouble,'" Mildred said.

Laura usually loved Mildred's homespun sayings, but this morning they were ringing hollow. "It's the Captain's job to keep us calm. Hopefully she's not downplaying the danger."

"It's her job to keep us safe," Ellen said. "I wouldn't want to be her."

A few days later, they were slammed with casualties again. Ambulances lined up, disgorging the wounded just in from the battlefield. Inside the triage tent, Laura took a deep breath as she surveyed the scene: a long row of cots filled with men, some missing limbs and soaked in bloody makeshift bandages the medics had applied in the field. Faces shot away. Sucking chest and abdominal gashes or the opposite: pinpoint entry wounds that likely led to massive internal injuries.

She gloved up and took her place at a station with Ellen, who'd been there for hours already, and Ellen was now bandaging what was left of a man's ear. "This one wants to go back to the front ASAP," she told Laura.

"I hear the Huns are bombing the crap out of these hospitals," the man said. "I want out of here."

"I can't imagine it's any more peaceful at the front," Laura said. It was hard to argue with him, though.

"At least we have foxholes there," the man replied. "Hey, you look familiar."

"I do?" Laura studied him more closely—dark hair, deep brown eyes, heavy stubble on his cheeks. "Sorry, I'm not placing you. We see so many boys..."

"Tunisia. I'm from Chicago, remember?"

"Oh, right!" Laura said, though she didn't.

"We talked about Italian food, our families. You gave me a lecture about...health issues." His face reddened.

All of a sudden, it clicked. The man had been sharing his sulfa pills with the other GIs to ward off gonorrhea. Then, when they got wounded and needed them, they didn't have enough. "Did you heed my advice?" she asked.

He laughed. "I did. I've got a girl back home, you know. A real doll. I said an Act of Contrition and cut it out."

"What's her name?" Laura asked. She knew she should move on to other patients, but she was touched that he had remembered her.

"Mary," he said, fishing a photo out of a battered tan leather bill-fold. "Her high school graduation." His voice cracked.

She studied the photo. Mary's pretty smile was innocent, untouched, like Laura had been herself not that long ago. "Gorgeous," she said. "You'd better behave yourself."

He tenderly replaced the picture, then clutched the wallet to his heart. "I can't wait to get home to her. Get married, kids. The whole nine yards."

"Let's see if we can salvage that ear, so you can hear her when she whispers sweet nothings," Ellen said. "Off you go to surgery." She motioned to a medic to take the man away.

"Thank you," he said, reaching for Laura.

"No offense, but I don't want to see you back here again," she said, squeezing his hand.

Ellen was wiping down their station with alcohol, getting ready for the next patient.

"You must be exhausted," Laura said. "Want me to take over?"

"Let's do one more together, then I'll go," Ellen said. "You're glad you missed this morning. So much trench foot." She wrinkled her nose. Everyone hated it. The men came in unable to walk on red, swollen feet from sitting in water-filled foxholes for too long. All they could do was give them warm foot baths and dry socks. After a short rest, most of them went right back to the front.

The next patient up held his right arm tight to his body in a makeshift sling. Ellen peeled off his tattered shirt, and they saw his torso riddled with shrapnel. He'd need a surgeon to pick it all out.

"Are you in a lot of pain?" Ellen asked him while Laura took his pulse.

"A little, but I'm counting my blessings," he said. "This shrapnel didn't kill me, at least not yet. My buddy wasn't so lucky—the shell had his name on it." The man was dry-eyed, stoic. Laura assumed he was still in shock and made a note on his chart. They saw much more of this here than in North Africa. *Battle fatigue*, they called it; the term sounded far too genteel for Laura's taste.

"Get out of here, before they bring in another one," Laura told Ellen. "Get some rest."

"That's gonna hit him later, about the friend," Ellen said, removing her gloves and mask. "He'll blame himself."

Later, on a surgical shift, Laura and Frances were assisting Dr. Pierce. A patient had a piece of shrapnel stuck in his aorta, acting like a cork. Once the man was sedated, Pierce took a deep breath. "I did one of these back home once," he said. "Hopefully, I remember what I did wrong." A rare moment of humility.

Frances kept track of the man's vitals. "Pulse 130, systolic BP 90 and dropping." Her voice was calm, but the numbers were alarming.

Pierce closed up the tear in the man's aorta, his stitches delicate and quick. "Moment of truth," he said, unclamping the artery. They all stood back. The repair held. Laura exhaled. She and Pierce had long since made their peace with each other. He still flew into rages now and then, but McCarthy was right: he was one of the best at his job.

Frances squeezed the blood pressure cuff. "BP 130 over 80. Damn, you're good, doc."

"I think he'll make it," Pierce said, removing his gloves. "Give him a shot of penicillin every four hours. And keep him far away from anyone with the gas gangrene." A lethal bacterium, the men picked up in the damp barnyards and farms of Italy, gas gangrene was the most dreaded and deadly of all complications, also ferociously contagious. Laura made the notation on the man's chart and sent him to post-op.

"I'm going out for a smoke," Frances said.

"Go ahead. I'll clean up here." Laura wiped down the table with antiseptic. Nicholas was working across the room. She didn't want to distract him—he had his hands deep into a man's chest cavity. A pang of admiration for him nearly brought her to tears. His steadfast calm had sustained her since they arrived in Anzio a month ago. He caught her looking and gave her the briefest wink before returning his eyes to his patient.

CHAPTER TWENTY-ONE

After weeks of relentless shelling, the endless flow of casualties slowed enough to give some of them a night off. After dinner, Laura and Frances were playing cards with Mildred and Avis. Foul smells wafted through the mess tent: a whiff of bootleg alcohol, the remnants of tonight's horrible creamed chipped beef dinner, cigarette smoke, and the reek of unwashed bodies—the frigid cold discouraged frequent showers. Around them, people were talking in small groups, some of the litter-bearers razzing one another over dominoes.

Over the speakers, Louis Armstrong sang "Basin Street Blues," which made Laura nostalgic for New Orleans—the music, the food, even her crazy family. Her parents' grocery store was just a short walk from Basin Street. She'd been away from home for a year now, almost to the day. New Orleans felt like someone else's life, sepia-toned and fuzzy around the edges.

"You still with us, Laura?" Frances tapped her finger on the table. She was the only one taking the game seriously, keeping score and quibbling over rules.

"Sorry," Laura said. She studied her cards and threw one in the pile. Her neck and shoulders ached from the hours she'd worked in the surgical tent.

"This game is like watching paint dry," Avis said.

Mildred tossed her cards in the pile. "Beats being slammed with wounded."

"I'd rather our guys break through the damned Gustav Line already so we can get out of this shit-hole," Frances said. "But I get your point."

A truck horn honked repeatedly outside, and everyone stopped talking.

Frances bent her forehead to the table. "Not again," she moaned.

Mildred held up a hand. "Wait...is that...Jingle Bells?"

Everyone rushed outside, some of them coatless. An open-backed truck skidded to a stop on the frosty ground in front of the mess tent, a makeshift Christmas wreath made from a shrub tied to its grill. Large gray canvas sacks filled up the truck bed.

Freddy Gomez hopped out from behind the wheel, a cotton-batting Santa beard tied around his chin. "Ho, Ho, Ho!" he shouted. "Our ship came in!"

"Mail!" Avis shouted. "It's a Christmas miracle!"

"Better two months late than never," Frances said. They hadn't received any mail at all since early December, when they were still in Naples. Not hearing from folks back home topped everyone's list of complaints, edging out the food and the weather—even the relentless nightly bombings.

Several enlisted men climbed into the truck and began handing the sacks down. People quickly formed a makeshift assembly line. Nicholas and Ellen emerged from the surgical tent with other nurses and doctors and jogged over, whooping for joy. "We were just finishing up and heard the honking," Nicholas said as he picked Laura up and twirled her around.

Back inside, two enlisted men and an MP started distributing the mail, shouting out names to cheers of delight. Laura sat with

Nicholas and Frances. Gomez showed off a snapshot to his friends at the neighboring table. His wife had given birth to their first child after he'd shipped out. As homesick as Laura was, at least she didn't have kids to miss.

"My son! Look how handsome he is!"

Gomez's pals pumped his hand and slapped him on the back. "Must take after his mom," someone joked.

Laura squeezed Gomez's shoulder. "Congratulations, Papa. Can I see?" He handed her the photograph. The baby was a miniature version of his father, with dark eyes twinkling and a little cleft in his chin. "He's perfect, Freddy. What's his name?"

"Carlos, after my father, God rest his soul." Gomez's eyes were bright with unshed tears. "My wife says they're calling him Carlito, little Carlos."

"You'll be throwing a ball with him in the backyard in no time," Nicholas said.

One of the enlisted men shouted, "Doctor Bruno!" Nicholas's smile disappeared as he rose, then pocketed a blue air-mail envelope without opening it. Laura felt a pit in her stomach. But of course, his wife would write to him. His marriage was all but over, he'd told her, the long annulment process taking its course. If he suffered any remorse for technically cheating on his wife, he kept that to himself. Soon, he'd be truly free, she reminded herself.

Finally, they called Laura's name, and the MP handed her a shoe-box-sized package from Aunt Inez, tied with brown paper and twine, along with a letter from Rose. Her heart raced as she scurried back to her seat. She tore open the package and found *biscotti*—a little crushed but still edible—a postcard of the French Quarter with a note from Aunt Inez on the back. She'd also sent a lovely little black hat with a frilly veil, two movie magazines, and a tube of red lipstick. Much as Laura wished her own mother had been more supportive, at least she still had Aunt Inez, her father, and Rose cheering her on. And Giovanni, wherever he was, if he wasn't still mad at her. She said a silent prayer to keep him safe.

"Jackpot!" Frances cried, reaching over to grab one of the magazines; Claudette Colbert smoldered on the cover.

Nicholas sat back down with a mug of coffee. Laura offered him a piece of biscotti, and he tapped it against the side of his mug. "Hard as a rock, just like my *nonna* makes." He dipped the cookie into his coffee. "Mmm. Tastes like home."

Laura placed the fancy hat daintily on her head of unruly curls. Would they ever again live in a world where they could dress up in pretty things? "I'm not sure I'll be needing this anytime soon, but that was nice of her."

"Hah! It looks good on you, though," Frances said. "Especially with those elegant fatigues you're wearing."

Frances opened a package from her sister-in-law. "Thank God. I was almost out." Frances said, opening up a small bottle of White Shoulders perfume and dabbing a little behind her ears. She'd told Laura she wore it when she cared for the men because it relaxed them and reminded them of home. Laura held out her wrist for a spray.

Nicholas excused himself and slipped out of the room. Laura knew he'd be anxious to read his wife's letter. She couldn't let herself dwell on that.

"Anything from Donny?" Laura was always tentative about asking after Frances's fiancé. But it would be rude not to ask; Frances was still holding out hope, despite his MIA status.

Frances flipped through the magazine. "Nope. This mail is from before Christmas, though, so anything he wrote could still be bouncing around...out there. Count your blessings, having your man right here with you."

That night, while her tentmates slept, Laura opened Rose's letter by the feeble glow from the kerosene heater and her pen light. The blue onion-skin envelope was postmarked November 29, 1943—three months ago. It started with early Christmas wishes, family gossip, and a report about her job at the Higgins shipyard. *I feel like every day we work here is one step closer to bringing you and Giovanni home safe. I worry so much, and pray for you both all the time. We had a postcard from him last week, from somewhere in the Philippines—a hula girl on the front, of course.*

Laura closed her eyes and held the letter to her heart, fighting back tears. Giovanni was alive and well—at least as of a few months ago. She unearthed some airmail stationery from her footlocker and wrote a brief letter back to Rose, carefully considering each sentence. The censors would read it before her sister did, but she had her own redactions to make. She wrote about Nicholas but left out the part about him being married. She wrote about the Higgins boats that delivered them to the beach here at Anzio but left out the part where the Germans were trying to bomb them into oblivion. She wrote about Frances but left out the part where her fiancé was still MIA in the Pacific. She didn't mention the crippling fear and homesickness—no need to add to Rose's worries.

She hesitated, then wrote a short letter to her brother, apologizing for hurting his feelings. Who knew how long it would be until they met again. *I hope we can put the past behind us. I love you very much and hope you're staying safe.* She knew it was more for herself than for him, that he had more important things to worry about now. But it felt good to write, to sign her name, and seal the envelope.

She had just clicked off her pen light when the red alert sounded. Mildred, Avis, and Frances were instantly awake, flinging off blankets and stepping into their boots. "God dammit!" Frances swore. Laura slid her fatigues on over her skivvies, not thinking, just executing on instinct and training, then she turned off the heater to douse the light. After a few minutes of urgent footsteps and shouts outside, an announcement came over the loudspeaker in between ear-splitting peals of the siren.

To your trenches immediately!

Frances took a sip from her silver flask before tucking it in her pocket. Avis gripped her miniature Bible and peeled back the canvas tarpaulin covering the trench that lined their tent. It did little to keep out the water and mud. Laura stuffed her half-full water canteen in one pocket and some hard tack in another. She grabbed her musette bag but looked at the small space inside the trench and thought better of it, removing Rose's Miraculous Medal and buttoning it inside the front pocket of her shirt.

Laura pointed her pen light down into the dark hole, her heart pounding and her throat dry, making it hard to swallow. Mildred climbed in first, immediately submerging her legs up to the knees in muddy water. She held out her hand to help the others down. They clung together in the trench, then pulled the canvas over the opening, creating a pitch-black tomb.

The wail of the siren all but drowned out their panting as the cold, muddy water seeped into Laura's boots. In the grave-like darkness, she squeezed her eyes shut; meanwhile, images of gruesome wounds she'd seen in triage and on the operating table flooded her mind as she imagined the damage the German bombs would inflict on them. Her left hand started to shake, and she stuffed it into her armpit.

Laura felt fingers on her wrist. "Deep breaths, kid," Frances said.

More images, like in a movie: her parents receiving a telegram that she'd been hurt, or worse. Rose breaking down in tears. She shook the pictures from her head. The trembling now threatened to overtake her whole body as she braced herself for the bomb impact that was sure to come. *Breathe. Breathe. Breathe.*

Laura burrowed closer to her friends, and someone took her hand. She prayed a silent Hail Mary, imploring the Blessed Virgin: *Protect us. Save us.* Avis prayed aloud, "Lord Jesus Christ, be near us in our time of weakness and pain. Sustain us by your grace, that our strength and courage may not fail."

"I hope God is listening," Mildred said.

"Of course he is," said Avis. "Pray with me."

"Y'all put in a word for me, would you?" Frances said. "I think God stopped hearing my prayers a long time ago. If it's time for me to check out, so be it."

They waited. Five minutes or thirty, she couldn't say. Suddenly, the siren stopped wailing, and the "all clear" announcement sounded over the loudspeaker. No bombs ever fell. Together, they pushed up the tarpaulin cover.

"Jesus," Frances said. "A drill?"

"Thank God," Avis said. "My feet are numb."

They climbed out one by one, stomped their muddy boots, and removed their helmets, then made their way to the mess tent. Inside, people talked in low murmurs, some laughing nervously. Captain McCarthy stood near the coffee urn with Ellen. Laura's feet were cold and wet, but at least she'd stopped shaking. Her heart still pounded, though, and she fought off the anger at being put through all that for nothing.

From the other end of the hall, Colonel Beaudet cupped his hands over his mouth. "Attention, please." The hubbub subsided. "The good news is this was just a drill. Congratulations on a smooth and orderly exercise."

Nervous laughter. "What's the bad news, Colonel?" someone shouted.

"At some point, we'll be in for the real deal," Colonel Beaudet said. He shared intelligence reports and plans to prepare for an expected German air assault. When the time came, most people would take shelter in their trenches, but Captain McCarthy asked for volunteers to stay topside and move the most severely hurt patients from their cots to the ground—dangerous, necessary work.

Laura shuddered. As bad as it was in the slit trench, the thought of working through the barrage was even more terrifying. Her hand began to tremble, and she stuffed it in her pocket. She felt like a coward, but even more, she wanted to live. Frances met her eye and shook her head. She wouldn't volunteer either. At least they'd stick together, but Ellen, Mildred, and Avis all approached Captain McCarthy. *Better women than me*, Laura thought.

CHAPTER TWENTY-TWO

The battle on the beachhead was unrelenting as the cold, wet winter dragged on. The Germans seemed determined to push the Allied forces back into the sea, and every day brought news of gains and losses in the muddy trenches. The work in the hospital tents was non-stop, with round-the-clock shifts and an unending flow of wounded men. The sun hadn't come out in weeks, and everyone was cranky.

Meanwhile, Frances got word that her fiancé Donny had been killed in action. No more pretending he might be found alive. Laura had tried to comfort her after Father Bill delivered the telegram, but Frances was inconsolable. "That was my guy, the poor bastard. We were going to get married." Since then, Frances had alternated between silent brooding and raucous partying. Laura was concerned, but Nicholas had advised her not to meddle: *She's a grown woman. She can look after herself.*

One day in late March, Captain McCarthy asked Laura and Frances to show some journalists around. Laura eagerly agreed, thinking it was important for the folks back home to understand what they were going through. But Frances said she wanted no part of it. "We're not here for public relations," she snapped.

Laura went to meet the journalists at the mess tent.

Across the room, she spotted the photographers, a man and a woman, weighed down with cameras and equipment bags. The woman's khaki uniform was tailored to fit, unlike the nurses' garb. She was clean, too, her face scrubbed and her high cheekbones making her look like a movie star.

The woman hitched her camera bag up on her slim shoulder. "Margaret Bourke-White," she said, extending her hand and introducing her colleague.

"I'm Laura Marino."

"Where are you from, Lieutenant?"

"New Orleans," Laura replied, touched to be addressed by her rank.

"I hear it's been pretty tough here," Margaret said.

"It has." Laura couldn't begin to explain Anzio.

"We don't want to get in your way," Margaret said.

"You're not. We need people at home to know what the boys are going through. We're glad you're here."

"Thank you. And I want them to know what *you're* going through, too," Margaret said. "Do you mind if you're in the photos?"

"I don't mind," Laura said, patting her hair into place as best she could, embarrassed by how dirty she was. She couldn't remember the last time she'd had a proper shower, her hair was an unruly mess of curls, and her fatigues were only as clean as brushing off a layer of dirt would make them. "But we're just doing our jobs here. We can start in post-op. It'll be a little less hectic."

"Great," Margaret said.

The post-op tent smelled of blood, wet plaster, and sweat mixed with oily emissions from the suction machine connected to two soldiers with tracheostomies. Bottles of plasma and saline dripped into nearly every man from lines pinned to the ceiling. Laura motioned to the row of cots. "This is the last stop before the evacuation department takes them to the port, then off by ship to Naples for further care and maybe a trip home." *If they were lucky*, she thought.

"Someone called that road to the harbor 'Purple Heart Valley,'" Margaret said.

"Sounds about right," Laura said. "We say a prayer every time we send them down there." The Germans targeted convoys of wounded trying to make it to hospital ships in the port. "Evidently, the Germans don't follow the laws of war the way we do."

The two photographers went to work. "Just go about your business," Margaret said. "Try to forget we're here."

Laura walked through the ward, checking on each patient. She stopped at one cot, bandages framing a man's impossibly young face, ghostly pale. Was he even old enough to shave? She laid her hand on his forehead, clammy and cold. He blinked up at her. She tried to find a pulse on his wrist. He reached out with a weak hand, and she squeezed it gently. Then he took his last breath. Laura checked his dog tags: Joseph Ahearn, Denver, Colorado. "Rest easy, Joe. I won't forget you," she whispered. Over her shoulder, Margaret's shutter clicked.

At the other end of the tent, Frances joked with those patients who could bear it, weak chuckles drifting across the ward. She shook her head at Laura.

"Vultures," Frances shouted. "Keep them away from me."

"No need to be rude, Frances," Laura said. She felt the heat rise to her face. "My apologies for my colleague. She's having a tough time."

"I heard that," Frances said, walking towards them. "This has nothing to do with me. I just object to the voyeurism. This isn't a zoo."

"Frances, please. They have a job to do," Laura said.

"Enough," Captain McCarthy had walked in during the exchange. "We're happy you're here," she said to the photographers. "You're putting your own lives at risk to document all this, and we're grateful. Nurse Harris, please go back to your work."

Frances was red in the face and walked away, mumbling curses to herself.

Everyone not asleep or on duty was in the mess tent a few nights later. A feeble warmth emanated from the portable heaters; the kerosene smell almost covered up the stench of semi-washed bodies, tobacco, the pungent latrines out back, and the antiseptic from the wounded patients. Laura stretched her arms over her head, trying to ease the aches from working multiple shifts. Nicholas, sitting to her right, rubbed her back lightly.

The movie soundtrack crackled through tinny speakers. Though Laura couldn't quite catch all the dialogue in the film over a patient's incessant cough, she didn't much care. She was grateful for a break and happy to be off her feet, watching a silly film about a handsome prizefighter in San Francisco. Errol Flynn as "Gentleman Jim," wearing only shorts, danced around the boxing ring on the improvised movie screen—a dingy white sheet so wrinkled the close-ups looked like a fun-house mirror.

Frances leaned over, her lips close to Laura's ear. "He's no Tyrone Power, but I'll take Errol naked from the waist up any day," she said in a too-loud whisper. "Maybe below as well." Her breath smelled of the "moose milk" she'd been sipping from her flask, a nasty concoction of canned grapefruit juice and medical alcohol. She was drinking too much and too often these days, but Laura was happy her good humor had returned, at least for now.

Nicholas cleared his throat, his face flushed. They'd had few opportunities for intimacy, but Laura knew that was on his mind, as it was hers. She kissed him behind his ear, and he shuddered. She'd nearly stopped thinking about the letter he'd received, which he admitted was from his wife. He was terse about the details, saying only that the annulment was in process. But Laura worried there was more he was keeping from her. Maybe his wife was fighting it; maybe his own family was against it. She tried not to press him for more.

In the next scene, Errol Flynn's family was eating dinner. "Real mashed potatoes!" someone shouted. Murmurs of approval rippled through the crowd. They were all so sick of C rations—and even worse, the K rations of hardtack and jerky when they were on the move. Laura thought about Rose's last letter, with its talk of everyday life back home. Her mouth watered, conjuring up family dinners, sipping Chianti from short glasses, the table heaped with delicious food. Whatever problems Laura had with her mother, Filomena Marino knew how to cook.

She recrossed her legs, trying to get less uncomfortable. Over the movie soundtrack, a faint *boom-boom*. Nicholas squeezed her hand. She held her breath along with everyone else, hoping it was just a random shot somewhere in the distant hills.

BOOM! Closer this time. The ground shook. The film stopped right in the middle of Errol's first kiss with his voluptuous co-star Alexis Smith. The sickening drone of German planes sounded overhead. The lights went out, and a collective groan went up from the crowd as the red alert siren wailed.

"Dammit," Frances said. "Just when they were going to get it on."

Captain McCarthy clapped her hands for attention. "Those of you who volunteered, get those boys to ground," she said. "The rest of you, roll into your trenches and be ready for the aftermath. It'll be all hands on deck afterwards."

Nobody panicked—the drills had prepared them for this moment—but everybody moved swiftly. Medics carried some of the patients away, while others in casts and on crutches made their awkward way out on their own.

Laura stood, wishing Mildred and Avis good luck. "I'm going to hit the latrine real quick," Frances said to Laura. "Meet you back at trench-sweet-trench."

Nicholas took Laura's hand in his. "You get in that trench and stay safe," he said. "If this escalates, I won't be able to focus if I know you're in danger."

The thought of that dark, muddy hole made her tense up. She hadn't told him about her panic attack during the drill. Maybe she should've volunteered to stay up top, too. She felt a surge of worry, thinking of Nicholas getting hurt. She wouldn't be able to bear it.

"I will," she said. "You be careful yourself. *Ti amo.*"

He kissed her hard on the mouth, then encircled her in a strong hug. "*Ti amo anch'io.*"

Just as Laura stepped outside, German flares turned the dark night to day in a fiery flash. Frances was smoking a cigarette near the latrines, her face lit in the red glow from the blast. She took one last drag and threw her butt to the ground. "To hell with them," she said. "They're just trying to scare us."

"It's working," Laura said. "Come on."

Back at their tent, they rolled themselves into their cold, muddy trench. A series of loud explosions echoed from the direction of the port. She envisioned those ships pulling anchor and heading back out to sea, the silver barrage balloons hopefully deflecting some of the low-flying Luftwaffe bombers. She prayed for the men shooting the anti-aircraft guns. Another wave of wounded would be headed their way soon.

After a few minutes, they heard planes passing over the hospital compound, unleashing anti-personnel bombs that whistled and crashed. The ground shook with another explosion, the closest one yet. The force of the blast rocked through Laura's body while fragments of jagged metal tore holes in the canvas above them. Outside, someone yelled, "They're hitting the ward tents! Motherfuckers!"

Laura clamped her hands over her ears, but the ringing was coming from inside her head, and she screamed. She rolled herself into a fetal position, shivering from a mix of cold and terror. Her heart slammed against her ribs. "I can't breathe," she said, gasping for air.

Frances held her tightly. "You're OK, kid. Pressure drop from the explosion. You've got the shakes. Inhale. One, two, three. That's my girl." It was the way they talked to their panicky patients.

Laura squeezed her eyes shut and bit her lip, feeling at once foolish and compliant. Still, she clung to Frances, feeling her strength and willing herself to calm down. She didn't know what she would do if Frances weren't here, if she had to face this alone. She couldn't remember ever being this scared—overwhelmed with fear and an utter loss of control. She prayed she'd be spared, then was immediately ashamed of her selfishness. She hoped Nicholas was safe with the others who'd volunteered to remain on duty. Blood pounded in her ears, letting her know she was still alive.

"I don't want to die," Laura said, hating her voice—she sounded like a child.

"Hey, nobody's dying on my watch," Frances said. "Not today."

Laura knew Frances couldn't possibly make such promises; even so, she clung to the tenuous truth of her friend's words. After what seemed like an eternity, the big guns went silent, though lighter artillery still faintly boomed in the distance. Laura panted, still short of breath. Frances slowly released her grip. Finally, the all-clear siren sounded.

All personnel to your previously-assigned stations. Mass casualty situation anticipated. All hands on deck.

"We have to go out there," Frances said. "They need us."

"I can't," Laura said.

"You can. Do you hear me?"

Laura checked her own pulse, still racing, and pressed her trembling hand to her thigh. She'd be no good to anyone until she calmed herself. "You go. I'll be out as soon as I stop shaking. Be careful. And don't tell Nicholas I lost it." She knew he'd run to her if he heard, and they needed him out there.

Frances put her hands on Laura's cheeks.

"Go," Laura repeated. "Don't worry about me."

"I won't," Frances said, lifting the canvas cover. "But in case I get blown up—I'm sorry for any times I was a bitch to you."

Laura remained in the trench for another fifteen minutes, trembling in the tense silence. Every inch of her ached, and her legs and feet were almost numb as she climbed out. She stumbled to the latrine, then to the pump, where she splashed water on her face, her left hand still quivering. They'd always been close to the fighting, but this felt different. The thin boundary between their hospital and the front had crumbled, leaving them exposed and vulnerable. She had to pull herself together. She'd signed up for this. Right now, men were dying in the tents.

She trudged through the damage in the dim glow reflecting off the snow, her ears still ringing. Twisted metal and mangled vehicles littered the pathway; the rubble of flattened tents still smoking in places. The stench of cordite from the bombs stung her nose and throat. Her foot kicked something under the snow—someone's helmet, lost in the chaos. She reached for it and held it to her chest for a moment, still struggling to take a full breath. She hung the helmet on a pole, hoping its owner was all right. Frances's voice sounded in her mind. *Breathe, just breathe.* Then Captain McCarthy's: *Do your job.*

In triage, nobody was giving orders, so Laura grabbed a mask and gloves to see where she could be most useful. Her eyes swept the room, searching in vain for Nicholas. Doctor Tolpin met her frantic gaze. "He's in surgery. He's fine. Frances is with him."

"Thank God," she said. "Captain McCarthy?"

Tolpin's eyes were intense over his mask. "Pre-op," he said, then cleared his throat. "They may need you there. Gomez was hit. And Ellen. Not sure if they'll make it."

The doctor's words landed like a punch in the gut. She ran to the pre-op tent and found Ellen on a cot, unconscious. Her face was deathly pale; blood seeped through the white sheet covering her. Avis was mopping Ellen's pallid, sweaty forehead with a cloth. "Sucking chest wound. She and Gomez managed to move all the post-op patients to the ground, then the bastards dropped a bomb directly on the tent. Some of the patients didn't make it. Ellen took some shrapnel. Pierce is getting ready to operate."

Laura's stomach churned. She couldn't breathe again. "I want to assist," she managed to gasp.

Captain McCarthy came up behind her. "No, dear. Mildred is already scrubbed in."

"Gomez?" Little Carlito's photo flashed in Laura's mind.

"Lost a leg, but he'll pull through." Captain McCarthy pointed to Laura and Avis. "You girls go get cleaned up and catch a little shut-eye while you can. We'll need you when the casualties start rolling in."

Avis placed her hand lightly on Ellen's shoulder. "Hang in there, honey. You saved a lot of lives." Ellen didn't respond. Laura kissed her clammy forehead.

Laura and Avis headed back to their tent. The battle still thundered in the distance. "You OK?" Avis asked, patting Laura on the back as they walked.

"Not really," Laura said. Ellen had been so kind, showing her the ropes back in North Africa. She could still see her, stunning in that emerald green dress at the Red Cross dance. "She's only twenty-four, the same age as me. She has her whole life ahead of her."

Avis's angular face was weary, with dark circles under her eyes. "Let's hope she does. I know it sounds selfish, but I couldn't help thinking, what if that was Mildred? If something had happened to her..." Her lower lip quivered. She wiped tears from her eyes.

Laura drew her into a hug, tears running down her own face now, thinking of Frances and Nicholas. Giovanni. "I know, I know. But she's safe. We're safe now." She hoped saying the words made them true.

Avis took a handkerchief from her pocket and wiped her face. "And poor Gomez, too. I'm so sick of this. I know Jesus said to love our enemies, but I hate those German bastards." It was the first time Laura had ever heard churchgoing Avis curse.

Back inside their tent, Laura tried to lie down, her left hand trembling. Her fear hardened into fury. Angry at the war, the Germans, herself. *I should've been out there.* She'd been feeling sorry for herself, missing home, hiding out in the trench. Weak and selfish. If she were a soldier, she'd be dead by now from her own cowardice. Before exhaustion took over and she passed out, she offered up a prayer for Ellen, wondering what kind of God would allow a good woman like that to suffer.

CHAPTER TWENTY-THREE

Laura woke up to the sounds of heavy equipment moving debris outside. Frances was still sleeping; Mildred and Avis were gone. Laura gathered her toiletries to clean up. At the water pump, she found a jagged hole in her kit and found a scrap of metal inside. Her pulse raced again. There, but for the grace of God.

In the mess tent, Captain McCarthy was eating by herself. Laura sat down with her tray of powdered eggs and dry toast. "How's Ellen?" Laura asked.

"Not good," the Captain said. Laura wondered when McCarthy had last slept. She looked weary, her hair a tangled mess under her cap, her usually rosy Irish face gray. Ellen was one of McCarthy's Girls. Laura knew the Captain was shaken up, though she would never admit it. "Pierce worked on her for two hours, but the shrapnel had passed through her lung into her abdomen. Massive internal injuries."

"Jesus," Laura said.

McCarthy brought a forkful of eggs to her mouth. "Triage is slammed already. We need you there ASAP."

"I'll go look in on Ellen, then I'll be right over," Laura said, then downed the last of her coffee.

"Make it quick."

A medic sat with Ellen in the post-op tent. "She was sleeping for a while, but she's starting to wake up now," he said, then lowered his voice to a whisper. "She doesn't look too good."

Laura put her hand on Ellen's wrist and took her pulse—too rapid. She felt her distended abdomen. Fluids were building up in her stomach. Ellen's eyes fluttered awake, but she was struggling to focus. Laura gripped her hand.

"Oxygen. I can't..." Ellen gasped. A heartbreaking little wheeze escaped her parched lips. Her face was ashen and sweaty.

"I'll be right back."

Laura ran to triage, where all hell was breaking loose. The smell of blood and flesh hit her hard. A sea of bodies crammed the tent, litter after litter filled with men with horrific injuries, many missing limbs, most mud-caked with gaping wounds. She didn't make eye contact with anyone, just grabbed an oxygen tank and ran.

Back in post-op, she put the mask over Ellen's nose and mouth. "Breathe, honey," she said. "Nice and easy. This'll make you feel better."

Ellen closed her eyes. "So tired..."

"Shh. Don't talk. Stay with me," Laura said. "Just inhale."

With every breath, Ellen's lungs made a terrifying rattle. Laura grabbed the chart hanging from the bottom rail of the bed. Someone had attached the chain with her dog tags and a rabbit's foot. Laura hoped it would be enough. She made a note on the chart. *Punctured lung?*

Ellen pushed aside the oxygen mask, trying to say something.

"We'd better leave the mask on, sweetie," Laura whispered, fighting back the tears welling in her throat. "Please fetch Captain McCarthy," she said to the medic. "She's in the triage tent. And Doctor Pierce, if he's free. Hurry."

The medic returned in a few minutes with McCarthy and Pierce. The doctor gently examined Ellen, then shook his head. His brow was furrowed, his face a mask of suppressed anger. Laura understood. He prided himself on tough cases, on being invincible in the surgical tent. And Ellen was one of their own.

"There must be something we can do," Laura whispered. McCarthy put a hand on her shoulder.

Pierce pulled down the blanket and examined the sutured incision over Ellen's chest. His signature stitches were perfect; Laura knew he'd done his best. He gently moved his stethoscope around. "Can you take a deep breath for me, Ellen?"

She sucked some oxygen weakly under her mask. The fear in her eyes broke Laura's heart.

"That's a good girl. One more, a little deeper now," Pierce said, his voice cracking. Laura thought back to that first awful triage shift with him, when she wondered what it would cost him to be kinder. Now she understood: maybe everything.

Ellen mumbled something through her mask, squeezing her eyes shut, tears forming on her lashes. Pierce backed away from her. "Just rest now," he said. "Don't fight it."

Laura took Ellen's hand. "We love you, Ellen, you know that, right?"

Ellen took a shallow breath, then was still. Pierce placed his fingers on her throat. "She's gone." He stepped back, punching at the canvas wall of the tent before storming off.

A few terrible moments passed in silence. Laura wept, too hollow to speak. McCarthy's face crumpled as she turned to the medic. Laura feared the Captain would break down. "Get the morgue guys over here, but tell them to keep her separate. Please."

He wiped at his eyes. "Yes, ma'am."

Captain McCarthy exhaled audibly, then squared her shoulders. "I need you in triage. Now," she said, gripping Laura's shoulder. "And dry your eyes. No crying in front of the boys."

Triage was so busy, Laura hardly had time to think about Ellen. Word spread quickly, and the other nurses made eye contact with each other, silently sharing their pain. She spotted Frances a few times, dry-eyed and silent. After several hours, Captain McCarthy rotated the nurses, sending Laura to the shock tent—as close as anyone got to a break.

As she slogged through the muddy snow, Laura suddenly remembered Ellen was dead and almost collapsed on the cold ground. She could still hear the buzz of aircraft and the booming of the big guns—*ours or theirs?* A deafening explosion shook the ground. She covered her ears and screamed. On the horizon, toward the harbor, a brilliant fire lit up the canopy of silver barrage balloons floating over the skyline. The Germans hit an ammunition ship, most likely. She hoped it took out some enemy planes with it. Better yet, all of them. They'd shown no mercy in bombing the hospital; whatever compassion she had was gone.

Inside the shock tent, Laura checked on each patient, smoothing thin blankets, patting shoulders, inspecting wounds. Most were asleep or unconscious. But the quiet only gave her mind more time to spin through alternative scenarios, ones where she could've done something to prevent her friend from dying. Ellen's face flashed in Laura's mind—happy and whole, her green eyes and kind nature. *Wisconsin nice*, they'd called her. She remembers how Ellen's calm competence helped get her through that first horrific night in triage, back in North Africa. "Just keep going," Ellen had told her. "Focus." Then the picture in her mind switched to Ellen's eyes above the oxygen mask, dying in pain, helpless and afraid.

A man with a bandaged head and gauze covering his eyes interrupted her thoughts. "Got any smokes?"

Laura fished a cigarette from her pocket and placed it in his mouth. Her hand was shaking again. He touched his cool, dry palm to the back of her hand, stilling it as she worked the lighter. For a moment, she let herself absorb his strength.

"Thanks, sis," he said in a rough voice, his accent vaguely southern. "This'll do. What was all the racket?"

"Something exploded in the harbor," she told him. "It's a long way from here."

Frances appeared in the doorway and motioned Laura over. "Captain wants me to take a quick inventory," she said quietly. "They put a call out to the Sixth Corps and the Seabees for blood donations. The port's a mess. No ships are getting to us anytime soon."

Laura let that sink in. If the Germans kept shelling the port, the hospital would be cut off from the rest of the world, unable to get supplies. Plasma, penicillin, bandages. Then, what? "How are we fixed for morphine? Some of these guys just need to sleep." She pointed to a man writhing on a cot.

"Should be OK." Laura administered an injection, and the thrashing man lay still within a few seconds.

Then the tent flap opened as two litter-bearers brought in a soldier and dumped him roughly onto a bed.

"Easy there," Laura said as the patient moaned in pain. "This is the shock ward. Is he in the right place?"

The men only shrugged and left without answering. She was peeved until she saw the swastika insignia on the soldier's jacket, a Nazi helmet above his ashen face, brown eyes pleading. "*Bitte, Fräulein. Helfen Sie mir bitte.*"

She cursed the litter-bearers under her breath for dumping this prisoner on her. She loaded up a fresh syringe with morphine and rolled up the German's sleeve. Before she could administer the shot, Frances pulled her back. "Nurse Marino, we're running low on morphine."

Laura was confused. "But you just said..." She was furious, thinking of the Germans bombing the port, hitting the hospital. But still, they were supposed to be nurses first. They'd taken the Nightingale Pledge: to do the best they could for those in their care, regardless of how they felt about them. "He's suffering."

Frances's blue eyes, usually bright and lively, were glassy and dead. Her voice came low and gravelly. "They need you back in triage. They're getting ready for casualties from the harbor explosion. I can handle things here."

Laura wanted to argue. She looked at the young German soldier. His eyes were closed, watering as he writhed in pain. But Ellen's terrified face flashed in her mind again, and she felt her will to help this man flag. Who knew how many Americans he'd killed? She wondered if Frances was thinking the same. And about Donny.

"Go," Frances said. They were the same rank, but it was not a request. Laura stared at her for a moment, then walked out into the darkness.

The following morning, the snow had turned to dirty slush as Laura joined a small group gathered next to a waiting ambulance. The air smelled of burning fuel and molten metal, the aftermath of the explosion at the port. The weight of the last few days pulled at Laura's bones the way the muddy puddles sucked at her boots: the unending flow of gruesome injuries, the relentless threat of the German bombs, the smell of burnt flesh in her nostrils. Ellen.

People milled around, eyes red and mouths grim, some smoking cigarettes. No one spoke. Ellen lay on a stretcher, her face pale but still pretty, as if she might wake up at any moment. She looked almost whole in her dress uniform, with gold studs in her earlobes and pink lipstick. The thought of Ellen's tent-mates carefully dressing her for this final ride made Laura tear up.

Freddy Gomez sat bundled up in a wheelchair, the stump of his missing leg heavily bandaged. Laura bent down to kiss his cheek. She hadn't seen him since the bombing. "I'm so sorry, Freddy."

"At least I'm going home. If we ever get off this damned beach."

Her left hand wouldn't stop trembling, and she kept it in her pocket. Nicholas patted her shoulder. "You OK?" She nodded, even though she wasn't. It was a difference between them. He always seemed able to weather the storm.

Father Bill said a few prayers in Latin over Ellen's body and read from his Bible. "Though I walk through the valley of the shadow of death, I will fear no evil: for thou art with me; thy rod and thy staff they comfort me." He talked about the enduring love of God, but Laura couldn't take in the words. So much senseless death. Where was God in this infernal place?

Just as the chaplain finished, the sky overhead filled with Allied bombers on their way to hit the German lines. Everyone cheered as the planes unloaded over the horizon and clouds of dust floated skyward. Laura wondered about the German soldiers who were getting blown up this time. Maimed, killed, not going home to their families. She tried to summon some sympathy, some instinct to forgive, to grant them their humanity. Instead, she found only bitterness and hatred, solidifying like a stone in her gut. *Bastards.*

Colonel Beaudet called for the group's attention. "I know you're all feeling numb and shocked. Ellen is the first loss from our company. Some of you have asked where she'll be buried. There's a temporary cemetery in Nettuno. Unfortunately, we can't risk the blockade in the port to ship bodies home. She was a good soldier, brave and selfless. I'm putting her in for a posthumous Silver Star."

Polite applause rippled through the group. A nice gesture, Laura thought, but cold comfort for her family, losing such a bright light, so young.

"And now, I'm afraid it's time for us to get back to work," the Colonel said.

Two medics loaded Ellen's body into the back of the ambulance and banged the doors closed.

As the crowd started to disperse, Captain McCarthy spoke up. "Hold on. I'd like my nurses to stay for a minute. Please."

Nicholas squeezed Laura's hand and walked away. Laura hugged one of Ellen's tent-mates, her face swollen with grief. Frances stood alone at the periphery of the group, looking off toward the hills.

Laura wanted to go to her but felt as if Frances had erected a wall around herself, so she went and stood with Mildred and Avis instead. They were both weeping quietly, which made Laura tear up again.

"I know you're all hurting," the Captain began, her face red and splotchy. "Father Bill is here if you need to talk." She gestured toward the priest, standing apart from them with his hands folded. Laura felt for him. He was always so alone here, with a singularly hard job. He took on all their suffering, but who heard his confession? Who comforted him?

"I'm not going to make a big speech," the Captain continued, "I just want to say…it's one thing to lose a patient, but quite another to lose a friend. One of us. Ellen was…" McCarthy's voice cracked, and she took a deep breath, "…a damn fine nurse. And a good human being. She didn't deserve this." Laura willed McCarthy to hold it together, for all of their sake. They needed her to be strong. If she broke, they all would.

"Ellen knew the dangers and made the choice to step forward, to answer the call of duty," the Captain continued. "We won't forget her, and we won't let the world forget her either. We'll honor her by doing what?"

Nobody replied. "Doing *what?*" The Captain repeated, hands on her hips.

"Our jobs," the nurses muttered, their voices disjointed. Laura could barely bring herself to say it, though she knew the Captain needed to hear it from them. "That's right. We do our jobs. Now, if you'll excuse me, I need to go write a letter to Ellen's parents."

McCarthy walked away. For a moment, no one moved, then people began wandering off to their next shifts. Laura locked eyes with Frances for a moment before Frances walked away without a word, heading toward the triage tent. Laura ran to catch up with her. "You OK?" She offered a cigarette to Frances.

"Not really," Frances said, lighting them both up. "Donny. Now Ellen. They took everything."

Laura stopped walking. "I'm still here."

"For now." Frances shook her head. "You have Nicholas. Family you like. A real life to go back to."

They walked a little further in silence.

"We'll get through this," Laura said. "You'll meet a nice fella, maybe here, maybe back home. Dallas and New Orleans aren't that far apart—"

Frances held up a hand. "I know you mean well, but please stop. Our lives were different before the war, and I'm guessing they'll go back to being different after."

"You don't know that."

"I do know," Frances said. "Not everything can be fixed."

They'd arrived at the triage tent, and Frances pushed aside the canvas flap. Laura finished her cigarette, feeling helpless. Maybe she didn't know Frances at all.

That night when they returned to their tent, Mildred and Avis were already asleep. Laura stripped off her fatigues and put on an old shirt of Nicholas's. She took her journal and a pencil from her musette bag, too keyed up to sleep, despite her exhaustion. She pulled the scratchy brown wool blanket over her legs, shivering in the damp cold. "I can't believe Ellen's gone," she whispered, as much to herself as to Frances.

Frances was rubbing cold cream on her face and neck. "Believe it."

The words hung in the air. Tears lodged in Laura's throat as she turned to the back of her journal and added Ellen's name to her list.

PART FIVE

New Orleans, 1951

CHAPTER TWENTY-FOUR

Laura walks briskly down Canal Street. The windows at D.H. Holmes and Maison Blanche are already decorated for Christmas, even though it's only the week before Thanksgiving. It's not as cold as it feels, but summer's humidity is now almost-winter's raw dampness. She flips up the collar of her coat, head down, anxious to get to Boyer.

She's spending all her free time with him now, hiding herself in a dark cave of pleasure, alcohol, pills, and guilt. She's already practicing the lies she'll tell her family at the upcoming Thanksgiving dinner she can't avoid. They think she's working on a special assignment at work—a cover story for why she isn't around much.

Inside the dark, smoky Chart Room, she stands still for a moment to allow her eyes to adjust. The jukebox plays Tony Bennett's hit "Because of You."

"Afternoon, Laura," Gerri says, placing a glass of red wine on the bar. Laura likes being known; Gerri makes her feel like a grown woman, out on her own in the world. No judgment.

Laura walks to the back of the room and puts her wine down on the table, where Boyer is standing. He kisses her on the mouth, and she shivers. "Hello, handsome," she says. She kisses him again, the feel of his soft lips now familiar.

"You're cold," he says, pulling her into a one-armed embrace. She hugs him tightly, soaking up his warmth and the spicy smell of his aftershave mixed with tobacco and whiskey, then scoots into the high-backed, black leather booth. He slides in after her, his thigh pressing hers under the table.

He's drinking whiskey, a half-full tumbler next to a lit cigarette smoldering in the ashtray. He lights one off the ember for her.

She takes a long drag, swallowing the smoke. "Thanks."

"How was work?"

"A little boring," she says. "I'm so tired of having to explain things to the new boss. I'm trying to make the best of the situation, but it's exhausting some days."

He rests his cigarette in the ashtray. "Such a waste of talent," he says. "You should be running the whole place." He always knows just the right thing to say, to make her feel special, wanted.

She leans back slightly, fighting an urge to slip her cold hand inside his shirt. Later. Instead, she takes a small bottle of pills from her purse.

"Thanks. Pull one out for me, would you?"

She shakes a pill from the bottle, and he swallows it with a sip of whiskey. He closes his eyes, relief already spreading over his face, though it'll be a while before it kicks in. It's wrong, what she's doing—stealing drugs from the hospital, feeding his habit. But he's so grateful. Plus, she tells herself, he is in genuine pain, his injury from serving his country. It's the least she can do to ease a soldier's hurt. Sometimes she needs a little extra help herself. Her nightmares have largely died down, but sometimes when she wakes up muttering in her sleep, he holds her and kisses the back of her neck, rocking her gently back to sleep. She does the same for him.

A sip of wine warms her on its way down her throat. "What did you do today?"

"Besides pining away for you? Not much," he says. "Stopped by the bookstore and the record shop. Then came here."

Until she heard his story, she found it a little suspicious that Boyer didn't have a job. When his mother died, just after the war, he and his sister sold the family house in Los Angeles, along with some antiques, and got more for it than they expected. After they'd split the proceeds, he booked himself on a cross-country train trip, got off in New Orleans, and never left. With the nest egg and his monthly check from the government, he lives simply but comfortably.

Boyer takes a drag off his cigarette. "You seem a little distracted," he says.

All of a sudden, her eyes are watery. "I'm sorry…"

He wipes the tears away with his thumb. "Tell me." She loves it when he says this.

"It's almost Thanksgiving. He'll be back in a few weeks."

Boyer shakes the cubes in his glass and sucks out the last drops of whiskey. He stares intently into her eyes, his mouth a grim line. "You know, just before I met you, I thought about walking into the river and letting it sweep me away."

"Arthur, please," she says. "We both knew what we were getting into…"

"I know. And I thought I could handle it," he says. "A nice distraction from my train wreck of a life. I didn't expect…this…you." Boyer's desire and love for her is so raw, so close to the surface, such a contrast to Nicholas and his surgeon's detachment.

She drains her wine glass and traces her finger along the back of his hand. "This hasn't been just a fling for me, Arthur. Please know that." Unlike Nicholas, he's willing to talk about the war, freely sharing his memories—the good times and the heartaches. She doesn't want to think about what happens next.

"I know, baby," he says, stroking her arm. "Not for either of us."

"Frances used to say, 'Squeeze that joy while you can, kid. You never know when this fucked-up life will snatch it from you.'" She thinks of Ellen, killed in an instant, of all the young men who died on their operating and triage tables, of Gomez, whose little boy must be around seven now, wishing his dad could run and play with him. Of Frances herself.

He's quiet, and she wonders if she's overstepped, dredging up the pain of his own loss.

"Let's get out of here," Boyer says. "I don't want to waste another minute not touching you."

CHAPTER TWENTY-FIVE

The French Quarter is quiet on Thanksgiving afternoon as Laura parks on Dauphine Street. It's a beautiful fall day, the sun peeking out from behind fair weather clouds and a pleasant breeze blowing up from the river. She carries the passable apple pie she made, a peace offering for the family she's been ignoring. She has a twinge of guilt as she thinks about leaving Boyer alone on the holiday. She'd promised to bring him leftovers after dinner with her family and said she'd make it up to him.

Loud talk and laughter are coming from inside the apartment above the grocery store. When she gets to the top of the stairs, the door flies open, and she's almost knocked over by little Marlene, waving the wishbone in her pudgy fist. Gregory is on her heels, and the two of them clamber past Laura, shrieking.

"Give it to me!" Gregory shouts. "I'm the oldest!"

"Catch me!" Marlene giggles. "*Ciao, Zia!*"

Rose yells from the kitchen, "Don't run on the stairs! *Piano, piano!*"

Laura shoos the children back into the kitchen, hugging the pie to her body. The aromas of turkey, garlic, and roasted artichokes mingle with the comforting scents of her childhood: her mother's talcum powder, her father's cigars.

Her mother bends over a large silver pot on the stove. "*Ciao*, Laura," she says.

Laura kisses her mother's cheek, a little damp from the steam. "Happy Thanksgiving, Mama."

Rose wears a ruffled apron over her dress. She takes the pie and hugs Laura. "Thanks for bringing this. Walter will be so happy. How've you been—haven't seen you in a while."

Laura steels herself, pulling up her carefully constructed lies. "Busy at work. I'm still on that special assignment."

"What's that about?" her mother chimes in.

"We're not supposed to talk about it," Laura says. "It has to do with the military." Recently, her mother has become obsessed with the communist menace; a vague reference to government work might satisfy her.

"Knock-knock!" Aunt Inez comes bustling through the door, her jet-black hair in an elegant updo, carrying two white Brocato's boxes tied with red striped twine. She wears a mustard-yellow silk dress with a fitted bodice and a flared skirt, a thin red belt at her waist, and matching leather pumps. At 50, Aunt Inez is well-kept and has a steady supply of beaus, a source of endless delight to her nieces. "I brought the *cannoli—now* it's Thanksgiving!"

"*Ciao, Zia*," Laura says, kissing her aunt on both cheeks. "You look gorgeous, as always."

"I have a date later."

Laura's mother shakes her head. "A date? On Thanksgiving?"

"So judgmental, Filomena," Aunt Inez says. "Maybe you're jealous."

Laura's mother laughs. "Why would I be jealous? I have your brother, after all."

Laura's happy to be back among this good-natured banter with the women of her family. She's almost forgotten how funny they all are.

"Can I set the table?" Laura asks.

"I already did it," Rose said. "But Gregory was helping, so you might want to check."

Laura walks into the dining room, which is the same as it has been for decades. The creepy statue of the Infant of Prague stares out from its nook in the wall. The shrine to Giovanni sits on the credenza, a lit votive candle flickering, just like at Rose's house. His loss is like a knife permanently lodged in her mother's heart. Laura squeezes away the tears that come to her eyes and tweaks the place settings. The big table is set with the lace cloth brought over from Sicily, which they only use for holidays, topped with a thin sheet of plastic to protect it. She opens a bottle of wine from the sideboard and pours herself a half-glass, downs it in two sips, then refills it.

Soon enough, her mother and Rose start bringing out dish after dish, and the table is crammed with food—turkey, mashed potatoes, stuffed artichokes, golden medallions of fried *cucuzza* squash. Laura thinks back to the war, how much they all craved real food like this.

Her father comes in with Rose's husband, Walter. "There she is," her father wraps her in a bear hug, and she sinks into his warmth. She doesn't doubt that her mother loves her, but her father has always been the affectionate one. Her brother-in-law kisses her on the cheek, squeezing her arm. Maybe today will be all right after all.

"Sit, everybody." Laura's mother says. "*Mangia tutti*. Who's saying grace?"

"Me! I want to say grace!" Gregory proclaims. He and Marlene are seated at a miniature table, off to the side. They all bless themselves and fold their hands as he stumbles through the prayer. Laura tries not to crack up laughing. After the amens, Laura's mother adds, "God bless Giovanni and Michael in heaven, and please, Saint Christopher, bring our Nicholas home safe to us." Laura swallows a lump in her throat.

Rose makes up plates for the children, whispering instructions to them about good behavior and promising *torrone* candy later, just like when she and Rose were girls, sitting at that same table with Giovanni. Dinner is the usual tumult, everyone talking at once, Laura's father teasing her mother good-naturedly. Walter talks about the latest goings-on at the water board. Laura measures her sips of wine, knowing she'll have plenty to drink at Boyer's later. She picks at her food and tries to stay focused, smiling and engaged.

"What do you hear from Nicholas?" Laura's father asks. "I worry for him, over there so close to those communists."

"I got a letter from him just the other day," she lies. "He's complaining about the food, but otherwise sounded good."

"Important work he's doing," Laura's mother says. "You're lucky to have such a good man."

"I'm proud of him," Laura says. She finds she actually means it, though her mother's comment cuts her.

After dessert—her apple pie warmly received—Laura volunteers to clean up, shooing away Rose and their mother, who did all the cooking. She's looking forward to the solitude, but Aunt Inez says she'll help too. "What about your dress?" Laura protests. "Isn't that silk?"

"Apron," Aunt Inez says, fastening one of Filomena's faded floral prints around herself. "You wash, I'll dry."

Laura laughs at the sight of her aunt in the frilly apron over her elegant outfit, then fills the sink with soapy water and starts washing the mountain of dishes and glasses.

"So, what have you really been doing the last couple of months? We've hardly seen you," Aunt Inez asks as she dries a plate with the dish towel.

"I told you, a special assignment." Laura keeps her eyes on the sink.

"I heard you. I'm not sure what that means, and it's none of my business," Aunt Inez says. "But you look a little too thin. I hope they're not working you too hard. You feeling OK?"

Laura's hand starts trembling; a glass slips from her grasp but doesn't break. "I have lost some weight. I don't know. I'm not sleeping too well." It's the truth that she hasn't been sleeping much, though not because of work.

"You must miss your husband," Inez says. "More than you're letting on."

Laura rinses her soapy hands. "Of course. But I'm fine, thanks. A little space from time to time doesn't hurt." She pauses. "I've also been a little blue since I got word that my best friend from the war died. She took her own life." She can give her aunt this much.

"That's rough," Aunt Inez says. "Remind me what her name was?"

"Frances," Laura says. Tears spring to her eyes. "She was a firecracker. Tough, so funny. You two would have hit it off."

Aunt Inez rubs Laura's shoulder gently. "It's so hard to lose a good friend."

They work in silence for a few minutes. After Aunt Inez dries the final plate, she pulls a pack of cigarettes from her purse, offers one to Laura, and lights them both up. "I'm sorry about your friend," she says. "You know, after my Roberto died, I went through a pretty dark time." Inez lost her husband to the Spanish influenza and has never remarried.

Laura takes a long drag, the smoke from her aunt's fancy cigarette sweeter than the Chesterfields she smokes with Boyer.

"You girls were too young to remember, but Giovanni knew your *zio* a little. My Roberto was such a good man. So smart, so kind." Aunt Inez looks out the small window above the sink, then shakes her head. "I was lost without him. He was the love of my life. And I shut out a lot of people, including your parents. I was drinking too much, staying out late in the clubs, hanging around with shady characters to numb myself from the pain. I made some pretty poor decisions—none of them permanent, luckily. I missed him so much. He left a hole in my heart."

"I'm so sorry," Laura says, knowing there's a message for her in there somewhere. Her aunt never talks about those days. "How did you climb out of it?"

"Slowly," Aunt Inez says. "Your father, for one. He took me aside one day and reminded me of all the good things I still had in my life. My business, the family, my house, even my animals. He knows me like nobody else."

Laura rarely thinks of her father as a man, a brother, a husband. But of course, he and Inez are close, having come over on the boat together as kids, speaking little English, making a life for themselves in a strange land.

"If something is going on with you," Aunt Inez continues, "Anything you need to talk about, you know you can come to me, right?"

Laura nods. Aunt Inez has always been there for her and Rose, the protector of a repository of secrets they couldn't tell their mother, and a source of adult advice about teenage crushes and the big decisions in their lives. It was Inez who'd backed Laura up when her parents objected to her enlisting in the Army Nurse Corps. A part of Laura wishes she could tell her aunt the whole truth, but that would be foolish. As modern as Aunt Inez's attitudes are, she'd been a devoted wife and would never condone the situation with Boyer. Even Laura can't defend it.

"Sometimes we forget to count our blessings," Aunt Inez says. "Even on Thanksgiving."

Laura considers this. Her aunt is right, but she's struggling to find the gratitude.

CHAPTER TWENTY-SIX

The Monday morning after Thanksgiving, Laura drives to work, taking small sips from Frances's flask at the red lights to help steady her nerves. The conversation with Aunt Inez at Thanksgiving rattled her. Nicholas will be home soon, and she'll have to make a decision. Of course, there is no choice. She'll welcome her husband home, cut back on the drinking and the smoking. Stop the pills. Maybe they'll try again for a baby. Boyer will be a fond, secret memory. The end is obvious. What she can't see so clearly is how she will get from here to there.

The car in front of her stops abruptly, and Laura slams on the brakes, swerving out of her lane and narrowly missing a parked car. Her head bumps the steering wheel, and she keeps her foot on the brake pedal, despite the honking horns from behind. "*Vaffanculo!*" She throws the Chevy into park and opens her door, then marches to the other car and bangs on the driver's window with the heel of her hand.

"Hey! You could've killed us! What the hell is wrong with you?"

The driver rolls down his window. "Calm down, lady. Didn't you see the kids crossing the street? What would you have me do, run them over so you can get wherever you're going a few minutes faster?"

Laura's left hand begins to shake. Two little girls are walking down the sidewalk, holding hands. She stalks back to the car, grateful no harm has come to them, or to Nicholas's precious car. Other motorists are honking incessantly now. She's embarrassed, infuriated. She climbs back into the Chevy and takes another swig from the flask before pulling out into traffic again.

The near collision has made her a few minutes late for work. At the nurse's station, Annie points to her watch.

"Don't start with me," Laura tells her, preempting the scolding. "I almost got into a wreck. Texas driver, of course." Everyone in New Orleans blames bad driving on Texans. She shakes her head and brushes past her boss, trying to make light of it. Texas. She still hasn't written back to Frances's mother.

Annie raises her eyebrows but doesn't comment. "We're understaffed today. I need you to do intake and outputs until we get caught up."

Laura goes through the morning robotically, measuring bodily fluids in and out, making notations on patients' charts. A bruise is forming on her forehead where she hit the steering wheel, and her whole head is throbbing. She goes to the pharmacy closet for some aspirin. Tammy's there with a clipboard.

"Damn, Texas driver almost got me killed this morning on the way to work," she tells Tammy. She points at her forehead. "I just need some aspirin."

"Glad you're OK," Tammy says. "That sounds scary. Here you go." She hands Laura the aspirin and then presents the clipboard. "Just initial here."

"For aspirin?" Laura asks.

"New procedures, I guess. Too many drugs are going missing. We need to sign for everything we take out from now on. They've asked me to coordinate it."

"News to me," Laura scribbles her initials on the form. She waits for Tammy to exit, then swipes a packet of morphine tablets, pocketing them in one quick motion. She turns around, and Annie stands in the doorway, her face red.

"I...I was just getting some aspirin for my headache," Laura says, displaying the two orange pills in the palm of her hand.

"And what else?" Annie asks, cool as a cucumber. "What's in your pocket?"

Laura freezes, a cold sweat breaking out in her armpits. "What are you talking about?"

Annie folds her arms across her chest. "I saw you, Laura. I repeat, what's in your pocket?"

"Nothing. Jesus, this place is getting like a Gestapo unit." She tries to move past Annie, but the smaller woman grabs Laura by the elbow.

"Show me."

Laura takes the morphine packet from her pocket and holds it out to Annie. "Just some morphine I'm taking down to post-op. One of the patients down there is having a hard time, so I..."

"And you've signed for it? What's the patient's name?"

"Look, I didn't know about the new procedure until Tammy just told me." She presses her shaking left hand against her thigh. "Shouldn't there have been some official notice?"

"Consider this your official notice," Annie says. "We're losing drugs around here at a rapid clip, and the bean counters have noticed."

"So, I'll sign it out. Where's the form?" She returns the morphine to her pocket.

"I repeat, who's the patient, Laura?"

"Boyer. Arthur Boyer. Amputee with phantom pain. Since when is it anyone's business how we administer meds? The Charity I know trusts its nurses."

Annie puts her hands up. "If people are stealing drugs, it's very much my business."

"*Stealing* drugs. I don't like to see patients suffer. Until now, that made me a good nurse."

Annie eyes her twitching hand. "A patient who's a known drug-seeker? Arthur Boyer is red-flagged. He's been turned away more than once from here and the VA. Do you have a personal relationship with him?"

"That's ridiculous. I'm a married woman." She'd slept at Boyer's place the night before; she can still smell him on herself. She wonders how Annie would know this. Maybe Phyllis has been paying closer attention to things than Laura thought.

"Stealing drugs is a fireable offense. It's not just that. People have reported you drinking on the job, appearing impaired at times. You've left me no choice. We're going to have to put you on leave while we decide what to do."

"Unbelievable!" Laura is livid. "Take your damn pills." She slams the pill packet on the counter.

Laura stops, her hand trembling uncontrollably now. People nearby cease their conversations and stare. Annie walks up behind her, calmly putting her hand on Laura's elbow, and Laura lets Annie steer her toward the nurse's locker room, where Tammy stands brushing her hair in the mirror.

"Give us the space, will you?" Annie says.

Tammy hurries out. Laura collapses on the small couch, buries her face in her hands, and begins to weep uncontrollably. Annie pulls a small stool over and sits near Laura's head, pushing her hair out of her face. "We're going to get you some help," she says.

"I don't need help."

"I'm afraid that's not up to you now," Annie says. "Keys."

Laura pulls herself together enough to gather her belongings from her locker, then hands over her car keys for Annie to drive. Worse, one of the med techs follows them to Laura's house so he can give Annie a ride back. Laura is mortified...and furious. As they near her street, Annie tells Laura she's called Rose, who was on Laura's personnel form along with Nicholas as "next of kin."

That sets Laura off. "You did *what?*" She dreads whatever will happen next, afraid Rose will overreact and might even tell their parents. Just imagining the shame of that makes Laura feel nauseated.

"Exactly what did you tell my sister?" she asks Annie.

"Just that there was an incident at work, and we thought it best that you go home for the day."

When they pull up to the house, Rose is at the front door. Aunt Inez stands behind her. Laura hesitates to leave the car. "Am I being fired?"

"Not today," Annie says. "But I can't make any promises. Suspended, for now."

Laura takes a deep breath. "Until when?"

"Let's see how it goes. I'll be in touch, Laura. You take time to get squared away."

Rose opens the car door and stands back to let Laura out, her face red, forehead wrinkled with worry. "Thanks so much," she says to Annie. "We've got it from here."

She leads Laura into the house. "Jesus, Laura. What in the world—"

Aunt Inez holds up a hand. "Later, *cara.*" She embraces Laura.

"I'm so sorry," Laura says. Her anger has simmered into shame. Suddenly, she's a little girl again, sobbing into her aunt's shoulder.

Laura surveys the trash-strewn living room and kitchen, the mess her life has become. She's supposed to be the role model. Now she's disappointed her little sister and her beloved aunt. "I need to take a shower," she says.

"Good idea," Aunt Inez says. "Do you need help?"

"I'm OK. You don't have to stay," Laura says.

"Yes, we do," Aunt Inez says.

Laura strips off her shoes and her clothes, leaving them in a pile on the bathroom floor. She's startled by her reflection in the mirror. Dark circles frame her puffy, bloodshot eyes, and red splotches on her cheeks. She runs the shower as hot as she can bear, scrubbing herself from head to toe. In the bedroom, she dresses in casual slacks and a sweater, stuffing her feet into slippers. She wants more than anything to crawl under the covers and sleep, but she's sure they won't let her. She takes a deep breath and walks out to the kitchen.

Rose is at the sink, yellow rubber gloves on her hands, washing a week's worth of dirty dishes. Aunt Inez is working her way around the room, emptying ashtrays and picking up trash. The wastebasket in the corner is full of spent butts and liquor bottles. Laura stands in the doorway, stunned, as if she's watching a movie of someone else's life.

"What the hell, Laura?" Rose says. "There are roaches in here. Old, moldy food in the fridge. Where have you been?"

"I...I told you...a special assignment."

"*Bullshit!*" Aunt Inez stands with a hand on her hip, pointing her cigarette at Laura. "We know there's no special assignment. Do you think we're stupid? That we didn't talk to your boss?"

Laura feels sick to her stomach but remains wary. How much do they know? Did Annie tell them about Boyer, too? She moves unsteadily to the kitchen table and sits down. She points to Aunt Inez's cigarette. "Can I have one of those?" Her voice is a whispering whine.

Aunt Inez takes a slim cigarette from the silver case in her purse, hands it to Laura, and lights it for her. Rose hands her a newly cleaned ashtray. Laura sucks on the cigarette greedily, as if it might save her. Rose pours freshly-made coffee for Laura and Aunt Inez, then goes back to work at the sink.

Aunt Inez sits down across from Laura, leaning her elbows on the table. "Out with it," she says.

Laura gulps some coffee. Her mind is reeling. She needs to provide a plausible explanation, but not the full story. "I told you about my friend Frances. I've been pretty broken up about that, and—"

"Frances, your friend from the war?" Rose asks. Laura had never told her.

Aunt Inez jumps in. "Dead," she says. "By her own hand."

"I'm sorry, Laura," Rose says, washing the last of the dishes and setting them to drain on the sideboard. "I remember reading about her in your letters. Why didn't you tell us?" She snaps off the rubber gloves and joins them at the table.

"Thanks. She was like a sister to me during those days," Laura says. Rose flinches at that. "I should've been a better friend."

"It's sad," Aunt Inez says. "But what else?"

Laura takes a deep breath. "Then I was passed over for a promotion. That woman who brought me home, she got the job I was supposed to have, so she's the new boss. A real hard-ass. Everyone hates her."

Aunt Inez shakes her head. "And that's why you've been drinking like a fish?"

"What? No." Laura is indignant. "Maybe I've been drinking a little too much, you know, to take the edge off. My friends from work and I...we've been hanging out at a bar downtown, blowing off steam." She's rambling, digging a deeper hole for herself.

"I heard you almost got into an accident," Rose says.

"That wasn't my fault. Some asshole from Texas..."

Rose and Aunt Inez look at each other. They're not buying it. "When does Nicholas come back?" Aunt Inez asks.

"In a couple of weeks," Laura says, and the reality of it hits her. Boyer. She wishes she were in his bed right now, losing herself in him.

Laura answers more questions from Rose and Aunt Inez, choosing her words carefully and deflecting as much blame as she can, implying that the hospital is overreacting. She's not sure she's convincing them; she just wants them out of her house.

"I'm fine," she tells them as they leave. "I just need some rest."

Aunt Inez narrows her eyes. "For the record, I don't think you are fine, *cara*. I know you're not telling us the whole truth either."

"But you won't say anything to Mama and Papa, right?" She can handle her aunt and her sister, but her parents would be a whole different story. She imagines her father's disappointment and her mother's glee over having been proven right, that Laura should be home raising a family, not out working.

Aunt Inez stubs out her cigarette. "I'm not promising anything. I won't lie for you, Laura."

Once they're gone, Laura takes a pill from the coin purse in her handbag and washes it down with cold coffee.

CHAPTER TWENTY-SEVEN

The next few days go by without incident. Laura stays holed up in her house, reading more of her war journal, listening to the radio, venturing out only for groceries, booze, and cigarettes. She tries to compose a letter to Frances's parents, but throws away every draft, none of her words adequate. In her self-imposed isolation, she tries to keep the house tidy in case of a surprise visit from her sister or her aunt. They take turns calling to ask if she needs anything. No one from work calls, and Laura is perfectly fine with that.

She's trying mightily to resist contacting Boyer. She'd never given him her home phone number or address, and knows he must be frantic, probably staking out the hospital, desperate to find her—and craving more pills by now. It needs to end, though. More time with Boyer will only pour gasoline on a fire she may not be able to extinguish. Still, alone in her bed at night, she misses him desperately.

It occurs to her she's repeating her mother's mistake: sleeping with a man she shouldn't be with, though Laura should know better. She's much older than her mother was when she met Father Tony. And her mother wasn't married at the time. She shudders to think what would happen if she got pregnant, as her mother did with

Giovanni. Father Tony transferred out of New Orleans shortly after the secret came out that he was Giovanni's real father. Laura wonders if he ever stopped loving her mother, whether Boyer would ever stop loving her.

A little more than two weeks before Nicholas is due home, Laura warms up leftovers for herself and pours a glass of wine, then another. The radio plays nothing but Christmas music, which only makes her more depressed, so she switches it off. After draining the bottle, she climbs into bed.

In the middle of the night, she sits bolt upright, disoriented. Her head is pounding. Her mouth feels like it's been stuffed with cotton. Fragments of the old war dream scatter when she rubs the grit from her eyes. Frances was there, though, she's sure of that. She can almost smell her perfume. And Boyer, but with both arms intact.

In the kitchen, she flips on the light, her hand shaking as she pours herself a glass of milk that she hopes will settle her stomach. The clock above the oven says 2:30. She'll never get back to sleep. Before she can stop herself, she dials Boyer's number and lets it ring a few times. He doesn't sleep well most nights.

"Hello?" he says. His voice is gruff and, she has to admit, sexy.

"Hey," she says. "Sorry to wake you."

He clears his throat. "I've been desperate to find you. Are you all right?"

"I just needed to hear your voice."

"Where are you?"

Laura takes a sip of the milk. "At my house. Things have not been good."

"Do you want me to come over?"

She hesitates. It's a dangerous and terrible idea.

"I'll call a taxi," he says. "Give me the address."

She gives it to him, not quite believing the words that are coming out of her mouth.

"Be there as soon as I can." He hangs up.

She taps her fingers on the phone and tightens the belt on her robe, then lights a cigarette. She holds the smoke in her lungs as long as she can. It's stuffy in the house, and she opens the front door, standing in the dark; the cold December breeze is bracing, the street quiet. All the sensible people are asleep. Multi-colored Christmas lights flash on and off through the window of her neighbor's house. She runs a hand through her hair but otherwise makes no preparations for him. He will have her just as she is, broken, dirty, shameful, alone—one last time.

Twenty minutes later, a black-and-white United taxicab pulls up in front of the house. She sees Boyer's silhouette lean over the front seat to pay the cabbie and thinks briefly about how she'll have to drive him home in the light of day. But she'll cross that bridge when she comes to it. For now, she steps aside as he crosses her threshold.

He closes the door, then reaches for her, drawing her to himself with his one arm wrapped tightly around her. He kisses her forehead, then her eyes, then her mouth. "I called the hospital, and they wouldn't give me any information—just that you weren't there," he says, hugging her close. "I was terrified something awful had happened to you."

"I don't want to talk right now," she says. "I just need you to hold me." She takes his hand and leads him to the bedroom, then sheds her robe and nightgown, and undresses him as fast as she can. He complies, silently following her lead. She's glad they didn't drink. She wants clarity now; she wants to map his body and fold it up for later, when she's lost.

After they've spent themselves, she lies with her head on his shoulder, the tangled, sweaty sheets twisted around their legs. The room is totally dark. She kisses him lightly on the collarbone, and he shivers with pleasure.

"Wow," he says. "That was…different."

"Sorry...I—"

"It was beautiful." He kisses her lips, slowly and tenderly.

She arches her back, thinking maybe they will make love again. She wants to. She wants him inside her forever, filling her. Knowing she can't have that makes the longing that much more acute.

"Run away with me," he says.

She laughs. "Sure. Where should we go?"

"Don't laugh. I mean it." He brushes his thumb against her nipple.

"Not fair..." She grabs his waist and pulls him closer.

"I love you, Laura. And I think you're in love with me too. What are we waiting for?"

"Well, there's my marriage." She hears the resignation in her voice.

He flinches. "You know he doesn't understand you the way I do, the way we understand each other. He never will."

Laura doesn't answer, thinking Boyer may be right about Nicholas. But could she really do that to him?

"People get divorced, begin again," he says.

"Not Catholic people. He's been divorced once already. It takes a long time to get a marriage annulled in the Church."

"We can be together in the meantime. I have friends down in Mexico. They need nurses, too. You can start over. We can be happy. I—"

She puts her finger on his lips to stop him from talking. "Sweetheart, it's a beautiful vision. A dream."

"It can be a reality. I have money, we can leave today."

For a minute, she allows her mind to follow that fantasy. Could she really do it? Run away from it all? Then she thinks of her sister Rose, the kids, her parents, and Aunt Inez. "My family is here. I can't just up and leave. I need to get my job back. They suspended me for taking the pills."

"I'm sorry," he says. "That's my fault."

"Shh. It's not. I did it willingly. I was taking them too, but I need to stop. And I need to stop drinking so much."

"We'll do it together. We can—"

"No, we can't," she cuts him off. It's true. Together, they'd never quit. They'd never want to. "Listen to me. Nicholas will be home soon. I have to face facts, not run away from my mistakes."

"Is that what I'll be to you? A mistake you made?" The dawn light is seeping in around the curtains now. She sees tears standing in his crystalline blue eyes and feels a sob rising in her own throat.

"Arthur..."

"You said it yourself: life is too short to deny yourself a measure of happiness. Isn't that what your mother did?"

"Oh, hell. Leave my mother out of this. She did what was right. Otherwise, Giovanni would've been..."

"Giovanni's not here now, though, is he? That kind of proves my point, doesn't it? What's it all for? Let's take joy where we can."

She regrets telling him the truth about Giovanni. She kicks the sheets off and climbs out of bed. "Don't talk about my brother," she says. "There's no happy ending here. This isn't a movie, this is my life." *My real life*, she almost said.

He gets up and pulls her toward him gently. "Then give me whatever time we have left until..." He takes her trembling hand in his, brings it to his soft, wet mouth, then slides it down his own body and pulls her back into the bed.

Boyer wakes up shaky. Laura digs out a pill for him, and he swallows it with his coffee. Laura's wearing one of Nicholas's old striped dress shirts over her naked body, the sleeves rolled up to her elbows. They are mostly silent through a hasty breakfast of cold cereal at the kitchen table. After multiple cups of coffee and too many cigarettes for this hour of the morning, Boyer puts his hand lightly over hers, his electric blue eyes rimmed in red. "I get it. I don't have to give up anything, but I'm asking you to give up everything. For the record: I'm not sorry. Not for any of it."

She's struck by his words—such a clinical summary of their situation—and wonders if she's sorry. No, she decides.

He stubs out his cigarette. "What happens now?"

She wipes at her eyes and forces herself to stand. "I'm going to get dressed, then I'll drive you home," is all she can muster.

He winces. "Home..." he shakes his head. "Home is wherever you are."

CHAPTER TWENTY-EIGHT

A week passes. She's seen Boyer a few times, but never at her house, only at his. They are careful not to discuss the future, savoring every minute they have left together. Laura is tidying up the house when the phone rings. "Is that you, Lieutenant Marino?" says the caller, in a strong Brooklyn accent Laura hasn't heard since she left Germany. A surge of emotion washes over her.

"It is. Captain McCarthy?"

"The one and only. It's good to hear your voice."

"What a nice surprise," Laura says.

"I was planning a cross-country train ride with my sister and wanted to see as many of you girls as I could. I was going to try to find you and Frances, of course. Then I got the news."

Laura takes a deep breath. "Just awful."

"I tracked down her parents. I couldn't believe it."

"How are they doing?" Laura asks, racked with guilt about not getting in touch with them. Now it feels like too much time has passed.

"Devastated, of course. Those calls never get easier." The Captain clears her throat. "I'm so sorry. I know how close you girls were."

Laura doesn't respond. The past tense feels so sad, so final. Worse, shameful.

"Anyway, I finally convinced Charity Hospital to give me your number. Had to pull rank."

"Oh?" Laura asks, trying to hide her panic. Had they shared any other information with her? The Captain would be so disappointed if she knew Laura had been suspended. Even now, Laura can't bear the thought of letting her down.

"So, sorry for the late notice, but we're due in New Orleans tomorrow afternoon, and I was hoping to see you. And Nicholas, of course. Dinner, maybe?"

Laura feels her heart quicken. Tomorrow? In the middle of all the turmoil? But she can't say no to Captain McCarthy. "Of course. And I'm off work for a couple of days, so that's perfect," she fibs. "Nicholas is away—doing humanitarian work in Korea. I'll tell you all about it."

McCarthy gives her the arrival time at the train station. After they hang up, Laura catches her reflection in the window. She looks a mess. She calls her hairdresser and makes an appointment for that afternoon.

The next day, Laura takes a long bath and dresses in a dark brown linen shift she hasn't worn in ages. She brushes on some makeup and smiles at herself in the mirror. Her newly-coiffed curls are shining; at least she *looks* healthy.

She drives to the station, not having been inside the terminal since Frances's departure from that disastrous Mardi Gras visit. Swarms of people jostle by, dragging their luggage and trying to calm crying children. Along the wall to the right, painters perch on scaffolding. The beginning of a large, colorful fresco emerges from the plaster, reminding her of the artwork at Charity, where, it occurs to her, she may never again set foot.

She spots them coming from the arrival hall, carrying small suitcases. Captain McCarthy drops her bag and crushes her in a tight hug. "Look at you!" she says, holding Laura at arm's length. "Pretty as ever. It's so good to see you, Marino."

"Bruno, now. Welcome to New Orleans," Laura says. The Captain has put on a little weight, and there are gray streaks in her auburn hair, but otherwise, she's the same. Solid and steady.

"This is my kid sister, Fiona," the Captain says.

"I'm Laura. So nice to meet you."

"Likewise," the sister says, shaking Laura's hand. Fiona is smaller-boned, with a pretty freckled face and light brown hair, but the resemblance is there.

Laura drives the sisters in a loop around the French Quarter, pointing out some of the highlights: the big department stores on Canal Street, the streetcar decorated with holly wreaths, and St. Louis Cathedral. She's careful to avoid Boyer's block.

She drops them off in front of the Hotel Monteleone with their luggage, then parks the car. In the lobby, she waits on a mauve-colored velvet settee next to an elaborately decorated Christmas tree. Laughter and music drift in from the Carousel Bar, and Laura wonders why she and Nicholas only come to the Quarter when they visit her parents, never just for fun anymore.

She loves this old hotel, with its ornate plaster moldings and chandeliers, founded by Sicilians from her neighborhood. Aunt Inez would bring her and Rose here for special dress-up *"zia* lunches" when they were girls. They always searched for the ghost of the little boy Maurice, who died upstairs in the 1890s and regularly appeared to guests. Laura hasn't thought of him in years and feels a pang of sadness, thinking of Michael, her own spirit child.

After about fifteen minutes, Captain McCarthy walks off the elevator alone, saying her sister's exhausted and won't be joining them for dinner. "She knows there'll be war stories," Captain McCarthy laughs. Laura is grateful not to have to navigate around a stranger.

They walk a few blocks down Royal Street to a Sicilian-owned restaurant Laura's been to with Aunt Inez. It's early, and only a few tables are filled. She drops her aunt's name, hoping word will get back that she's been there, looking well, and having dinner with her old friend from the Army, like a civilized person.

After they order and have glasses of wine in front of them, the Captain asks about Nicholas. "He's a big-shot surgeon here, I assume?"

Laura takes a deep breath and tells her about his position at Charity and his assignment in Korea. "Wow, he went back to a war zone?" McCarthy asks. "That's a good man."

Laura considers this. "Yes. Well, they're out of harm's way. At least I hope so."

"I remember how happy we all were when the two of you got together, like you were meant for each other. No kids?"

Laura tells her a short version of what happened with Michael. The Captain's never been married and doesn't have children of her own. Laura is grateful when she offers a quick "sorry for your loss" and changes the subject.

Over salads and antipasto, they reminisce about their comrades from the war. Ellen, Freddy Gomez, the doctors they loved and hated. Pierce is now the chief surgeon at Bellevue in New York City, McCarthy tells Laura, and Father Bill is back at his chaplain job in St. Louis. It feels good to remember her friends, how they weathered the tough battles together. They laugh at some of their memories, like the time Gomez wore a Santa suit when the mail finally came to Anzio. Laura feels a sense of relief and calm she hadn't expected at having her mentor here—a fellow witness to what they all went through.

The Captain has stayed in touch with Mildred and Avis, who live on their own little farm in Oklahoma. Mildred is enrolled in veterinary school after fighting for her GI Bill benefits. "I hope Avis is still singing," Laura says.

"She is. Leads a church choir." McCarthy scribbles their address and "MAVIS" on a cocktail napkin for Laura, who vows to write them. "You were all such good nurses. You made me proud. You still do."

Laura's not so sure she still deserves to be included in that number, but she raises her wine glass in a toast. "We had the best Captain. To the McCarthy Girls!"

The waiter arrives with their dinners—veal piccata for Laura, trout almondine for McCarthy. The Captain eats a forkful of the tender fish. "Oh my God, this is so good. Beats the hell out of hard tack and creamed chipped beef on toast."

"Frances called it 'shit on a shingle,'" Laura says, laughing.

"Accurate!" The Captain chuckles, her round Irish face suddenly blotchy with emotion. "I can't believe she's gone. She was larger than life."

Laura takes a sip of her wine; she's been doing her best not to drink it too quickly. She shares what few details she got from the letters, wiping tears away.

"Had you seen each other since the war?" McCarthy asks.

"Once," Laura says. "She was here for Mardi Gras back in '48. But it was kind of a catastrophe. Her stupid boyfriend, too much booze, my impatience. We lost touch after that." She pauses. She doesn't mention the apology letters from Frances that she ignored. "I had no idea how bad things were until I heard from her mother."

McCarthy carefully puts down her fork. "I had my own dark moments when I came home. I kept thinking about everyone who didn't make it back. Going over and over what I could've done differently, better."

"You can't think like that," Laura says, even though that's exactly how she thinks. Maybe Captain McCarthy has nightmares, too, although she can't picture the Captain as anything but confident and strong. "We did the best we could, that's what Frances would say."

"I know. And I'm OK now. Most days," McCarthy says. "We're only human. We faced down not just the enemy, but a nearly impossible job day after day, under the worst circumstances. It was inevitable that it would all catch up with us eventually. It was my job to keep it at bay while we were on duty. I understood the assignment. We owed that to our boys."

"How did you get past it? The dark times, I mean," Laura asks, hoping for a simple prescription.

"I'd be a liar if I didn't admit I still have my tough days from time to time. But I was lucky I had a lot of family support when I got back. Fiona's been great. And there are a bunch of us nurse corps veterans at my hospital. Good women. We take turns bucking each other up."

"I wish I had that," Laura says. "I don't know about New York, but the VFW here doesn't allow women. We're not even treated like veterans." She tries to contain the anger and hurt that wells up in her. "Early on, after I came home and was struggling, I did talk to my doctor about it. He basically patted me on the head and told me, 'You'll be fine—women are strong. After all, it's not like you were in combat.'"

"Idiot," Captain McCarthy says, mopping up the last of her almondine sauce with a slice of bread. "It was war. Nobody ever gets over it completely. The men don't either. We just learn how to cope, or some of us do." She closes her eyes, and Laura knows she's thinking of Frances. "But you've managed to carry on. And at least you've had Nicholas to confide in."

Laura hesitates, knowing McCarthy is fond of Nicholas and respects him as a doctor. "We almost never discuss the war. He says I shouldn't dwell." She chooses her words carefully. The Captain might be the only person left who won't judge her, who will always have her back. She doesn't want to add McCarthy to the list of people she's let down. "I've worked hard, Captain, tried my best to put all that behind me."

"Of course you have."

"I was up for a promotion at work, but didn't get it around the same time I found out about Frances. I guess you could say my own dark days returned. Even the Anzio Shakes."

"I remember," the Captain says, patting Laura's hand.

"They brought in a new supervisor," Laura continues. "Army nurse herself, but that hasn't worked out very well for me." She considers telling the truth about her suspension, but can't bring herself to say the words.

"I wish I lived closer," McCarthy says. "Is there really nobody you can talk with?"

"There is someone I met a few months ago, a fellow veteran. He lost an arm in France." Laura stops herself. She hasn't told a soul about Boyer, but she has to tell someone, and if not McCarthy, then who? The Captain had seen it all during the war. "But I really shouldn't be spending time with him. It's complicated."

McCarthy cocks her head to the side. "I see," she says coolly, sipping her wine. "So why are you spending time with him?"

Laura reaches to refill her own glass, but the bottle is empty. "He listens. When I'm with him, I feel a little less alone." She squeezes her eyes shut. She's never thought it through, but saying those words out loud, she wonders if that's fully true, or if Boyer just helps her keep her guilt and pain about Frances at bay: the booze, the pills, the sex, the lies. An even worse thought occurs to her: she's punishing Nicholas. Or maybe it's even simpler: Boyer is broken, and she wants to fix him.

"We all need someone to hear us," McCarthy says.

Laura wipes fresh tears from her eyes, conscious that other diners in the restaurant are now glancing their way. "The truth is, I haven't done my job. I should've intervened with Frances before it was too late. I left her behind."

"Look at me," the Captain says, gripping Laura's chin with her meaty fingers. "What happened to Frances is not your fault. But what happens next is 100% up to you. You need to back away because you may not even know where the edge of the cliff is. One more step, and it might be too late."

Like Frances, Laura thinks a little frightened that her friend's suicide no longer seems unreasonable. At least she's at peace. "I don't know how to do that," Laura admits. "Pull back, I mean."

"You do. Use your skills. Just like in triage. Take things one step at a time—solve the worst problem first."

In the hotel lobby, Captain McCarthy pulls her into a bear hug, the older woman's warmth and wisdom shooting directly into Laura's battered heart. A part of her wants to stay there, to have the Captain take charge and tell her what to do.

"You give my love to that good-looking husband of yours when he comes home, all right? And come visit me in New York. I'll take you two to Ebbets Field for a game."

Laura nods. "I'd love that."

"And do me a favor."

"Anything."

"Stop beating yourself up. We survived. That's what our boys fought for, what we worked so hard for. So, there's nothing to feel guilty about. You're still a good nurse. I mean that. Be grateful and get back to work. That's an order, Miss Marino."

Laura straightens her back and salutes. "Yes, ma'am."

At home, Laura kicks off her shoes and lights a cigarette. She stands at the open screen door, staring out into the quiet neighborhood as she smokes. Elsewhere in the country, cities are buried in snow, but here the evening air feels tropically warm, like a soft blanket. She watches as the purple and pink sky surrenders to shadows. Insects buzz around the porch light, flinging themselves at the brightness. *Solve the worst problem first.* The Captain was right—without even saying it directly, her guidance was clear. The affair with Boyer must end.

Back inside, she pours herself a whiskey; downs it in one shot. She doesn't trust herself to tell Boyer goodbye in person. His grip on her, their mutual bond—physically and emotionally—is too powerful. She's come to crave him the way he needs the pills.

She dials his number and leans her back against the kitchen wall. He picks up on the first ring, as if he's been sitting by the phone. Waiting.

"Laura," he says.

"How did you know it was me?"

"Nobody else ever calls."

His words make her so sad that she almost can't go through with it. His own pain is so great that at times, she can forget about her own. She takes a deep breath. "Arthur," she begins. "I've been thinking a lot since our last conversation—"

"Why don't you come over? We can talk it through together."

"I can't do that," she says, as gently as she can.

"Can't? Or won't?" He's not going to make this easy for her.

He's breathing hard, but doesn't speak. She closes her eyes and pictures him standing in his kitchen, the little cat winding around his legs, an open book, and a tumbler of whiskey on the coffee table. "Both, I guess. I'll just say it: I can't go on like this. Maybe I'll regret it—"

"You will. We can have a beautiful life. I promise you."

"But I told you, I can't just run away."

"It's not running away. It's making a choice."

"I'll hurt too many people."

"But it's OK to hurt me?"

His wounded tone of voice slices into her heart. "Arthur, please don't—"

"Why not? We love each other, Laura. We're good for one another. You know that. Come over here and tell me it's not true. Tell me to my face."

She blinks back tears. She's not sure they are good for each other. But he's right, she could never say that with him standing in front of her. "I've made my decision. I'm sorry."

"Are you?" His voice sounds harsher now, cold.

She slides down the wall and stretches the phone cord to sit on the floor. "Of course I am. I know the pills—"

"It's not about the pills. It was never about the pills. What we have is real. I know you, Laura, things he'll never know."

"Don't bring him into this," she cuts him off. "I'm so grateful for what we had, Arthur. I'll always carry you—"

"Stop. Spare me the sentimentality. I don't need your pity. Goodbye, Laura."

He hangs up. Gone. For a minute, she can only stare at the linoleum. She stands up, returning the phone to its cradle. She holds onto the receiver, as if he may call back. A part of her wants him to. She's hollowed out, too empty to cry. The breeze from the open front door makes her shiver, and she closes it against the night.

CHAPTER TWENTY-NINE

Three nights later, Laura moves through the house, absent-mindedly putting things away, shutting off lights. Boyer's voice still rings in her ears. *We love each other, Laura. We're good for one another.* She wonders what he's doing at that moment, whether he's thinking of her, too. Flashes of their time together run through her mind. The lovely dinner on his balcony that first night, his touch, the revelation of a passion deeper than she ever knew was possible, born of their shared war wounds. The desperation in his eyes when the pain came. The risky thrill of being with him brought the adrenaline rush of living on a knife-edge—the way it had been in-theater. But he'd also provided a measure of compassion she didn't know she craved. At least some of what he said was true. He understood her anguish as nobody else did—not even Nicholas.

She brushes her teeth, studying her face in the mirror. She's lost weight, and her cheekbones are sharp, her eyes bloodshot. She had herself fooled for a while, convinced she deserved the thrill Boyer gave her, that she could drink on the job and handle it, that other people were to blame for her failures. But she knows the truth now:

their relationship would have burned her life down if she'd allowed it to. And still could, depending on what happens once Nicholas gets home.

She switches on her bedside lamp and pulls her war journal out of the nightstand drawer. She'd been going through it page by page, trying to rekindle the memories she'd locked away for so long, but now she flips forward to the summer of 1944, as the war raged on, still no end in sight.

She's surprised at how messy her handwriting is on these pages—unreadable in places. Most of the entries are terse. *Finally free of Anzio. Ships got us out—why didn't they come sooner? I've never been happier to leave a place.* Later in the summer: *Promoted to First Lieutenant. They got Denny in the mess tent to make me a cake out of SPAM. We pretended it was chocolate.*

She skims through tedious notes about daily life, then comes to a significant event, remembering the relief she felt. *Annulment finally came through. I feel the same about him now as I did before he was officially free. Am I a bad person?* She wishes she had written more, but remembers how tired they were all the time. In early September, yet another false ending: *The Brits captured the port at Antwerp! I'm sure it'll be over soon.*

She shakes her head. How wrong she'd been.

PART SIX

Italy, September 1944

CHAPTER THIRTY

The sun was barely over the horizon when the nurses climbed into the back of the trucks. The hard wood of the benches dug into Laura's thighs as their convoy rumbled through the Italian countryside. The air was fresh with the lingering scent of damp earth after an overnight rain, and the olive trees lining the road shimmered silver green. The sun shone as if nothing had happened there, as if nothing had been lost. But the landscape that survived the Allied bombs told a different story.

They drove slowly past a house reduced to a pile of stones, patches of chicory and purple-flowered thistle poking up through the rubble, possessions scattered about—kitchen utensils, an iron bedframe, a child's toy wagon. Further down the road, a ruined church, the back wall blown away, part of its roof open to the sky, the steeple still intact. Some houses stood, but most were damaged. She wondered about the families who'd left, and the ones who hadn't. When did it become too unbearable to stay? And how had those left behind managed to get by? How long before their lives returned to normal? Would they ever?

As they traveled through small villages, the GIs tossed candy to the ragged children who ran alongside the trucks, waving and laughing. Laura blew them kisses and shouted, "*Ciao, bambini!*" She wished they could stop so she could hug them all, imagining what they'd been through, never knowing peace in their short lives, until now.

"At least it'll be a change of scenery?" Mildred piped up over the rumble of the truck engine. She was always the one trying to cajole them out of their cynicism, but even Mildred sounded doubtful. Laura tried to catch Frances's eye so they could laugh like they used to. At something. Anything. But Frances just pulled on her cigarette, her face inscrutable.

They'd set up six different hospitals since leaving Anzio. Laura was worn out, attempting to locate a reserve of energy. Their joy after the liberation of Rome and the Allied invasion of Normandy last June had given way to the grim reality that the war was far from over. Nobody would be going home any time soon. The disappointment gnawed at them in their exhaustion throughout the sweltering Italian summer. At least they would be safe from the fighting in this new assignment—far behind the front line.

They were headed to Cinecittà. The Allied Military Government had taken over Mussolini's massive propaganda film production complex just outside of Rome and transformed it into a refugee village. It would be the first time their unit would be working mostly with civilians—displaced Italians, and escapees from German forced labor camps and occupied territories.

The trucks pulled up to a long concrete building, and the nurses climbed down. They'd been told they'd have a real bunkhouse inside a building. After months in muddy tents, they were looking forward to walls and a floor. Their excitement was short-lived. The women fanned out, examining the rows of rusty iron bunk beds in the barracks. The place resembled a prison. Laura put her duffel bag down on a lower bunk, trying not to think too hard about the stains on the thin mattress. She assumed Frances would take the adjacent bed, as she had so many other times. But Frances walked right by, chatting and joking with a few other nurses. She carried her belongings to the opposite end of the room without looking back.

They set to work. The nurses were sprayed with DDT to ward off the lice, typhus, dysentery, and TB rampant among their new patients. Laura was concerned about the skull and crossbones on the side of the truck, but Avis told them they used DDT all the time on her farm back home.

They were quickly able to replicate their usual field hospital inside a converted soundstage, and the next day, Laura worked with Mildred and Avis to establish a system for processing the refugees, who'd been patiently waiting for them in nearby barracks. Frances went with Nicholas and the surgeons, stationed in another area of the massive building.

The patients came to them, guided by GIs. There were old men and women, young mothers corralling small children, all of them in tattered or ill-fitting clothes, looking scared and gaunt. Except for the Italians, most of them didn't speak any language Laura could decipher; it was hard to communicate, so she stopped trying. She did her best to be gentle, to smile and look them in the eyes, to acknowledge their humanity. But the work reminded her of triage back at the front—catch and release. They didn't need her pity; they only wanted their lives back.

They'd been settled in for a few days. Laura was on her way to refill her canteen at the water point when she heard incoming planes, and she panicked. There were no foxholes or air raid shelters here, so she made a dash for a row of vehicles, throwing herself to the ground and rolling under a truck. As she curled herself into a ball, the Anzio

Shakes returned with a vengeance. She took short, painful breaths and shook violently as the planes passed overhead. *Why is nobody else running? Where is the red alert?* She braced herself for bombs that never came. She felt like she was losing her mind. She heard screaming but realized it was coming from her own throat.

After a few minutes, she crawled out from her hiding spot, dusted herself off, and went back to the barracks without filling her canteen. Frances was coming out of the building as Laura approached, still trembling.

"What is it, kid?" The old nickname Frances hadn't called her in months. Laura dissolved into tears, and Frances drew her into a hug. "Hey now, what the heck?"

"I can't...stop shaking," Laura told her. "I thought it was the Luftwaffe...I'm sorry, I'm so sorry..." She felt ashamed for hiding, for being weak—just like in Anzio.

Frances led her inside to her bunk. "Sit," she said. "It was just the Russians. That's why you didn't recognize the engines." She pulled her flask out of her pocket. "Here, take a swig. It's the good stuff. It'll steady your nerves."

A part of Laura didn't want to need the alcohol, Frances's antidote of choice. Still, she took a long swallow. "Thanks," she said, then kicked off her boots and lay back on her cot. The whiskey burned her throat, but the shaking did subside. "It was like a nightmare, only real."

"It's over now. You're all good." Frances smoothed Laura's hair off her forehead like she would with a patient. It was the most tender thing Frances had said to her since Laura couldn't remember when. Laura touched her wrist and felt her pulse slowing. She recognized the heavy footfalls before she saw him. Nicholas.

"Laura? I heard you yelling." He rushed to her side and knelt by the cot, putting his palm on her forehead. "Oh my God, are you OK?"

"Just the shakes," Frances said. "She'll be all right."

But Nicholas ran his hands over Laura's arms and legs, as if checking to make sure nothing was broken. Laura started weeping again, unable to stop the tears.

"I'll give you two some space," Frances said, turning toward the exit.

They trudged through their days, treating more diseases than wounds. Many of the patients were malnourished, and it broke Laura's heart not to be able to feed them the food they'd been deprived of for so long. Too much too soon would make them sick. Even through the depression, her parents' grocery store guaranteed that food was never in short supply in the Marino home; never had she gone without. Some of the patients they saw were too far gone to save—weakened by malnutrition and dying from infections that should've been prevented. Laura thought there must be a special place in hell for the Nazis who'd used starvation as a weapon of war.

Medical supplies ran short—nothing new for Laura's unit—though she wondered why they couldn't be resupplied, with liberated Rome so close. They halved the doses of antibiotics and sulfa, saving them for the gravest cases. They enlisted refugees with medical training and others with practical skills from their lives before the war. Civilian carpenters fashioned splints and braces from scrap wood, and a group of Polish women organized themselves to tear up old sheets and boil them to use as bandages. Nobody asked questions when Italian refugees with connections to the local black market procured eggs and other produce, even bringing back grappa they could use as disinfectant in a pinch.

There was little time for relaxing beyond a few hours of sleep and hasty, tasteless meals of army rations. The work was tedious; even so, Laura was grateful not to be treating the types of gruesome battle wounds they'd encountered since landing in North Africa. Now and then came a rare moment of joy. When a new baby was born, the nurses fussed over the squalling child and his exhausted mother. *Someday I'll be one of them*, Laura thought. "Isn't he precious?" she asked Frances.

"I'm not much of a baby person," Frances replied. "I'm going to get a beer. I'll catch you later."

Laura had seen her drinking and playing cards in the canteen with a rough-looking crew of enlisted men and a few of the younger nurses. Frances never seemed impaired while on duty, only hungover. She was always functional, all the same, always a good nurse. At times, she was exceptional, able to focus amidst chaos. Laura envied those nerves of steel, wishing them for her own. But not other things, like the interchangeable young men Frances picked up and kept around until she got bored and sent them away.

I don't know what's going on with Frances, Laura wrote in her journal. *She seems broken. I don't know how to fix her.*

That first month, they processed the backlog of refugees, shipping the more serious cases to a better-equipped hospital in Rome. As other patients grew strong enough to travel, they were sent on their way. Laura was never sure where, but she hoped they'd be able to rejoin loved ones. Some wouldn't be so lucky.

The patients who spoke a little English told her stories of being uprooted from their homes, corralled into ghettos, held in deplorable conditions in makeshift camps where some were made to watch family members put against a wall and shot in cold blood. Parents had been separated from their children, some lost forever. Laura wondered how these people made it through, whether she'd be strong enough to survive under the same circumstances, or come out whole again. Sometimes she thought of her own parents and the family they'd left behind in Sicily and would never see again. They never talked about it, except to say, "Life was hard there. We had to leave."

One day, after they'd been paired on a surgical rotation, she and Frances snapped off their gloves and walked out together. She often worked some of the same shifts as Frances, but they rarely kept company outside of work. Frances had different friends now, and Laura spent most of her free time with Nicholas. It was a beautiful autumn day, the air crisp and the sky a deep blue with just a hint of winter to come. Frances offered Laura a cigarette as they headed back toward the barracks.

"How've you been?" Frances asked.

Laura was a little startled. "Fine, I guess. You?"

"Bored out of my mind."

For a moment, it felt like old times, the closeness they used to have palpable between them. Laura had so many questions bottled up for Frances, anxious to find out what was really going on with her. "It's strange not bunking with you next to me anymore."

"I thought you'd had enough of my antics."

Laura stopped walking. "What do you mean?"

"You know what I mean," Frances said, not stopping.

"I do miss you." Unexpected tears caught in Laura's throat as she trotted to catch up. "I've never been closer to anyone in my life, except my little sister."

"And Nicholas."

"That's different."

Frances took a deep drag from her cigarette and exhaled a smoke ring. Where she'd picked up that trick, Laura didn't know. Perhaps the card players. "This isn't high school," Frances said. "We're in a war. It's hard to make room. You're in a serious relationship—I get it. I was engaged once."

Laura felt defensive but didn't want to say the wrong thing and pour salt on Frances's wound. "Things don't have to end because I'm with a guy," Laura said. "It's not finite, friendship."

"Isn't it?" Frances asked, pausing in front of the barracks. Instead of opening the door, she headed off in the opposite direction.

"Where are you going?" Laura called out.

Frances raised a backhanded wave. "Catch you later."

CHAPTER THIRTY-ONE

New Orleans, 1951

Laura skims the subsequent journal entries, searching for Frances's name but finding few mentions. Instead, she'd written note after note about Nicholas. She cringes as she reads them; she sounds like a schoolgirl with a crush. *Just knowing he's in the same room makes me happy. Sometimes I can't believe he's mine.* There was more to it than the undeniable physical attraction. His steadfast commitment to her, to them. And his dedication to his job, to quietly being the best—it inspired her. Back then, she didn't fully appreciate how he treated her and all the nurses, sharing the credit and making them equal members of his team. Even now, with all her experience, the doctors at Charity rarely treated her that way.

She wonders how much the war had to do with their falling in love—feeling so alive in the face of so much loss and death. If only they could've bottled that passion. If they were to meet now, would she feel the same way about him?

She turns the page and stops. *September 16, 1944. Giovanni.* She'd drawn a small heart, broken in two, next to the notation. She closes her eyes, remembering. Father Bill had taken her aside after breakfast that day as she laughed and joked with the girls. From the look on his face, she knew something was terribly wrong, even before he held out the dreaded yellow envelope. She hadn't saved the telegram. She didn't need to. Her father's words are forever burned into her memory: *GIOVANNI KILLED IN ACTION. MAY GOD KEEP YOU SAFE, CARA. PAPA.* Captain McCarthy said she was sorry, but there was no way Laura could go home to be with her family without leaving altogether, and she couldn't do that. She had a job to do, a mission to complete. Nor could she imagine being apart from Nicholas.

I'm the oldest child now, she'd written that day. The thought had terrified her; the unbearable burden of it. She remembers curling up into a ball on her cot, unable to move. McCarthy gave her two days off. Nicholas came and went, holding her while she wept.

After the third day, it was Frances who appeared at her bedside, ordering Laura to get up and shower. *Don't dishonor your brother's sacrifice by wallowing here in the dark. Get your behind out of this bed.* When Laura didn't move, Frances gripped her by the shoulders. *You're not the first person who's lost someone, and you won't be the last. We have a job to do.*

CHAPTER THIRTY-TWO

Sperlonga, Italy, September 1944

In late September, Nicholas arranged a day off and borrowed a jeep to drive them to the beach town of Sperlonga, about an hour south of Rome. They strolled through the steeply terraced cobblestone streets, dodging bomb craters. The sound of hammers rang out as people worked to clear debris and restore their houses. Shopkeepers greeted them with warm smiles and "*Buongiorno,*" while watering pink bougainvillea and potted palm trees that reminded her of New Orleans.

"What are you thinking about?" Nicholas asked, giving her hand a gentle squeeze.

"My sister Rose. I wish she could see this place. She'd love it."

"I can't wait to meet her. And your parents, of course." Giovanni's absence from the conversation made Laura wince. It had been two weeks since she'd received her father's telegram, and she was still caught by surprise every time she remembered he was gone. Forever. Her chest tightened, and her left hand trembled briefly, the way it had in Anzio.

"They'll love you," Laura said. She held back on saying anything else. Though the annulment had been finalized, they hadn't talked much about the future, beyond a stray daydream or two.

They had lunch in a little café in the piazza, then drove down a steep, winding lane, barely wide enough for the jeep to pass, and parked. Ahead lay a white sand beach framed by high cliffs. They kicked off their shoes and walked hand-in-hand along the water's edge. They were alone, except for a few tiny brown shorebirds, darting in and out of the wavelets in search of food. The sea was crystal clear, an impossible shade of turquoise, and it reminded her of the miraculous oasis they'd visited back in Tunisia.

"Laura, can we talk about something serious?" Nicholas placed a hand on either side of her waist, holding her steady in front of him. "I know I don't bring it up much, but my old life in Boston—I'm anxious to put it behind me."

Laura held his gaze. "You mean your wife?" She'd always been afraid to mention the subject. She wished she could better understand what had happened between them, how their relationship had gone so wrong.

"My *ex*-wife," Nicholas corrected. "She's not a bad person, and you'll never hear me say anything against her. She's just not what I needed in my life. I think I knew it even before we got married."

"Then why did you?"

"It was expected." He paused, pressing his lips together. "And I was too much of a coward to do anything about it."

"You're not a coward," Laura started to argue. He'd done so many brave things in the operating room, heroic even.

He put his finger on her lips, gently. "Please let me finish. This isn't easy for me, and I only want to say it once."

She kissed his fingertip.

"I'm obviously no longer in love with her, if I ever was. But I also know there are some hard feelings, and not just with her and her family—also with mine."

Laura's heart sped up a bit. She'd been worried Nicholas's family might think of her as some kind of homewrecker.

"I think it's best we put some distance between them and us," he continued. "I think we should live in New Orleans when we get home. Do you understand what I'm saying?" He bit his lower lip. "I can't wait to start our lives together. If you'll have me, I want us to get married. Please say yes." He squeezed his eyes shut.

She held her breath: the chance to build a stable life, something new, in the city she loved, with her family nearby; he was offering her all of it at once. She couldn't hold back the tears. "Yes," she said, smiling up at him. "*Ti amo.*"

He brought her hand to his lips, kissing her palm, his eyes still closed. "*Anch'io ti amo. Sempre.*"

CHAPTER THIRTY-THREE

Germany, May 1945

The 48th had commandeered a sports stadium near Cologne, Germany, hoping it would be their final time setting up a makeshift hospital. It was starting to feel like the war was finally winding down. They'd all been saddened when Roosevelt died—the only president Laura had known in her adult life. She had nothing against Truman, but it pained her that FDR didn't get to see things through to the end. And she grieved for Eleanor, a particular hero to the nurses. In her journal, she'd noted victories almost every day: Iwo Jima and Okinawa. *Too late for Giovanni,* she'd written. *Mussolini hanged upside down in Milan, with his mistress.* When she'd heard the grisly news, she felt no remorse. They were monsters.

Laura spotted Father Bill sitting alone in the mess tent, hunched over a magazine. His face was red, and he ran a hand through his thinning hair, clearly agitated. Though she'd stopped going to services after Giovanni died, she was fond of the chaplain. He was usually so even-keeled; she rarely saw him upset like this.

"Have you seen this?" he asked. He quickly flipped the magazine closed—*Life.* The cover photograph showed three men looking directly at the camera—one with his bandaged hand in a sling—a small caption in the lower left read: *The German People.*

"Yes," she said, sitting down next to him. The magazine had made its way through the nurse's quarters. The pictures—by the same woman photographer she'd met in Anzio—were seared into Laura's brain. Gruesome images from Buchenwald, Bergen-Belsen, and other camps, liberated just the previous month. Emaciated bodies stacked like cordwood. The former prisoners, dressed in tattered clothes, their eyes sunken and cheeks hollow. She'd come close to vomiting. Mildred and Avis had sobbed into each other's arms.

Now, she waited for Father Bill to say something, anything to have it make sense. When he didn't, she couldn't stop herself. "With all due respect, Father. Where was God when all this was going on?" She'd read that Patton had ordered the townspeople to enter the camps to help, to witness what they'd allowed in their own back yards. "And those Germans living right outside the camps as if nothing was out of the ordinary? How could they not know?"

"It's hard to imagine they didn't," the chaplain said, shaking his head.

It wasn't enough for her. "Good Christians, I suppose. What happened to 'do unto others'? How could God let this happen?" She held back from saying it was Satan's work, that evil seemed stronger than good.

"Some things," he said, tapping the magazine, "defy explanation. We believe, despite those unknowns. That's why they call it faith."

Laura waited for more, incredulous, feeling her face flush. "So, you're saying there's no answer? Not even from the Bible?"

"I'm afraid not." He flipped the magazine over. On the back cover, a bride and groom held Chesterfield cigarettes while gazing out a window onto a bucolic vista. "It's enough to make anyone question their beliefs. Even me."

Laura sat back, surprised at his honesty. He'd worked so tirelessly in the tents, praying quietly over the sick, comforting the nurses, and ministering to the dying. But he was just a man, after all. She had tools and medicine to fix people. He only had words and stories.

Father Bill handed her a cigarette, then lit it for her.

"You know, I never smoked before the war," she said.

He inhaled a long drag. "Neither did I."

On a picture-postcard day in early May, Laura and Frances climbed with Mildred and Avis to sit on the top level of the bleachers, a favorite spot where they could survey the countryside, now so peaceful. The sky was a deep blue with just a few puffy clouds blown by a fresh spring breeze. The air smelled of lilacs and the lily-of-the-valley that had sprouted up throughout the compound. Birdsong rose from a nearby grove of linden trees, a music Laura swore to herself she'd never again take for granted after the unnerving silence between bombings in Anzio.

Frances lit a cigarette and reached out to light one for Laura. The recent German surrender in the Netherlands made everyone feel that the end of the war was really in sight, and the conversation turned to post-war plans. Mildred and Avis said they would stay together, move back to Avis's hometown in Oklahoma, and help her parents out on the farm. Mildred was even talking about going to veterinary school. It made Laura happy to think of them there.

"Aren't you afraid of what people will say?" Frances asked.

They laughed. "After what we've been through?" Avis asked. "Let them talk. Sticks and stones."

"We're going to live our lives the way we want to," Mildred said. "It's nobody else's business."

Laura inhaled. She admired their certainty; they knew who they were and how they wanted to live. Fearlessly.

"What about you, Laura?" Avis asked.

Laura paused. All she knew was she wanted to be home—with Nicholas—to be safe, to be happy. But the horizon was fuzzy to her, and she wasn't sure what her life would be like on the other side. "I can't wait to get Nicholas back to New Orleans. I hope my Papa likes him." Nobody could ever replace her brother, but bringing Nicholas home and having another man in the family might help fill the void.

"Of course he will," Frances said, gazing off toward the horizon.

"You must be anxious to see your folks, too, Frances," Mildred said. "Get back to Fort Worth and hit those honky-tonks."

Frances took a long drag off her cigarette and shook her head. "Not really."

Laura was taken aback. All anyone wanted was to go home. "Haven't you had enough of all this?" She gestured to the compound below, muddy ditches in between rows of gray tents.

"It's hard to explain," Frances said. "Maybe I'm crazy, but *all this* is me now."

"This isn't real life, though," Mildred said.

"Seems plenty real enough to me," Frances said.

"Sure, but it's not forever," Mildred said.

"Thank God for that," Avis said. "I never want to drink powdered milk again." She stood, helping Mildred get to her feet. "Come on. I need a walk. See you back at the barracks."

Frances waited until Mildred and Avis were out of earshot. "I'd never say it to them, but I think they're in for a little more resistance than they expect."

"The rules are different here," Laura said. She thought about Frances's drinking, the card games, the soldiers she went with, craving thrills. And her own rule-breaking relationship with Nicholas. She didn't want to think about any harm coming to Mildred and Avis.

"Or maybe there are no rules here," Frances said.

"You sound like you're enjoying the war," Laura said.

"Not exactly," Frances said. "Don't get me wrong, I hate the fighting and pray we never have to go through this again. I'm glad the Krauts are almost done. I hope we beat the Japs real soon. But it's different for me. You have Nicholas, your family back in New

Orleans. Mildred and Avis have each other. There's nothing for me back in Texas. No one."

Laura knew she meant Donny. She assumed Frances had gotten over him. How naive. "What about your parents? Your brother?" Laura twitched a little, thinking of Giovanni. Rose had written that their mother was sleeping in his bedroom now, inconsolable.

"I think they were relieved when I went to war. Glad to get rid of me."

Laura couldn't imagine that. For as much resistance as her parents had given her about signing up, they'd just wanted to keep her close and safe. She understood that now. It had been over two years since she'd last seen them. Whatever anger she'd once felt toward them was gone.

"I'm sure that's not true," Laura said. "You're their only daughter."

"You don't know them. In their defense, I was already a handful, always in trouble," Frances said, shaking her head. "The thought of moving back into my childhood bedroom, after the places we've been? A jail cell. I'd probably run off with the first lunkhead who paid attention to me, get knocked up, and end up with a houseful of brats."

"You could work, find a nursing job," Laura said.

"At the local clinic, treating runny noses and broken legs? After what we've done over here? No, thank you."

Laura exhaled the last of her cigarette and flicked the butt to the ground. Frances wasn't wrong about what they'd been through and what it meant. Laura was proud, but she craved the normalcy Frances seemed to dread. Personally, she'd take being bored over dodging bombs any day.

"Maybe you could make a fresh start somewhere else," Laura said. "Come to New Orleans. You'd love it. Charity always needs good nurses. We could—"

Frances held up a hand. "Thanks, but no. This is the first time in my life I've mattered, that I've made a difference. I'm not just a witness to history, I *am* history. Once it's over, it'll never be like this again, so I'm in it for the long haul. After that, I'll figure it out."

Laura wanted to object, but Nicholas's words echoed in her mind. *She's a grown woman.*

CHAPTER THIRTY-FOUR

When victory came at last, Laura was alone in her tent, jotting notes in her journal. *Russians marching through Germany. Fighting is over in Italy.* The end of the war finally felt inevitable. Avis came in, breathless. "Did you hear?"

"Hear what?"

"He's dead. Hitler. Hung himself in his bunker. Eva Braun, too."

Always with their mistresses, Laura thought. "Good riddance to both of them."

Avis punched her in the arm. "Party in the canteen tonight!"

That evening, Frances met Laura at the door to the mess hall, wearing a slinky red dress. Her blond hair hung loose and reached halfway down her back. Laura wore the rose-colored dress she hadn't worn since the Red Cross dance in North Africa. "Looking good, kid," Frances said, adjusting Laura's dress so it showed more cleavage. It was almost like old times.

Inside the mess hall, they found the party in full swing. The radio was playing the Andrews Sisters' "Victory Polka." Mildred and Avis sat at a table, handing out small American flags that had appeared out of nowhere. Laura scanned the room for Nicholas, but he hadn't arrived yet.

Frances grabbed champagne from a tub full of ice—a gift from some GIs, who'd liberated it from a Nazi hiding place in a nearby cave. She popped the cork, took a long drink right from the bottle, then handed it to Laura. She took a swig of the champagne.

The music stopped abruptly, and the crowd hushed. A BBC announcer introduced Winston Churchill. Everyone froze in place, listening with rapt attention as the prime minister spoke.

"In the long years to come, not only will the people of this island but of the world, wherever the bird of freedom chirps in human hearts, look back to what we've done, and they will say 'do not despair, do not yield to violence and tyranny, march straightforward and die if need be-unconquered.'"

A cheer went up in the room; Laura attempted to grasp the enormity of the moment. No more listening for the menacing roar of enemy engines overhead or explosions in the distance. No more parade of sick and wounded, fresh from the battlefield, missing limbs, gaping holes where organs should be. The music came back on— Glenn Miller's "In the Mood"—and the dance floor erupted with whirling couples, jitterbugging and swinging, dipping and pressing themselves together in a sweaty, delirious blur. As much as she ached for home, she tried to lock the image in her mind, knowing she'd miss these people forever. And for a strange, terrible moment, she understood Frances. She didn't want the war to end just yet.

Nicholas walked in wearing his dress uniform. The collar was a little frayed now, but he'd pinned his service medals over his heart. He folded Laura in his arms. "It's over, sweetheart," he said into her ear. "Time to start our real lives." Laura pulled him out to dance, trying to stay in the moment.

After everyone was good and tipsy, Captain McCarthy raised her glass, calling for quiet. "An Irish toast," she said, with a touch of the brogue that showed up only when she'd had a few drinks. "To those we have loved and lost along the way. May their memory never fade, and may we meet again in a better place."

Laura squeezed Nicholas's hand. She could feel the tears stuck in her throat, thinking of Giovanni and Ellen, of all the boys who came into their wards and never made it out.

"Here's to you, Captain," Avis shouted, raising her drink.

"Hear, hear," the crowd answered. Laura downed her champagne in a single gulp, and someone next to her refilled her glass.

"To victory in the Pacific," someone said. Laura found Frances across the room and raised her glass. Frances had tears standing in her eyes; she raised her bottle back, and they both drank. It was their own wordless toast to Donny. And Giovanni.

The tributes went on: to the Allied victory, to Roosevelt and Churchill and Truman—even to Stalin. "To home," Mildred said finally. She kissed Avis's cheek tenderly.

"*To home*," everyone repeated. Avis led them in singing along to "Happy Days are Here Again." Nicholas slung an arm around Laura's shoulders. Under its weight, she felt her future safe and secure, and leaned into his chest. He would be her home, her anchor, her peace.

The nurses met for an all-hands meeting the next afternoon in the canteen. Most of the remnants of the raucous party the night before were gone, though there were a few cigarette butts still floating in stray cups of flat champagne. When the Captain clapped her hands for attention, the noise made Laura's head throb; it had been a long time since she'd had that much to drink.

"Some of you already know what's next for you personally," McCarthy said. "Raise your hand if you're booked on Thursday's transport out, and onward to serve in the Pacific." A dozen women raised their hands. Frances, standing erect, her lips pursed, chin forward, was the last to lift her arm.

Laura looked over at her, but Frances kept her gaze straight ahead, stone-faced. She'd as much as told Laura her plans when they talked on the bleachers, but now it was coming to pass. Frances would be gone from her life.

"Let's give them a round of applause," the Captain said.

"What about you, Captain?" someone shouted as the clapping died down.

"Me? I'm headed back to Brooklyn on the next magic carpet out of here. I've got a hot dog, a cold beer, a seat with my name on it in the bleachers at Ebbets Field."

Applause rippled through the group. "Go Dodgers!" someone yelled. It hit Laura hard. Soon they'd go their separate ways. Mildred and Avis would be heading home. Frances would be off to God-knows-where, back to the front lines in the Pacific. It was all coming to an end.

"If any of you find yourselves in the Big Apple, you look me up," the Captain continued. "The drinks at McFeeley's Pub are on me. It's been the privilege of my life to serve with you." More applause came, and Laura wiped away a tear. "When times get tough in the future—and they will—don't forget what we did here. We made it through. We did our jobs. We helped save the world."

After more chatter and tearful hugs for those who'd be leaving them, the nurses started filing out. "Hey!" Laura called as she trotted to catch up with Frances, reaching for her arm. "Why didn't you tell me?"

"Like you said, a fresh start."

"More war?"

"They need nurses over there. And I need to see this mission through to the end. I don't expect you to understand." She started to walk away.

"Wait..." Laura reached out, holding her arm.

"Don't make this tougher than it needs to be." Frances unpeeled her fingers. "I'll see you later."

The morning of the first departure day, the whole company turned out to see their comrades off. It was a bright, sunny day, summer just around the corner. Weeds and wildflowers sprang up along the side of the road, and the scent of pine trees wafted in from the nearby forest, clean and fresh. Nicholas stood with the doctors. Frances kissed him on the cheek, making him laugh at some wisecrack Laura couldn't hear.

Laura had come to know and mostly love these doctors, nurses, medics, litter-bearers, and MPs. There were lots of long hugs and promises to write, to get together state-side. People surrounded Captain McCarthy; Laura waited for her turn. "I don't know what to say," she stammered. "Thank you, Ma'am. You've taught me so much."

"You were a good nurse to begin with," McCarthy said. "The Charity girls always are."

"You made me a better person," Laura said. "I'll never forget you."

"Don't get all mushy on me, Marino. You Italians—so emotional." But tears welled in Captain McCarthy's blue Irish eyes as well, and she pulled Laura into a hug. "You take care of that man of yours—he's a keeper. And come see me in New York, you hear? Maybe I'll even come down to New Orleans someday."

Laura smiled through her tears, then joined Mildred, Avis, and a few others lined up next to the truck Frances would board. Time expanded, then compressed. Training camp seemed like a million years ago, but also like just yesterday. Laura had been so intimidated by the tall, brassy Texan. Now Frances made her way down the row as if it were a receiving line, collecting hugs. She wore her neatly pressed dress uniform, her hair in a smooth chignon tucked under her cap, makeup perfect, vital, and animated.

To Mildred and Avis, taking one of each of their hands, Frances simply said, "Be happy, you two." They surrounded her with a hug.

When she reached Laura, Frances tipped her head with an exaggerated pout of her Victory Red-painted lips. "I feel like Dorothy in 'The Wizard of Oz.' And you're the scarecrow."

"Gee, thanks," Laura said, though she knew what was coming.

"I'll miss you most of all, kid," Frances whispered, hugging Laura tightly. She reached into her musette bag, pulled out her silver flask, and tucked it into Laura's hands.

"You're giving me the Good Thing?"

"Consider it a loan. Some of my worst decisions were made with that in my pocket," Frances said. "Maybe you'll have better luck with it."

"I'll hold onto it for now. You'll come see us in New Orleans, right?"

"I'll come for the Mardi Gras," Frances said. "You know me, I'm always up for a party."

The truck engines rumbled to life, coughing out clouds of diesel exhaust. There were so many things Laura wished she had time to say. "Be safe," she managed.

Frances grinned. "Why start now?" She stepped up into the truck with the others, then looked back over her shoulder and blew a kiss. The drivers beeped their horns as they filed out of the camp, dust swirling around their tires. Laura clutched the flask, watching until the convoy disappeared from view.

Nicholas came up from behind and put his arms around her. "Don't worry," he said. "We haven't seen the last of her."

CHAPTER THIRTY-FIVE

New Orleans, November 1951

The alarm clock reads almost two a.m. She should be fast asleep by now, but Laura's mind is buzzing. She puts on her slippers and brings her glass to the kitchen. She eyes the half-full wine bottle and feels the familiar pull—one more might numb her mind enough to sleep. Instead, she washes the glass in the sink and pours herself some water. She looks out the front door. Outside, the street is deserted. She pictures Frances as she was on that last day, boarding the truck in her dress uniform—the model Army Nurse Corps poster girl. So happy to be off to the Pacific, more alive than Laura had seen her in months, heedless of whatever danger lay ahead.

Back then, she'd thought Frances was just running away from whatever awaited her at home—and maybe she was. But she was also fearless, prepared to see the war through until the bitter end, to stay in the thick of things. *I'm in it for the long haul,* she'd told Laura. *Those boys need me.* She'd done her job for as long as her country needed her. No matter what happened after, nothing would change that.

In the Pacific, Frances continued tending to the wounded and the dying. In the end, though, nobody tended to Frances, especially when she got home, and she couldn't save herself. Laura hadn't understood the depth of her friend's grief back then. The war, Donny's death. Now Laura thinks Frances probably brought some damage with her to training camp, and a need to escape whatever it was. But she also brought her strength, sharing it with the rest of them, joking her way through the chaos. Quips like armor. Impenetrable. Finding some release from the pain of the moment with booze and sex. It was all they could do then. Laura cringes at the thought of her own self-righteousness during the war and again later, during the disastrous Mardi Gras visit. Frances was just trying to numb the pain, to feel alive amidst the daily onslaught of loneliness and grief. Wasn't that all Laura herself was after with Boyer?

Frances had not only refused to let Laura fail, but she'd also made her a better nurse. *You're the best person I know*, she'd written in her farewell letter. Laura wants to find that version of herself again, if only to prove her friend right. She closes the journal and turns it over, opening it from the back, reading name after name. *Gardiner, Sheetz, Morrow*. The fatal honor roll of so many who didn't make it home. She counts ten pages, from North Africa in 1943 through Ellen and others in Anzio and beyond.

She finds a pen in her nightstand and, in the space below, writes, *Frances Harris*.

PART SEVEN

New Orleans, 1951

CHAPTER THIRTY-SIX

As Laura tidies up the house the next morning, Rose calls and invites her over for supper that evening. Laura resists the urge to decline. She hasn't seen her sister since that awful day with Aunt Inez, but she's done hiding. She gets herself cleaned up and presentable, finding a pretty red blouse in the back of her closet that Rose had given her last Christmas.

Her sister greets her at the door, wearing a Santa-themed apron over her simple beige dress. Her dark curls are caught up in a bun at the nape of her graceful neck, and she has a dishtowel slung over one shoulder. Laura bends to hug her, holding on for a long minute. Her little sister is petite, yet solid. "Good to see you," Laura says, shaking off uninvited tears that lodge in her throat.

Rose's house is decorated with pine boughs on the mantel and wrapped gifts under a tree strung with cranberries and popcorn. The display of holiday cheer is jarring; Christmas is just a week and a half away, but Laura hasn't given it a second's thought. A red candle flickers in front of the framed photo of Giovanni on the mantel, forever young, in his Army uniform. Laura touches her fingers to her lips and then to the picture, speaking to her lost brother in her mind. *Mio fratello perduto.* In the years since the war, the pain of her brother's death sometimes ambushes her. The holidays are always hard, but now she grieves for the loss of the man he would have become, of the many evenings like this they might have shared.

Laura wipes at her eyes and follows Rose into the kitchen, where the aroma of tomato sauce and garlic—their mother's recipe—makes her stomach rumble. "It smells delicious in here."

Her sister pours her a glass of red wine. If she notices Laura's tears, she lets them go. "I'm almost done," Rose says, transferring the cooked rigatoni into a silver colander in the sink to drain.

Laura walks to the window. Rose's children are playing tag in the yard; Walter sits near them in a lawn chair, serving as referee. Rose never left New Orleans, staying close to their parents. She had adventures too—her wartime romance with an Italian prisoner of war, the Higgins bookkeeping job. But ultimately, she settled down into the exact life their parents had wanted for both of them: marriage, children, a home of their own, savings. Their immigrant American dream. Laura used to think Rose's life was boring. Uninspired. And yet, her sister seems so happy—at peace.

Rose brings a wooden spoon to her mouth to test the sauce, then sprinkles some salt from her hand into the pot. "Last time I saw you, things were pretty rough."

Laura sits at the table. "Not my finest moment. But I'm better now." She takes a small sip of wine, then puts the glass down, pacing herself. That day comes back to her in bits and pieces. She's grateful to Rose and Aunt Inez, but embarrassed that they had to intervene. She wonders how long it will be before they trust her again.

"I'm sorry we were so hard on you," Rose says.

Laura runs a hand through her hair. "I'm sorry too. I was going through a rough time, my friend dying, and all. But that's no excuse."

"We were afraid for you. Afraid of...," she pauses. "Losing you."

Laura bites her bottom lip, a little anguished that her baby sister has to worry about her. It's supposed to be the other way around. "That would never happen."

Rose pats Laura on the shoulder, then hands her a fistful of silverware. "I remember you writing about Frances in your letters. I can't imagine anything like that happening to Marie. We're so different, but we've always stood by each other, through thick and thin, since fourth grade."

Like sisters, Laura thinks. Was it really just a few years that she and Frances were together? "War has a way of compressing time, bringing people close," she says, setting the table. Each day back then was so long, so packed with life and death. "You and Marie are lucky to have each other."

Rose tastes the sauce once more before adding the rigatoni. "We are," she says. "Your letters were a big deal to me back then. Your life was so glamorous."

"Glamorous?" Laura laughs, thinking of the sand fleas in North Africa, the mud in Anzio, their filthy bodies and clothes. Rose's letters sustained her during the war, tethering her to home.

"Sure," Rose says. "You were so close to the action—dodging bombs, saving lives. All I did was push numbers around on a ledger."

"Your work was important, too. Plus, without your boats, we couldn't have won the war."

Rose covers the pots to keep them warm. "We all had our part to play, I suppose. It's why we won." She unties her apron and hangs it on a hook. "Hey, I don't want to ask in front of Walter, but what's going on with your job?"

"Nothing," Laura says, finishing her wine. "I haven't heard from them."

"But you're going back, right?"

"I'm not sure it's up to me."

"Do you want to?"

"What else would I do? Nursing is all I know."

Rose is quiet for a moment and sits down at the table. She folds her hands, leaning toward Laura. "Sounds like you're at a crossroads."

Rose doesn't know the half of it, Laura thinks—all the poor decisions she's made over the last few months. "I guess so. You're lucky you've never gotten yourself into a spot like this."

"Luck has nothing to do with it." Rose dips her chin slightly, pressing her lips together. "It's not like I haven't had choices to make in my life. Hard choices."

"That guy you were seeing while I was overseas—the Italian POW."

"Sal," Rose says, a small crease appearing between her eyebrows. "That was one."

"Do you ever miss him? Or have regrets about sending him away?"

"What's done is done," Rose says. "Why do you ask?"

"Just thinking about consequences. Silly, I know. Maybe it's just the holidays making me feel sentimental."

"Not silly. But the answer is no, I don't regret it. Sure, I think about Sal sometimes—my first love—, but he's married with a family of his own, living with his parents on their farm in Italy. Marie's husband, Vincenzo, keeps up with him. Sal's made a good life for himself, and so have I. We're both where we belong."

Laura wonders where she belongs, whether she can move on from the sugar high of Boyer, so thrilling in the short run but so destructive—like the war itself. She no longer wants the chaos, if she ever did, yet she isn't ready for Rose's tame life either. She wants her own, one that she makes for herself. "That's good. People move on, I guess."

"Yes, but it's more than that. Life is made up of decisions. It's up to us to make the best of it."

Her baby sister used to come to her for guidance when they were growing up, Laura thinks. Now Rose is the one full of wisdom. "Mama and Papa did, I guess," Laura says. Laura thinks of their mother, the choices she'd made, the regrets she lives with, and sometimes takes out on her daughters. And their father, choosing to raise another man's son, to embrace him as his own, only to lose him.

"Some wounds can fester—especially the secret ones," Rose says, as if reading Laura's mind. "What's this really about? Is there something wrong between you and Nicholas?"

Laura hesitates, reluctant to admit to the strain in her marriage. "No. We haven't been in touch much since he's been away. The mail is slow over there, I guess. He'll be home soon."

"Well, if you're looking for something to keep you busy while you're off work and waiting for him, I know Mama and Papa could use some help at the store. They've been stretched a little thin since Carmine left."

"I didn't know," Laura says.

"He left about a month ago. Merchant Marines. Finally getting his chance to serve." Their cousin Carmine had worked for their parents for years. His poor eyesight had kept him from the war, and he was always bitter about it. "They'd never ask, but with the holiday rush and all, I'm sure they'd love to have you around."

"It's been a long time since I've worked at the store."

"Not much has changed," Rose says. "Still the same old Sicilian ladies demanding their thin-sliced capicola. Papa's Italian songs on the radio. I'm sure it'll come right back to you."

"I'll think about it," Laura says. She'd worked at the store all through high school. The notion of hanging around there now makes her a little queasy, like going backwards.

Walter comes in the back door, still in his Sewerage & Water Board work shirt and gray trousers. "There she is," he says, grinning broadly.

Gregory and Marlene push past their father to get to Laura. "*Zia! Zia!*" they squeal. Laura bends down and gathers them up. They are warm, smelling of grass and dirt, their little arms clutching her. She releases them reluctantly and hands them lollipops she'd purchased at the grocery store. The children thank her and scramble to their seats at the kitchen table.

Rose pours wine for herself and Walter, then reaches the bottle toward Laura. "*Basta*," Laura says, putting a hand over her glass. "I'm good for now, thanks."

When Laura arrives home, she empties the mailbox. Along with a few bills and Christmas cards, there's a small package addressed to her, no return address, and no postage. She dumps the other envelopes on the kitchen table, resisting the twin urges to pour a drink and light a cigarette. When she opens the package, a small paperback slides out. Her mouth goes dry. It's the tattered copy of *The Heart Is a Lonely Hunter* that Boyer had been carrying the first day she met him. He must've dropped it in her mailbox while she was at Rose's. She searches the package but finds no note, only words on the flyleaf: *'The way I need you is a loneliness I cannot bear.' John Singer.* And underneath: *Off to Mexico. Wishing you peace.*

He hadn't written her name or his—it would be dangerous for her to keep the book if he had. She brushes her fingertips over his words, tears in her throat, but not in her eyes. Mexico. She'll never see him again. She tucks the slim volume into a row of others on a shelf in the living room. For a moment, the book's spine seems to glow.

She shuffles through the other mail and spots an envelope with a Brooklyn postmark. A Christmas card from Captain McCarthy, a jolly Santa smoking a pipe on the front. *Wishing you both a very merry Christmas! Love from New York City, Bridget McCarthy.* On the facing panel, the Captain had written: *Visited with Frances's parents on my way west. I'm sure they'd love to hear from you.* Laura swallows hard, then replaces the card in its envelope.

In her bedroom, she takes her journal from the nightstand drawer and shakes out the photo of her and Frances tucked inside. She'll get a frame for that. She puts the Miraculous Medal aside. Maybe Rose would like to have it back. Then she takes the journal and Frances's silver flask up to the attic and places the Good Thing and her words back in her old footlocker and closes the lid.

CHAPTER THIRTY-SEVEN

Two days later, the bell over the door at Marino's grocery store tinkles as Laura walks in. She spots a shiny new cash register, but other than that, the store is the same as always: bins of beans and rice, canned goods lining the walls, every inch packed with something good to eat, the familiar smells of cheese and meat, mixed with the sawdust on the floor. On the radio, Louis Prima takes a trumpet solo. The Army banner still hangs on the wall: a blue star for her, as one who came back, Giovanni's star gold, as one who didn't.

"Look who it is!" her father shouts from behind the counter, his white butcher's apron straining over his tummy. He's waiting on a customer, Laura doesn't recognize, with a bright red scarf tied over her gray hair. "That's my daughter," her father says to the woman. "She's a nurse down at Charity. Saved a lot of boys' lives in the army. Africa and Europe."

The customer raises an eyebrow. "You mean in the war? You were there?" she asks, her English accented with the old country.

People are always somehow surprised. "*Si. Buongiorno, signora.*"

Laura's father finishes wrapping the woman's package of cheese and hands it to her. "*Grazie*, Mrs. T."

"*Dio vi benedica*," the woman says to Laura, making the sign of the cross as she leaves. "God bless you."

The store is quiet. "Is everything all right?" Her father's brow wrinkles.

"*Bene*," she says, a little ashamed that she's been absent so long that her father assumes something must be wrong for her to show up. "Rose told me about Carmine. Thought you might need an extra pair of hands. I have some time between now and when Nicholas comes home next week."

"Well, we could certainly use the help," her father says.

Her mother comes out from the back of the store, thin and wiry as ever. She runs a hand through her shoulder-length brown hair, streaked with more gray than Laura remembers. "*Ciao*, Lauretta! We haven't seen you in so long!" Her mother kisses her on both cheeks. She smells of onions and flour, a hint of her lavender soap underneath. "You're not working today?"

Laura takes a deep breath. She doesn't want to add to her parents' burden. "That special assignment I told you about is over, and they gave us some time off for Christmas."

"We're proud of you, *cara*," her father says. Laura winces but knows it's kinder to let them believe what they want. "Fil, Laura's here to help out today."

"*Va bene*," her mother says. "Come back to the storeroom. There's an extra apron on the hook." Laura is relieved to find her mother in a cheerful mood. Holiday sales must be up.

In between customers, they assemble a care package for their families in Sicily—hard salami, packets of spices, macaroni, and a sack of rice. Things are still tough there, six years after the end of the war. It feels good to move, to lose herself in the steady momentum of tasks. She misses her job, the useful work she used to do every day. While they work, Laura collects the latest gossip—a neighbor's daughter is pregnant, no father in sight, and Aunt Inez's new boyfriend. "Younger than the last one, if you can believe that," her mother reports.

Laura begs off staying for dinner; she longs for the quiet of her own house. Her mother packs up some food for her—bread, salami, fontina cheese, Aunt Inez' olive spread. "And your favorite," her mother says, adding a packet of her homemade biscotti. "Still the best in the city."

"It is, Mama," Laura says, genuinely touched, and kisses her mother's soft cheek. "Thanks for everything. I'll see you tomorrow."

Her mother heads upstairs as her father flips the "open" sign on the front door to "closed." Laura helps him tidy up, straightening the meats and cheeses in the big glass-fronted deli case. The radio blares the latest news about Korea, and her father reaches over to turn it off.

"Rose told us about your friend from the war," he says in a low voice. "Sorry to hear it. I know it's hard. I've lost a few good friends myself. Boys I knew from the village. And Giovanni, of course." He waves his hand at the Gold Star banner.

"Thanks, Papa," Laura says. "You would have loved Frances. She would've made you laugh like hell." It feels impossible to say more without breaking down completely.

"In Sicily, we'd say *se ti ricordi di lei, lei sarà sempre con te*," he says. He presses his hands together and shakes them at Laura. "If you remember her, she will be with you always."

"I could never forget her," she says, her voice breaking. "She helped me through, you know?"

Her father nods. "I do, *cara*." He hugs her, and she falls into his chest, remembering his embrace when he saw her off at the dock back in 1943. She was twenty-one years old and had never been further than Baton Rouge. How she longed to get away from them then, to prove herself, only to ache for home the whole time she was in the war. She breathes in her father's warmth for a few moments before pulling herself away. "*Ciao*, Papa."

"*Vai piano-piano*." Go easy-easy. Her father's been saying that to her all her life. If only it were so simple.

CHAPTER THIRTY-EIGHT

The day Nicholas is due to return, Laura is up with the sun. His train is due in at four o'clock that afternoon, which gives her time to clean the house from top to bottom. She hangs freshly washed laundry on the clothesline in the back yard, where it billows in the unseasonably warm breeze. Once the house is sparkling, she takes a long bath, carefully applies her makeup, and styles her hair. Looking at herself in the mirror, she examines her face for any trace of infidelity. She adds a spritz of perfume behind her ears and at her wrists, and wears a green shirtwaist dress, one of Nicholas's favorites.

Inside the arrivals hall at Union Passenger Terminal, one of the fresco panels she'd seen when she picked up Captain McCarthy is now nearly finished. The images are bold and provocative: a Sister of Charity tends to an emaciated Black man on a stretcher, two lovers embrace on the verge of a kiss, a baby angel floats, a halo around his little head.

The hulking black locomotive huffs into the station, belching soot and smoke, its wheels screeching against the metal rails. In minutes, the passengers begin to climb out, laden with luggage and holiday gifts. People around her jostle for a glimpse of their loved ones. A toddler breaks away from his mother, shouting, "Maw-Maw!" and waddles toward a gray-haired lady carrying a large teddy bear. The grandmother squats down, and the boy throws his little arms around her neck, which makes Laura smile.

She searches every face, looking for Nicholas. For a moment, she worries he's changed his mind about coming back to her. Then, seemingly out of nowhere, he's there, walking toward her. He looks a little thinner than when he left, and his sandy brown hair brushes his collar. He's dressed in casual slacks and a dark green sweater she's never seen before, and there's a growth of stubble on his grinning face. He drops his old Army duffel bag and enfolds her in a tight hug.

"Aren't you a sight for sore eyes?" he whispers.

"Welcome home," Laura says, fighting back tears. She breathes in his familiar musky scent. Her whole body is quaking now.

He holds her at arm's length, looking her up and down. "You're shaking. What's wrong?"

"Nothing." He hands her a handkerchief from his pocket, and she wipes her tears away. "I'm just so happy to see you." She's flooded with relief. Until this moment, she wasn't sure how she'd feel to be with him again.

He picks up his bag. "Let's go home, Nurse Marino."

Back at the house, Laura closes the front door behind them. His presence is disorienting after all her time alone in the house. "You must be hungry," she says. "I have some pot roast from Mama. Why don't you take a nice, hot shower, while I warm it up?"

"Sounds good," he says. "I'm feeling pretty grimy. The trip back was grueling." He heads into the bathroom down the hall. In the kitchen, she unwraps the roast and puts it in the oven to warm. She sits on the couch, trying to slow her breathing. *You can do this. Keep it together. He's your husband.*

The shower stops running, and Nicholas is whistling, as if he'd never left. He comes back out as she's setting the table, dressed in khakis and a white t-shirt. "That felt great. The showers over there left a lot to be desired," he says, with the clean-shaven smile she first fell in love with back in Tunisia.

He sits in the same seat Boyer sat in less than a week ago. She shakes off the image and sets out two plates of pot roast with potatoes and carrots. She pours him a glass of wine, a smaller one for herself. He digs into the food, eagerly forking a bite of meat into his mouth. "I have so much to tell you. The people I worked with were fantastic. From all over the country."

She picks at her dinner as he describes medical work, the well they helped to rebuild, serving food to the American GIs who cycled through. "I had surgical rotations, but sometimes they threw us into triage," he says. "Gave me a glimpse of what you went through. Exhausting." He mentions his team members by name and seems really fond of them. She hasn't seen him this animated in a long time, and envies his energy, the kind of charge that comes from being given a difficult task and rising to meet it. She has a fleeting thought about the nurses he worked with there, a ripple of jealousy to which she's not entitled. Perhaps he'd been tempted. How awful it would be to lose him that way—the way he almost lost her.

After dinner, he pours whiskey for them both, and they sit on the couch. She takes a small sip, letting its heat sit on her tongue, and puts her glass down. He touches her under her chin, lifting her face and kissing her deeply. She relaxes into his embrace, startled by how much she wants him. She'd been afraid she wouldn't, that her time with Boyer had somehow ruined her. But the old attraction reemerges. Physical, yes, but something more—a deep kind of longing.

Nicholas downs his whiskey in one gulp. "Let's go to bed."

Laura lies on her back on the mattress, her eyes closed, drowsy with pleasure. Nicholas is propped up on an elbow, stroking the inside of her arm, which is making her tingle all over again. "What are you thinking about?"

"I was remembering that day in Sperlonga," she says. She pictures the beach, the gentle waves lapping the shore, his earnest declaration of love. "We were so young."

"Only six years ago," he says. "But I know what you mean. Another life."

"It was. I still love you that way," she says, as if speaking it aloud will make it truer.

"I love you too, Laura." He pauses. "I remember watching you at Cinecittà one day. You were helping a young mother adjust to her newborn. She was Italian, and you spoke to her so tenderly."

The sweet, tiny babies had brought so much joy, after all the death and destruction. "I didn't realize you were there," she said.

"You didn't see me. I remember thinking how lucky I was not just to work with you, but to love you. For you to love me. It almost made me cry. That was when I knew."

It's gotten dark; she's glad he can't see her face anymore. "After you left, I dug out my journal from the war. I've been going through it while you were away, trying to remember."

"Do you think that's a good idea?" he asks.

"I don't know. I just needed to. Forgetting hasn't worked very well for me."

He rolls onto his back with a sigh. "I remember you scribbling in that notebook. Frances used to kid you about it."

She rests her hand on his chest. "She always thought I was writing about her. Sometimes I was, apparently. A lot about you."

"Poor Frances," he says. He's quiet for a moment. "You were a good friend to her."

Laura isn't entirely sure that's true, though for a time, it was. Her journal had shown that. A thought crystallizes in Laura's mind: she could've been a better friend to Frances, especially after the war, but she couldn't have saved her. The only one she can save is herself. "I miss her so much. I've *been* missing her, just haven't allowed myself to think about it. I'll never have another friend like that."

Nicholas finds her hand and holds it. "I've missed you, too."

"You mean while you were in Korea?"

"Even before that," he says. "Even right now, lying next to you. Like I still can't get close enough, like how we used to be. I know I pulled away, especially after we lost Michael. I didn't know what to do, and it paralyzed me. I'm a surgeon. I'm used to repairing people."

She thinks about what her sister said, about decisions. She can't fix the past. All she can do is try to make things right going forward. "I want to do better," she whispers. "To be close again."

"I want to do better, too. I may not always get it right, but I want to try. We'll find our way back together. A fresh start."

She kisses his chest and lays her head in the crook of his shoulder. Within minutes, he's snoring softly.

The next morning, she puts slices of bread into the toaster, then pulls eggs from the refrigerator. She tries to hold onto the warm glow from the night before, but Nicholas is dressed for work, and she needs to tell him about her suspension before he hears it from the hospital grapevine.

He fills his mug from the percolator on the counter, then sits at the table. "What we said last night about a fresh start," he says. "I was thinking, maybe we can both take a break and sign up for another stint in Korea. They need all kinds of help over there. It's a broken place, but a beautiful country. I think you'd like it."

She cracks the eggs into a frying pan. Flashes of light behind her eyes make her shake her head. "Back in a war zone? I don't know if I could handle that."

"We were nowhere near the front line. It was more like Cinecittà. Mostly civilians, some GIs, but no mass casualty situations. Plenty of supplies." He laughs. "Warning, though: the coffee is still as bad as ever."

She turns from the stove, needing him to say it. "You'd really want me with you?"

"More than anything. I won't go again without you." He offers a small smile. "You don't need to decide right now. Just consider it."

"I will," she says, thinking of the possibilities. Working alongside Nicholas. A new place. Just a job to do—the one that matters most.

"They're forming up another team right now. We'll just need to get you a letter of recommendation from Charity. Maybe ask about it when you go in next?"

The dream evaporates as quickly as it had formed. She plates the eggs and toast, and tightens the belt around her bathrobe. "I don't actually have a next shift," she begins, sitting across from him, and suddenly wishing she were properly dressed. "I'm on leave."

His brow furrows. "What do you mean? Have you been sick?"

"Nothing like that. It's just..."

"Just what?"

"I've had kind of a hard time at work while you've been gone."

He shakes his head. "I sure didn't miss that while I was away. Hospital politics? More budget cuts—"

"I got suspended," she says before he can go on.

He puts down his fork, his eyes locking on hers. "What for?"

"They put in some new rules about signing out medications. I should've known, but apparently, I stepped over a line."

He stays quiet, pushing his plate to the side and leaning toward her. "I don't understand. What actually happened?"

She takes a deep breath. The old urge to blame someone else is there, but what happened was her doing. No one else was suspended, only her. She puts her shaking left hand in her robe pocket, willing it to be still. "I provided morphine to a patient without accounting for it, and they reprimanded me."

"That doesn't sound worthy of a suspension," Nicholas says.

She chooses her words carefully, omitting what he didn't need to know—that she was drunk at work, that the patient was Boyer. "The new boss, she's a veteran herself. Kind of a stickler for procedure. Probably looking to make an example of someone."

"I would think her being a veteran is a *good* thing," Nicholas says in an even tone. "That you two would have a connection."

"You'd think," she says, remembering how Annie had sought her out in the courtyard, how she'd revealed her story. Annie had been trying to connect; instead, Laura had pushed her away. "I might have had a bad attitude after they didn't give me the promotion. And I might have been hungover at work once or twice. I'm sure that didn't help. You'll probably hear about it, so I wanted you to know."

He drains his coffee. She refills his mug and sits down again. "This is serious, Laura."

"I know." She tells him about Captain McCarthy's visit and how her advice helped her think things through.

"I wish I had been here for that," he says. "I wish I'd been here to help you, too."

She nods. The whole thing wouldn't have happened like it did if he were here—no Boyer, no binge drinking, no taking drugs from the hospital. But it also occurs to her that she might have been a ticking time bomb anyway. The pressure was building. One way or another, a breakdown was inevitable.

"So, what now?" he asks.

"I haven't talked to them since, so I'm not sure where things stand. I really want to go to Korea with you. I think I can help. It would be good for me, for us."

"You'll need a clean reference. Can you appeal the suspension? There must be a way. I can speak to—"

She holds up a palm to stop him. "No," she says, a little too forcefully. She can't always be relying on him to fix things. To fix her. "I mean, please don't. I'll handle it myself."

CHAPTER THIRTY-NINE

After Nicholas leaves for work, Laura calls the hospital to make sure Annie will be there. She thinks about what Frances taught her in an early pep talk: that the only way through a mess is to put the last shift in a box and move on. Like the soldiers had to. After she washes up and dresses, she takes the streetcar to Charity. It's a strange sensation to walk into the hospital in civilian clothes. She waves and says hello to the security guard at the front desk, to the janitor, mopping up a spill in the cavernous lobby. They smile at her, warm and friendly, perhaps a little confused that she's not in uniform. Upstairs, the new wing is humming, full of patients, modern and clean. Even so, Laura has a pang of nostalgia for the old ward, shabby though it was.

Shoulders back, chin up, she knocks on the open door of Annie's office. "Good morning. Do you have a few minutes to talk?"

"Laura! What a surprise." Annie stands and shakes Laura's hand. Her short blond hair is combed straight back, the tiny scar on her eyebrow pulsing. "Please come in and close the door."

The small room is tidy and uncluttered, with a few papers neatly stacked in a tray on the desk. Light cascades through a high window. Hanging on the wall is a photo of a group of nurses in fatigues, with palm trees in the background. Laura picks out Annie, a little shorter than the rest. The nurses are dirty and exhausted-looking, but Laura sees their camaraderie, arms slung over each other's shoulders, loose and smiling. "Your squad in the Philippines?"

Annie rests her eyes on the photo with a knowing smile. "The best," she says. She gestures to the chair opposite her desk. "I was going to reach out. How've you been?"

"You were right. I needed a break. I've done a lot of thinking lately, took a hard look at my life." Laura knows it's what Annie wants to hear, but it's also true.

"It's tough to see when you're in the thick of it," Annie says. "Sometimes with people who don't necessarily have your best interests at heart, you can lose your way, if you know what I mean."

She means Boyer. "Those people aren't in my life anymore. In fact, my husband just got back. You'll probably run into him. Nicholas Bruno. He's a surgeon here."

"I've heard the name." She pauses. "And the drinking?"

Laura fights off a little defensiveness, reminding herself that she expected this question. Annie is only doing what Captain McCarthy asked them to do—her job. "Cut way back."

"Good. Not everyone needs to go cold turkey like I had to. But it's good to be aware. Honest." Annie doesn't sound as preachy as she did before. Just sensible. Caring. Or maybe that's what she was then, and Laura just couldn't hear it. "I assume you're here because you want to come back to work?"

"I do," Laura says. "But I have another opportunity."

Annie shakes her head. "Please don't tell me Touro's trying to hire you. We lost two nurses to them last week."

"Nothing like that. My husband just returned from a humanitarian mission in Korea. A displaced persons camp. He's signing up for another stint and wants me to come with him."

"I read where things are pretty rough over there. Lots of refugees. Do you think you're ready to go back to a war zone?"

"He says they desperately need medical help. And that it's far from the action. It would be for three months, starting in early January. I'd need a clean reference from you."

"That's soon." Annie raises her eyebrows. "And after that?"

"I'd love to come back, if you'll have me," Laura says.

Annie sits back, sighing. "One of the steps in AA says we have to take full responsibility for our past acts."

"Look, I know it's a lot to ask," Laura says. "I haven't made the best first impression."

"If I give you a reference and you fall short, that's my reputation. And for any other Charity nurse who may try to follow you as well. You understand?"

"I do."

"I'll need you to promise we'll never have that kind of situation again," Annie says. "And that if you have any...setbacks...any issues at all, that you'll come to me *before* things get out of hand. Let me be clear: there will be no suspension if there's a next time."

"You have my word," Laura says, looking Annie in the eye. "Thank you."

Annie makes a note on a pad of paper in front of her. "I'll write the letter. We'll call it a sabbatical. You're a good nurse, Laura. Everyone says so. We just need you to be more a part of the team."

They shake hands. "I hope we can start over when I get back," Laura says. "Clean slate."

"I'd like that," Annie says, keeping her grip on Laura's hand. "Understand, I'm doing this for you because others did this for me."

Outside the hospital, Laura pauses on the front steps. Across the street, Joe's has a big Christmas wreath on the front door. An inviting glow shines through the window. She hasn't been inside since Joe saw her there with Boyer. She considers crossing over, just for one beer. So easy. Instead, she heads to the streetcar, knowing she has an important call to make.

At home, she digs out Captain McCarthy's Christmas card with the Harrises' phone number. After several rings, a woman answers.

"Mrs. Harris? This is Laura Bruno, um Marino. Frances's friend from the war. You sent me a letter a while back." The line goes quiet on the other end, and for a moment, Laura worries that she's made a mistake in calling.

"Oh, my goodness, Laura," the woman says. "It's so good to hear from you."

Laura is almost undone by Mrs. Harris's Texas twang, an echo of Frances's voice. She twists the phone cord around her finger, squeezing her eyes shut, as she delivers the words she's rehearsed. "I'm sorry I haven't been in touch. I know it's been a difficult time."

"It has." Mrs. Harris's voice cracks, breaking Laura's heart.

Laura fights the urge to tell Mrs. Harris all the things she wishes she'd said to Frances. She's afraid that if she starts talking, she'll never stop. "I was thinking I might take a trip to Texas," she says instead.

"We would love to meet you," Mrs. Harris says. "It would be like having a little piece of our Frances back."

"Frances was the best friend a gal could ever hope to have." The words are out before Laura can stop them. "I wouldn't have made it through the war without her."

That evening, when Nicholas comes home from work, Laura tells him about her meeting with Annie.

"The next group is leaving right after Twelfth Night," he says, pulling her close. "Are we in?"

"Yes," she says. "There's just one thing I have to do first."

He stands back. "Another problem?"

She considers the question. For a while, it had seemed like a problem. Now it seems like part of the solution. "I need to go to Texas," she says, and recounts her conversation with Frances's mother. "I know what my parents went through, losing Giovanni." She needs to pay her respects at Frances's grave, to tell her friend goodbye. That last part just occurred to her, or maybe she just couldn't bear to picture it before.

"Of course," he says. "We can take the Chevy on a road trip. I'll try to get a couple of days off before we leave for Korea."

She takes his hand. "Thanks, but I need to do this on my own."

CHAPTER FORTY

A few days after Christmas, Nicholas takes her to the station. On the platform, passengers are already boarding the train. Laura checks her purse several times, making sure her ticket is inside. It feels strange to be the one leaving. She adjusts her hat and fidgets with her outfit.

Nicholas squeezes her hand. "You'll be fine," he says.

"I just don't want to say the wrong thing." She wants to let them know what a special person Frances was. How much she meant to so many people, to her, about the lives she saved.

"You won't," he says. "Just say what's in your heart."

"Maybe I'll tell them a few war stories."

"A few. But I don't think they need to know *everything*," Nicholas laughs. "Frances was a little wild over there."

"We all were," Laura says, remembering those early days in Tunisia, speeding across the desert in the jeep with Nicholas, making out on a blanket in the dunes, drunk on bootleg hooch and new love.

"We had to be," Nicholas says. "It's how we got through."

The engine chugs to life, and the conductor shouts from the doorway, "All aboard! Louisiana Eagle, number twenty-one westbound.

Baton Rouge, Alexandria, Shreveport, and Fort Worth, Texas. All aboard!"

Nicholas bends down and kisses her. "I love you. Be safe," he says.

Laura smiles, remembering Frances's parting shot back in Germany.

"What?" he asks.

She shakes her head. "Just something Frances said. *Ti amo.*"

On the train, she finds her berth, a roomette she's grateful to have to herself for the overnight journey. She hoists her suitcase onto the overhead rack and takes a seat by the open window. Nicholas finds her and blows a kiss; she knows he'll be waiting for her there in two days when she returns. The locomotive emits a long, loud whistle, then the train lurches forward. For a disorienting moment, it feels like the platform is moving away while she's sitting still. Then she realizes she's the one picking up speed.

–THE END–

AUTHOR'S NOTE

In my first novel, *The Italian Prisoner*, the main character Rose Marino received letters from her big sister Laura, who was serving overseas in the Army Nurse Corps. In conducting the research behind those missives, I waded through many journals, letters, oral histories, and non-fiction books about nurses in the service. I was disappointed there weren't more novels written about the nurses who served in World War II, outside of a few excellent books about the nurses who were captured as POWs in the Pacific. A couple of books about the Red Cross Clubmobile girls, including Luis Alberto Urrea's wonderful novel *Good Night, Irene* are nurse-adjacent. *Triage* is intended to give those brave nurses who served in North Africa and the European Theater their due.

Over 70,000 American nurses served in World War II, and 222 of them died in service. Six nurses died in Anzio, including Ellen Ainsworth. In 2024, I was honored to visit her grave at the Sicily-Rome American Cemetery and Memorial in Nettuno, Italy. Unlike subsequent wars, there were no helicopters in World War II, so hospital units were stationed very close to the front lines. Nurses, doctors, orderlies, medics, chaplains, ambulance drivers, and other personnel were often in harm's way and witnessed unspeakable carnage.

Unfortunately, when the American nurses returned home, they were often not recognized as full-fledged veterans. While they were allowed to utilize the G.I. Bill for education, they were denied VA medical benefits. When they sought help to deal with the effects of the trauma they'd suffered, the women were often told to just get over it and move on.

This book is, of course, a work of fiction. The characters, action, and dialogue were inspired by the many books, articles, oral histories, and films I consulted as part of my background research. Laura's unit, the 48th Evac Hospital, is a composite drawn from what I learned about several hospital units. The 48th Surgical Hospital (later re-named the 128th Evacuation Hospital) was with the first amphibious landing of U.S. troops in North Africa in 1943. The 56th Evacuation Hospital was in Anzio. I took some liberties with the timeline for the sake of narrative clarity. For example, sharp-eyed New Orleans history buffs will note that the Conrad Albrizio frescoes in the Union Passenger Terminal were not completed until 1954, when the new train station opened. If you'd like to learn more, I encourage you to check out the references link on my website www.elisamariesperanza.com.

In addition to the primary source research, I gathered first-hand accounts from contemporary nurses, particularly those who'd served during the COVID-19 pandemic. The words they used and the stories they shared were reminiscent of nurses' wartime recollections I'd read from World War II through Korea and Vietnam, to more recent conflicts. I should also acknowledge Kristen Hannah's runaway bestseller *The Women*, about the Vietnam-era Army nurses. I'm grateful that she turned her considerable audience on to the stories of these unsung she-roes.

As I write this message, the weight of history is very clear and present. These are dark days in the United States of America, when many of us are resisting our country's slide into the same kind of assault on democracy and humanity so many sacrificed to fight against in the 1940s. The medical personnel in WW2 were, of course, part of the vast Allied presence in the European and Pacific Theaters who fought, suffered, and died to liberate the world from fascism. What's past is prologue, as Shakespeare wrote.

World War II was the first war in which more men died from combat than disease, and the nurses never received the credit they deserved. I hope this book will provide them a small measure of recognition and, by association, acknowledge the hard-working, selfless professional nurses who serve our communities every day.

ACKNOWLEDGEMENTS

My first debt of gratitude goes to you readers. Thank you for reading this book, and for reading in general. We all know reading fosters empathy, and the world certainly needs more of that. Much love and appreciation to the human beings who bring books to you, especially those who work as independent booksellers. (RIP, Gail Calato of Two Fish Books in St. Bernard Parish, Louisiana. You are missed.) Thanks also to librarians everywhere, especially those fighting against censorship. To those of you in one of the dozens of book clubs and organizations I've spoken to over the past four years—*grazie mille*, and I hope to see you again soon.

In researching for this book, I consulted a wide variety of sources and linked a list of references on my website for those who want to take a deeper dive. Nurses, doctors, historians, military veterans, academics, and others with personal connections to this story were an invaluable source of information and insights. They provided color commentary about Charity Hospital in New Orleans, mass casualty situations, medical procedures, World War II history, and trauma response. Some also served as beta readers*. Big thanks to: Bevin Beaudet*, Dr. Danila Bracaglia, Ron Capps*, Chris Dier, Dr. Noel

Difillippo, Paula Fortier, PhD, Antonia Glenn, RN, Joan Guccione, RN, Laura Guccione, Kim Guise, Lista Hank, RN, Marianne Hartmann, RN, Anna Lee Ingalls, RN, Vahe Katros, Lora Kostka, RN, Kevin McCaffrey, Robert Miller, Linda Morrison, EdD RN, Dr. Elizabeth Norman, RN, Miki Pfeffer, PhD, Donita Qualey, RN*, Emma Reid, Betsy Reifsnider, PhD RN, Robin Rivera*, Kristen Melberg Schwartz, Rita Sudman, Elaine Taylor, RN, Bruce Tobey (RIP), Lisa Tourtelot*, Michele Visconti, PhD RN*, and Nanci Zhang, MPH, RN*.

Say what you will about social media, but I'm indebted to the good folks in the Facebook groups "Ain't there (dere) no more" and "If you trained at Charity, then you will remember," who shared such great information about a number of topics, including Joe's Lounge. They led me to a delightful conversation with Joe's son, Charles Raviotta. I also got some great material from the Charity Hospital School of Nursing Alumni.

After the release of my debut novel *The Italian Prisoner*, I was so grateful to be welcomed into the community of writers, especially in New Orleans and on Martha's Vineyard. Much of this book was written during Sunday quiet writing hours at the beloved Featherstone Center for the Arts in Oak Bluffs—thanks to Literary Arts Director Mathea Morais and CEO Ann Smith for all you do to support writers and artists on the island. Thanks also to Kate Feiffer for including me in the Islanders Write family.

Big thanks to fellow authors I admire so much. Maurice Carlos Ruffin—both personally and through his excellent Substack "Sitting in Silence," has been a source of inspiration, friendship, support, and relentless positivity. Jami Attenberg, through her Substack "Craft Talk" and #1000WordsOfSummer provided literary sustenance throughout. Thanks also for words of wisdom and encouragement along the way from Dr. Martha Boone, Alan Brickman, Geraldine Brooks, Ron Capps, Martha Hall Kelly, Vincent "Chip" Lococco, Emily Mayhew, Marie McCurdy, Andrea Myers, W. Christy Smith, and Greg Cope White. Shout out to my original #1000WordsOfSummer squad, the F&S Writers Collective (IYKYK). The advice and validation I received from Luis Alberto Urrea and the team at the Spannocchia Writers Workshop was the lynchpin I needed for *Triage* to click into place.

This book is dedicated to my sisters, by which I mean my actual sisters: the artist Kathleen Speranza, Marianne Speranza Hartmann RN, and our dearly departed little sister Laura. I also mean all my fabulous women and women-identifying friends from the (many) stages of my life and career. To all the nurses and women veterans out there, I salute you. The Women Warriors Book Club in New Orleans generously shared their insights at a pivotal early stage in my research. I can't overstate my gratitude to the Washashores Writers Collective, the special sisterhood Brenda Horrigan and I co-founded in 2021 that has grown into an invaluable support network and source of strength and joy.

Special thanks to Jessica Kinnison and Allison Alsup, co-founders of New Orleans Writers Workshop, where it all began. As my fabulous developmental editor/coach/book whisperer, Allison has unleashed an encore writing career beyond my wildest dreams. I've learned so much from her guidance and patient tutelage. If you haven't yet read her debut historical novel *Foreign Seed*, you need to put it on your to-read list.

I made an affirmative decision to indie-publish this book under my own micro-press for many reasons. You can read about that on my post "Going Indie" in the archive of my Substack "The Bricklayer's Daughter" at elisamariesperanza.substack.com. I'm grateful to the Burgundy Bend Press production team for this project: book designer Kim Leaird, proofreader Abby Remer, cover artist Jon Langford, photographer Cheryl Gerber, and website designer Shayna of Bright Bunch Designs. For the audiobook, I was excited to work with voice actor Debi Tinsley (who did such a great job on *The Italian Prisoner*) and Grammy-winning recording engineer Chris Finney.

I'm grateful for the love and support of all my friends and family throughout the long journey to launching *Triage* into the world, including Bryce, Ruby, and Iko. Last but certainly not least, big love to my Alpha Reader, my *chef de cuisine*, and my partner in all things, Jon Kardon.

ABOUT THE AUTHOR

Elisa M. Speranza is the author of two historical novels, *Triage* (2026) and *The Italian Prisoner* (2022), a finalist in the Faulkner-Wisdom Creative Writing Competition. She is board chair and an instructor for the nonprofit New Orleans Writers Workshop and has been a featured author at the Tennessee Williams & New Orleans Literary Festival, the Louisiana Book Festival, Islanders Write, and the Salem LitFest. She is the co-founder of the Washashores Writers Collective on Martha's Vineyard and writes "The Bricklayer's Daughter" on Substack.

Originally from Boston, Elisa lives with Jon Kardon in New Orleans and Oak Bluffs, Massachusetts. For more information, please visit: www.elisamariesperanza.com